# RELEASE TO FREEDOM

by Armand P. Ferland

# RELEASE TO FREEDOM

Armand P. Ferland

Railroad Street Press
394 Railroad Street, Suite 2
St. Johnsbury, VT 05819

Published in the United States by Railroad Street Press, St. Johnsbury, Vermont.

ISBN: 9781936711109


1.   Fiction

Jacket design by Susanna V. Walden.

First Edition 2011

Railroad Street Press
394 Railroad Street, Suite 2
St. Johnsbury, VT 05819
(802) 748-3551
www.railroadstreetpress.com

Dedicated to
Dorothy

Who has cared for me for more
than four decades,
and given me HOPE

# One

The room's walls were cold and hard with only one color, yellow, outlining the formerly grey cinder blocks of the wall. The pattern of each new block covering one half of the ones under it to maintain stability and strength as the walls formed the small room. One wall of the room had two steel frames bolted into the walls to form a bunk bed style sleeping platforms. One wall had a metal door that was welded to its jamb with a four by six inch viewing port about five feet from the floor. Opposite to the door was a stainless steel toilet/sink combination that was bolted to the wall and floor and open to the entire room. On the same wall, was two small shelves bolted into the corner to keep personal stuff on. The rest of the eight by twelve foot room was open. On the sleeping platforms were two hard, foam mattresses that were about three inches thick and did little to soften the steel platform under it. On the bottom mattress, I was trying to figure out what I was doing there and wondering what to expect in the near future.

This was the first of many days that had been scheduled for me by a federal judge. The federal prosecuting attorney thought that I would enjoy the surroundings as I contemplated my brash actions directed at others in society. I would be allowed to join a guest list of nearly eight hundred other guests as we shared three meals a day and other complimentary activities such as lockdown. I tried to deny the offer but my personal lawyer had little success except for getting some charges dropped and thereby lowering my minimum time to serve. My accommodations were medium security as I had not hurt anyone physically with my actions. I had never been near a prison before and I was placed with a man who was recognized as being calm and helpful to other inmates as an instructor for me to prison etiquette.

Don had given directions on what part of the room I could occupy as well as where to place my stuff. The word was that there were definite boundaries within the walls of the cell we would share. Don said, "I will tell you what to expect as far as times of the day. We will be allowed out into the yard for exercise for one hour in the morning which you have missed and again this afternoon. We will be going for meals at six-forty-five in the morning, eleven-thirty, and five-thirty. We will get twenty minutes in the mess hall and then we are expected to get everything cleaned up and return to our cell block. I will tell you more later on," as he climbed up onto the top bunk and started to look at a magazine.

From outside the cell, the constant barrage of orders on the intercom was annoying if not discomforting. The simple closing of cell doors reverberated in the tomblike cellblock as well as the voices that echoed to the point of being indistinguishable of origin and unintelligible in meaning seemed to never end. I picked up a book that I had brought in to the prison with me and started to thumb the pages to where I had left off reading. I was not able to even begin to read what was on the pages as the thoughts racing through my head plunged me into a chasm of fear in my mind. I had never been afraid of anything in my life and that was what led me to begin taking more and more risks but there was a part of this reality that was beginning to put a fear in my soul.

I began to remember a time a little over a year ago. I was doing construction in the area in which I lived. I often took jobs on the side that were not big enough to be of any interest to my boss and did them on nights and weekends. I had aspirations of going totally on my own some day and was using some of the money from the side jobs to buy specialty tools for my use. I was going to go and meet a mister Jones the friend of a former client who wanted to meet me and ask me what parts of a job I could do for him. I should have known there was something strange going on when he wanted to meet somewhere other than where the work was going to be done. We were meeting in a warehouse type building in the middle of town. I had been told what door to use and how to find the office once inside. I was not yet used to look for things that were not of face value and had a naïve trust of people. I was not ready for the con job that was laid on me. The man that I saw sitting at the desk with blueprints laid open was wearing tailored clothes and nice shiny shoes. The light blue shirt was offset by a nice mixture of burgundies in a print tie. The jacket hanging on a hook looked like fine wool and matched his trousers. The man gave the appearance of well-to-do with stylish hair and manicured nails. Mr. Jones started by telling me how pleased his friend had been with my work and my take charge attitude. He went on to compliment me about the timeliness and conservative price that I had gotten for my work. He went on to say that I gave all indication that I could ask more for my work and could probably lead a crew as a boss. Mr. Jones laid it on heavy but in a way that stroked my ego also. He asked me if I was interested in becoming independent with him as a silent partner in starting a new construction company.

We left the warehouse and went to a nice restaurant in town that would not balk at the casual attire that I was wearing. I had after all left my house to price some work for Mr. Jones and the blue jeans and work boots would have been fine for that. I had never been to this restaurant before but it was obvious that Mr. Jones was well known there. He was led to a table that was fairly well concealed from the entrance but he still looked around the room one time before he sat down. He ordered us a drink of choice and I simply showed my tastes by ordering a house tap beer while he had a club soda. He gave us time to look at the menu but never looked at one himself. Once I had ordered my meal, he casually brought the talk back to the question that he had asked me before. He asked me the scope of work I had done in the past and if I could do bigger estimates from blueprints. I assured him that I had done some larger scaled jobs in conjunction with my current employer and that I was often left to interpret blueprints on my own. He laid on some more of the ego statements similar to those he had said earlier. He said that he could find places that needed work to be done from his many associates that were in the area. He said that I could share part of the office space and warehouse where we had met earlier. He said that I could draw a salary until I could live on the percentage I would be making from the jobs. His one stipulation was that he would be involved in every bid that we would put out to the public so that he could keep his hand on the finances. He was interrupted by our meals being brought and I was surprised at the fact that he had not ordered a meal out loud.

I had taken the opportunity to think about giving him total control of the money part and simply drawing a salary. I made mention out loud to Mr. Jones that I used the income from these side jobs for some of the pleasures that I provided for my family. He asked me what I was drawing from my current employer and then was told that my salary could easily start at twice what I was getting now if I considered the profits from the work. The company would buy the tools that we needed and as the boss, I could hire people with some of the tools that we did not have and still make a profit on the work and time that they produced. He assured me that that was how the world of business was run. I was doing a lot of listening and dreaming in my head as I listened to the man. I would also take an occasional bite from my plate and sip on the second beer in front of me as I listened. The talk was slowing down when he asked me if I wanted to go and see the first job that he wanted to bid on.

We left the restaurant without ever receiving the check from the waitress. I thought that he may be running a tab as well as they seemed to know him. We went to another part of the city and went into a building that was just a shell. We drove around it first as Mr. Jones told me that a friend of his wanted to convert this building into office space on the middle two floors and wanted to make luxury apartments on the top two floors. The bottom floor was going to become storefronts for tenants. He said that the plans were all submitted and approved by the city. The owner wanted to start work as soon as two weeks from today. I am sure that Mr. Jones caught my apprehensive look as I thought of being ready to start this size of a job in two weeks. Mr. Jones assured me that we could make it come together with no problems and that this job would not require a solid estimate to get rolling. He told me that his friend had the banks approval for the entire project and that making timely draws on the work in progress was part of the total contract. Mr. Jones then asked me if I was ready to become a businessman and boss. I simply told him that I better get looking at the work to be done as we walked into the building.

The ride back to the warehouse did not have much talking involved as I was deep in thought and had some intimidation about the whole thing. Mr. Jones simply smiled and drove back through the early evening traffic. We went back to the office that the afternoon had started in and received a multipage set of blueprints from Mr. Jones. He told me that he did not need an answer before I had spoken to my wife. He told me that if I showed up at the office at four-thirty the next day we could finalize the agreement. He told me to think about all the things that I would like to buy for my wife by becoming a businessman. Things you never dreamed you could have. Think it over and get back to me tomorrow because my friend wants to get started right away.

I was brought back to reality by Don jumping down from the top bunk and stating that we would be called out to the mess hall in about three minutes. He just stood by the door and suddenly all the doors in the cellblock opened at once and we lined up by the door leading down the hall. We were lined up single file and led down to the round-a-bout where the control room for all of the prison was. When we were all ready to move at once, the door opened again and we went around to the other side of the circle. Once we were all within the circle, the door to the cafeteria opened up and in we went. We had not been allowed to talk in the hall but everyone started as we got into the seating area. We filed around the back wall of the cafeteria and came to where the trays were being filled for each of us. We could get a portion of bread, vegetables, potatoes, and what appeared to be a mushroom burger with lots of greasy gravy but no bun. There was also a cookie if you wanted it. We then passed by a drink table where we served ourselves and then were seated randomly. I went to the table that Don chose and soon met some of the other inmates in our cell block. Don quickly looked at me and told me that we would be marched out at the end of our twenty minutes whether we were done eating or not. I looked for a salt and pepper shaker but was told they were not allowed. Once I tasted the food on my tray, I decided that salt and pepper could probably not help what it was supposed to be. All four of us at the table spent the first few minutes making sure that we ate what we did not want to forfeit at the end of the twenty minutes. As the trays became freed of their items, the talk began about things that we could look forward to for the rest of the day. After the meal, most of them wanted to go out into the exercise yard because of the nice weather today. We would be allowed one hour this afternoon and they had been outside for an hour before I had arrived to my cell. This would be the only time that more than one cell block could be in contact with some of the other cell blocks. I was told that once we were removed another couple of cell blocks would use the yard.

I took the opportunity to ask how we got assigned to a cell block and if we could ever expect to be moved. I was told that within a couple of weeks I would get a chance to partition for a particular cell block of my choice. Don said that there were jobs that went with each of the cell blocks such as wood working or metal working. I might have to wait for an open bed but usually the first request was honored. I was also reminded that if I got into any kind of trouble I would be sent to the "hole". The hole was prison slang for solitary. It was a single occupant cell where your meals were brought to you and you only saw daylight for about one hour per day. I was told that it was the kind of place where a person might lose his mind in the quiet but foreboding cells. The guard then called out that we had one minute to put our trays back and line up for the return trip.

# Two

Don said that we had about one hour before we would get to go to the yard because another pair of cell blocks was already out there. They had eaten earlier and were out there already.

I got back onto my bunk and had the sudden added realization that I could not discuss any of what was happening around me with my wife. We were both accustomed to talking about the good things and the bad things of our day. I started to remember how we had been discussing taking a well deserved vacation to Aruba around Christmas. We certainly had the money to do these kinds of things since I had gone to work for Mr. Jones. Mr. Jones, what a joke on me. I found out as my world was crashing in around me that his real name was Tony Gatzee. He was blood kin to the Mafia in our area and I was his sucker. I made myself stop thinking about Tony and pictured my wife in her most recent bikini. I knew that I was really going to miss her and the boys. Even after more than ten years of marriage and two children, Bonnie was the center of my life and we had grown a mutual relationship that seemed to have no end to how high we could take it. We were both health conscious and had a home gym we would use together in the evening. Bonnie only weighed two pounds more now than when we were married. Often when she had come to the work sites where I had been employed, the men who did not know that she was my wife would be giving her the once over and even doing some cat-calling. Her blonde hair, long legs, and size six body were noticeable from near and far. My life when I had been employed as a carpenter had been much more physical than it had become when

I became the boss. It didn't take long to notice that I had to watch what and how much I would eat as well as increase my activity at home. We had done all this so that we could enjoy each other for the rest of our lives in activities we both enjoyed. It was just the two of us for several years when we would hike some area mountains or canoe around a lake. I had appreciated the fact that my wife was willing now to bring our sons, Ryan and Tyler, on these trips although we could not yet resume all that we used to do or as often.

Bonnie had not taken the trial very well and now all the promises from me that it was all going to work out had become a lie. We had several months to adjust things in our home so that Bonnie would be able to maintain living in our home. The government tried to seize our home and all that we possessed when they closed down my new business for money laundering. The memories of how I had been duped into believing that I could create such a successful startup construction company were very humbling. My lawyer was able to combine leverage for some of my testimony and the fact that we had owned the house for five years before the start of the company. He argued that the funds used to maintain the house were not exorbitant and had not been derived from the money laundering income.

Don startled me again when he came back off from his bunk and said that it was time to go into the yard. Just as with lunch, the doors in the cell block opened as one unit and we all milled over to the exit door. The afternoon yard time was mandatory so everyone went outside. The other two cell blocks had come back in and were nowhere to be seen. The two cell blocks totaled one hundred and sixty men who were not necessarily friends. Once I was outside I got a chance to take a look around the activity compound as it was called. Two of the sides of the compound were the walls of cell blocks that rose up nearly twenty feet. At the top of the walls, was a row of coiled razor wire approximately five feet in diameter. There were some sporadic items caught in the wire such as a part of a shirt and a couple of soccer balls that had become impaled in the wire. The wire was held by large tee shaped angle brackets every few feet. The other two walls were of chain link fencing that rose up equal to the walls of the building and then were topped with the same amount of razor wire. In the center of the chain link walls were guard towers that had a constant visualization of the yard and everyone in it. There appeared to be two armed guards with high powered assault rifles in the two towers. I was just starting to distinguish what was on the ground when Don touched me on the shoulder and startled me. He told me that no one was allowed to climb anything in the yard for any reason and if caught trying to scale one of the fences I could expect to be shot by one of the guards in the towers. He pointed out some areas with some partial barricading surrounding areas like the basketball court or weight lifting equipment. He said that if any trouble started in an area, the barricades would close each section off to contain the problems. Inmates would then be processed for any activities that could get them restrictions from the yard or even get the hole. He stated that any assault in the prison was as punishable as on the outside and could tack on several months or years to your time to serve.

We had begun to walk around a little as Don was telling me these things. I suddenly found that I was being yelled at by an inmate fluent in profanities. I tried to understand what was going on when Don told me that I had walked into the path of a horseshoe tossing game. By the time Don was able to tell me what the problem was; the rather large inmate was striding toward me with his fists clenched. The man was in my face and we were starting to draw attention when Don stepped between us. He told the guy to calm down before everyone got into trouble and managed to explain that I had never been here before. The inmate took one look at me and then around the yard and saw that two guards were already on the way over to us carrying some restraints and mob controllers. He quickly backed up a couple of steps. He left me with some parting instructions on prison etiquette and also that we could meet again. After the yelling stopped and the inmate went back to his game, the guards came over and spoke to Don and I. Don simply told them that I was totally new to the compound and had made a mistake that was not appreciated by the other inmate. They both told me that it would be to my benefit to learn about the compound as quickly as possible so as to not get into trouble accidentally because I would receive the punishment just the same.

The two guards left Don and I standing where we were so we moved over to speak to some inmates Don knew. I looked up at the towers and saw that we had been the center of attention by the high guards also. I looked at the inmate who was back at his game of horseshoes and was paying me no mind. The two new inmates that we were talking to knew Don from when they were together in the other cell block. I did not know if it was proper to ask these other inmates why they were in or how long their sentences were. I thought that they might overlook any incorrectness of it if I asked it as a general question about the prison. I was told by Don that it was not correct to ask directly but over time everyone knew what the other inmates were in here for and how long. Don said that it was common practice by the guards to goad someone they were having trouble with by using the slang for a crime and mention how many more years someone may have to enjoy their company. These comments were usually embellished with offers to see other sights such as the hole. He said that you will soon figure out that the guards love to add mental cruelty into the lives of the inmates. He said that I would learn the pet peeves that some of these guards had toward different crimes and the people who had committed them. He said that the warden had to keep certain criminals in secluded areas to allow for their safety such as sexual predators of children. He said that the violent criminals were more respected amongst the population here than the ones who preyed on kids.

We were still standing there talking when a couple of the inmates began to fight in the corner near us. In just a matter of a few seconds, there was a ring of onlookers cheering them on as the blood of one began to flow from his temple area over his right eye. Whistles started blowing and the sounds of partitions moving into place made us look for a place to stand that was further away from the action. By now there were several guards on the move with all kinds of equipment and lockdowns for the prisoners. When we were last able to see the two men, there was blood on both of them but there was no way to tell if it was all from one or if the other had gotten a laceration as well. A new loud buzzer started to go off and Don said he knew that was coming. He said that we were all to go immediately to our own cells or be subject to punishment as bystanders. I saw no reason to look for trouble so I joined the rest of the population that had not been partitioned off and were quickly going back to our cells. I did take a quick look up as I was nearing the door and I could see the guards with their weapons ready to fire into the yard where the fight was still going on. What will happen to them I asked Don as we neared our cell. It will depend a lot on how much trouble they have in getting everyone back under control. It could be that only the two fighters will get disciplined or it could go to all of the ones who were watching the fight as well. If it really gets serious and they have to use gas or something like that we may be kept in lockdown during our normal yard time for a few days. Like I said before, the guards use mental cruelty more than physical restraints because they don't have to work as hard to achieve order.

I was lying on my bunk after the evening meal that was as delicious as the noon meal and wondering how I was going to survive the rest of my time. The evening hours brought on a chill to the concrete castle I was visiting and I wished that I had a bigger variety of clothing with me. I had received a sheet and light blanket to use from the admitting clerks and got under them to keep warm. I spoke out into the cell and asked Don what time things would become quieter that evening. He told me that it never really got quiet but the lights would go dim at ten o'clock. He said that the time from eight to ten was when inmates would do the jobs they were given to keep the cell block cleaned down. The assignments lasted for one week and then others would get your assignment for a while. There are areas that will get mopped and there are walls to be scrubbed in the showers and general seating areas. He said that the cell doors would be open from eight to ten and we could watch TV or do or join odd games in the common area with other inmates. I sensed that it was going to be a very long night.

I dozed off somewhere after the lights were dimmed at ten o'clock. I had joined the others in watching a mindless rerun of the "Dukes of Hazard" because the other inmates wanted to see Daisy Mae in her short shorts. The following show was a reality show where the audience was expected to believe that the participants were the only people with intelligence. From my point of view, I would rather have had a chance to tuck the boys into bed and lie down beside Bonnie in our warm bed. I had not dozed long when I was awakened by the slamming of a cell door somewhere. I laid there in bed trying to remember where I was for a minute. It all came back to me very quickly and then I just rolled onto my back and stared at the bottom of the top bunk where Don was laying.

My mind went back to the day that I had told Bonnie about Mr. Jones's offer and how it would change our lives. I did not know at the time just how prophetic those words were going to be. She had listened to my repeating all the promises that I had been given. She took a candid look at the blueprints I had placed on the table and asked me if I could really do the scope of work required. She was quick to remind me that we were doing quite well the way our lives were. She asked me if I thought that we would enjoy the life that the new responsibilities would bring. I told her that the new income will mean no more side jobs on my own and would allow me to be home with her and the boys more instead of less. She said that we would both have to wait and see if that was true. She asked me if I trusted Mr. Jones with control of the money and assured her that I would have complete access to the books. She reminded me that I would have to give my current boss a notice of leaving for at least a week if not two in case I had to eat crow in the near future and ask for my job back. I snapped at her for the vote of confidence. She told me that she trusted me completely but she had no idea who Mr. Jones was and if he was honest. She had then gone to bed alone and left me looking over the blue prints. I had now come to rue that impulsiveness I had given in to.

I decided to give my current boss a notice the next day. He was more than polite and offered me congratulations on going on my own. He accepted the notice of only one week and told me that he would hire me back if it did not work out on my own. I did keep the information to myself that I was going to have Mr. Jones as a silent partner. I came to regret that as much as anything I had ever done because I later learned that my old boss knew that Mr. Jones was really Tony Gatzee and pure trouble. After the day's work was done, I went to meet Mr. Jones at the warehouse. He went to a small refrigerator that I had not noticed the day before and got me out a beer. He handed it to me and offered me a chair. I told him that I had given my notice that day and was ready to rock and roll into the business world. He congratulated me on making the choice and asked me if I had time to go to the building with him then. I noticed that he was dressed similarly as he had been the day before and still wanted to go to the work site. He told me that he was going to introduce me to the building owner there and then we were going to the restaurant to go over some of the details. We got into his luxury car again and were soon at the building. I noticed that the car that we parked beside was also a luxury car but had a sportier look to it. We walked right in a door facing the street and to the back of the building. We came to a small area that was working as a makeshift office and knocked on the door. A voice from inside told us to come it. The room was well lit though poorly furnished except for a vintage desk and an overstuffed chair diagonally placed in the room. A man was in the process of standing to his feet and coming to greet us when we opened the door. A smile came over his face as he said hello to Mr. Jones and called him Tony. The two exchanged handshakes and a man type shoulder hug and then stepped apart. Mr. Jones told me to meet Mr. Frank Gavin, the owner of the building. I shook his hand firmly and then took a step back to see what I could see. Mr. Frank Gavin was a man that was smaller in stature than Mr. Jones but had a little more age to his features and a pudgy little belly. The hand that I had shaken had not seen physical work for a long time. The clothes were similarly tailored as well as stylish hair showing the introduction of gray. A top coat hung in the corner near the end of the desk where a phone was placed. There were not many papers on the desk but there were depictions of the building with its new store fronts hanging on the wall in a frame. Frank saw me looking at the print and asked me if I was going to build his project. I assured him that I was going to make him proud of what would be the finished project. He smiled and slapped me on the shoulder nearest him. That's a man after my own heart Frank said to Mr. Jones.

We talked a few more minutes in the office and never did go into the building that night. The two of them said we could talk some more over drinks and a meal and we were soon on our way again. Upon arrival, we were taken to the same table as the night before. No one ordered anything but we were all brought out something to drink to our tastes. I felt that I was getting the opportunity to begin living a lifestyle that I could get used to. I looked at the menu as the two men spoke and ordered a chicken dinner when the time came. Frank ordered some sirloin tips with stuffed mushrooms and again Mr. Jones did not order out loud. The talk went to what unions we would have to use as tradesmen were needed and the men asked me if I was used to getting union people involved in the work projects I had done in the past. I assured them that I knew who had to do what but that I had not ever been the one to bring them on board. Mr. Jones said that he would help me get the first few involved and was sure I would get the knack of it very quickly. The two men asked me if I would join them in a bottle of wine as a little celebration of kicking this project off. We were soon getting some wine poured for us by the house wine master. He quietly walked away after setting the remaining wine in ice at the empty space at the table. A toast went up to the start of something big and prosperous. A second toast was offered up to future projects together. The timid part of me was thinking that that might be a little premature at this stage.

The meal was even better than the night before but it might have been helped by the flowing wine. The other two gentlemen seemed to linger over their food more than eat it. I on the other hand was hungry from a day of working and wanting to put some food with the alcohol. We had been talking for two hours about anything but work when I asked if we could call it a night so that I could go and see my family. Mr. Jones apologized for the thoughtlessness and we were soon at the warehouse so I could get my truck and go home. The two of them went to bring Mr. Gavin back to his building and his car.

The boys were already in bed when I got home that night and Bonnie was a little short at the thought of my having been drinking and then driving home. I tried to use the lame excuse that it was not my idea and how the men had wanted to celebrate a little. Bonnie just said that she did not have anything to celebrate about yet. I was lying there remembering this and thinking that I wouldn't be home to put the boys in bed for a long time to come.

# Three

I must have dozed off more soundly after that because I was awakened by the turmoil of getting ready to go to breakfast. I had not heard Don at all during the night but I heard his feet hit the floor and then he was urinating across the room. This lack of privacy was also going to take a little getting used to. There was a little area on the stainless steel unit that worked as a sink for washing your hands and getting water to brush your teeth. There was a stainless steel plate on the wall that was supposed to work as a mirror as you shaved and combed your hair. I was starting to understand why so many of the inmates had short hair and I made a comment to Don about my assumption. He told me that I was partly correct but that the hair was often used as a restraint by the guards or even other inmates in fights or assaults. I asked him what he meant by the assaults and if yesterdays fight had been one. Don said that there were areas of the prison where you could be without protection from gang related sexual assaults on other inmates. That was not a pleasant thought and I asked him what areas were the most vulnerable. He told me that it was not talked about but the laundry area was noted for times of trouble.

Breakfast was a similar ritual to the other meals but you could pick from hot items such as oatmeal or cold cereals. You had to like them the way they tasted naturally because you were given one packet of sugar for either one of the meals. The milk was obviously from powder and was served from a vat that kept it constantly stirred right beside a similar machine that gave you orange juice or the juice of the day. I was thinking that if any food was ever tainted around here that a lot of people were going to get sick because there was nothing so far except the sugar that was packaged. I joined Don with a couple of new people that morning that were obviously mad at another inmate and were talking about retaliation against him. As we all left to return to the cell block, one of the men looked me right in the eye and told me that if I spoke to anyone about their conversation I could be next. He did not wait for an answer from me before he left the table. Don simply said that you had to learn when to be quiet around here and it wasn't always smart to talk about some things the way they were. He said that the walls had ears and people were always found out about in this place if they spoke to anyone and then broke the rules.

When we got back to the cell block, it was open door time and the TV was on again. The today show was on and people were commenting about the progress or digress of the war in the Middle East. Don said that we would be allowed into the yard in about one hour for an hour as we had been yesterday afternoon. I did not know anyone in the common room except Don so I went and found a chair by itself and watched a little of the news as we waited to go outside. The early morning sun was cheering and warming as I slowly looked for a place where I could do something physical and loosen my aching muscles. I spotted a group of men who were playing basketball with too many players already but was invited to join in. It didn't take long to figure out that the game was being played a little more physically than is allowed on the courts on TV. I took a couple of elbows before I made my first shot at the basket that went cleanly in. I dropped back to see how some of the others were reacting when I noticed the two from the breakfast table. They used the game to get one of the other inmates knocked onto his back and then stomped on his hand as he tried to get himself up. In the turmoil of the game, it all looked innocent except for what I had heard at the table. I watched in silence as the injured man approached a guard to get his hand attended to in the infirmary. The man who had given me the warning walked by me and looked me in the eye again as the game resumed. I had to wonder if that was going to be the end of the disagreement or if it would continue in some other venue later on.

The yard time ended more peaceably than yesterday and we went in by the short blast of the time buzzer. Both cell blocks went in and returned to their appropriate cells. I had gone into my cell to lift up my shirt and see how many of the elbows I had taken that had left their marks. They appeared to be no worse than a two by four that might have fallen or hit me. A guard suddenly appeared at my door and told me to follow him quietly with no explanation whatsoever as to where we were going. I started to wonder if the walls really had ears and wanted me to tell what I knew about the incident in the yard. We waited by doors as the guard called for the doors to be opened by the people in the control room. We went out into the roundabout and went into an area that clearly stated prison personnel only at the door. The guard waited for the door to open and there was a man there who was not in uniform. The new man told the guard that he would call central when he wanted to have me transported back to my cell block. I was led into a room that only had two doors and a desk in it. The man sat behind the desk and told me to sit down across from him. He reached into a briefcase beside him and then turned and introduced himself to me.

"I am John Clark and I am going to be your case manager as you spend your time here with us," he said. "I will be a combination of liaison, advocate, and man from hell. I will be the person you will contact when you want to change cell blocks for any reason. I will be the person who will ultimately keep track of your total days here and if you ever get good time, I will hold that information. I can take any information you want to give to any official here in the prison and I will be your agent in getting you in touch with your lawyer if the need arises. There are times here in prison where a lawyer can be provided and help you face any allegations from within or without these walls. I will be the person that will get in contact with you if there is any outside news such as a family sickness or death and be your advocate in getting you transportation if it is required and possible. Let me inform you now that you will not get to your great aunt's funeral. I will also be the person who will be contacted if you get into trouble here. When a guard writes you up for anything, I get to see a copy and it goes into your file. I am responsible to the warden and must have your file as up to date as possible if he asks to see it. I would like to now go over with you all your personal information and the charges that you are serving time for currently."

We went over all the basic stuff about me and Bonnie. He had Ryan and Tyler named as sons and their ages. He took a minute to tell me about Angel Tree and how they gave gifts in place of me for my sons at Christmas. We discussed the charges at length for which I was serving and told him my lawyer was trying to appeal my conviction as to no prior knowledge. He told me that he would contact my lawyer and tell him how to get a message to me. We talked about what cell block I had considered and I told him I had no idea what was available. He asked me to verify that I was a carpenter and I assured him I was a master carpenter in the local union when I was arrested. He suggested the cell block that had a wood working shop as the first place to try for. He stated that doing something I was familiar with and good at would help pass the time here as well as giving some purpose to the time I was here. We ended the conversation with his telling me where to find the forms to contact him and that he had up to forty-eight hours to answer me. He told me to contact him with any questions and reminded me that I could make it easy on myself here or the guards would help me not enjoy the visit. Now let's get you back to your cell before lunch.

I found myself in the quiet time after lunch in my bed and thinking about my family. Bonnie and I had not been apart for more than an overnight since we had met in college. I had never missed seeing the boys in twenty four hours in the past and had been a part of all their birthdays, holidays, and school activities. What had blinded me to the truth so badly about Tony Gatzee? I remembered the first time that Bonnie and I had gone camping in the nearby National Forest. We had been like any young lovers and had been a little adventurous out by the lake. We had made love together as the sun came up in the Eastern sky and then gone into the lake for a swim without getting back into our clothes. We were just getting back out of the water when we heard a young voice tell her mommy to look at the people without clothes. We quickly got covered as the mother took her child in another direction. We laughed at getting caught as we took apart our tent and started the hike back to our car. Bonnie was always willing to having fun times that did not hurt anyone. That was not the only camping trip that we had to remember where we left an area quickly. I believe the one where we decided to tease a baby skunk until mama got our attention from the bushes taught us a little about nature's protective ways. That time we ran into the lake with all of our clothes hoping to get the smell out before it set into the material. We were able to laugh about that in about two days when the smell on our bodies started to dissipate. I had not thought that I was in danger of losing times like these when I went into the agreement with Tony Gatzee. I thought that we would have even greater memories to share.

The first day on the job with Mr. Jones was when he told me that his friends called him Tony. He supplied me with a cell phone as he asked me if the name for our company could be Able Construction. I told him that I was agreeable to the name and said that we would have to register with the state before the unions would work with us. I had gone to the city offices during the morning and registered the name and legal address for our company. At the time it never dawned on me why Tony would have me signing most of the legal documents for the company. He told me that I would be listed as the president of the company when his lawyers filed for the company to become an LLC. Tony was going to take the position of Chairman of the Board for Able Construction. We also signed a previously prepared contract for the work with Frank Gavin. I was to begin doing the layouts of the two office floors the next day. We were also to meet with some of the subcontractors that would be doing electrical, plumbing, heating, air conditioning, and some of the minor subs like the solid waste people at the work site at nine a.m. in the morning. As the work progressed, we would find a sheet rocker, painters, and masons for the stucco exterior. The permit for the building retrofitting called for most of the equipment and materials to be handled from the buildings own parking lot in the back and only when the front was being revamped could we block the sidewalks for a short time and with as many safety barriers as we needed. The entire project was scheduled to be completed in twenty-two to twenty-six months from starting date and was expected to cost fourteen million dollars. The kind of numbers I was not used to playing with. Tony told me that the same accounting firm that he was using for another business had agreed to take us on as a client. At the time I was so out of my league that I was being agreeable to everything he suggested.

The meeting the next day at the work site was almost a rerun of Tony telling me what we were doing. The subcontractors were all handpicked by Tony and there were very few questions from any of them about my inexperience or our new company. He was on a first name basis with most of them and assured me that none of them would disappoint me any more than they had for him in the past. There was the exchanging of phone numbers on a sheet of paper that was then copied and given to each of us. I was also given the name of several material suppliers in the area with a preferential order to a couple of them. I then ran around town establishing accounts and ordering some materials to be delivered to the site. Bonnie told me that she was sure I could do this as we lay in each other's arms that night. I remember giving her a macho line from a movie to keep from telling her of my insecurities.

# Four

The days in the cell block started to become habitual. I spoke to Don on a regular basis and tried to keep out of trouble everywhere. I was now also speaking to a man named Danny who seemed to have the ability to keep a low profile here in the cell block. I did get a message from John Clark that I was going to be visited by my lawyer on Monday around two in the afternoon. I wasn't given a clue about why the meeting was being called but I let myself hope that there was going to be a change coming up. One day in the yard I was minding my own business near the weight lifting bench when two inmates started fighting beside me. One of the inmates was thrown onto my by the other and I was written up for pushing the guy off from me by the guard who only saw me push him and not the start of the fight. I started to argue my case with the guard but he told me to shut up or get a double violation for the non-compliance with an officer as well as fighting.

I spent a lot of time thinking about Bonnie and the boys. We were not allowed to have visitors for the first two weeks upon arrival to the prison. I got to speak to her one Sunday afternoon and she told me that she had received a letter stating she could start visiting me on Tuesday evenings and she intended to come the day after I was to meet with my lawyer. Bonnie asked me if I knew yet what the lawyer was coming to speak to me about. I had to tell her that I still did not have a clue as to why he was coming. I got to speak to the boys and it broke my heart when Tyler asked me when I was coming home. I could only tell him it would be a little while yet before I could come home.

I also had time to think about the sequence of events as they progressed as Tony and I opened our business. I remembered more about some comments made by two of the subcontractors about how they were to write the invoices for payment from Mr. Gavin. I did not find it strange that our company was to have the invoices written in our company name but the fact that they had to give a duplicate copy for Mr. Gavin was not standard. They all did it like it was normal business for them when they worked for Tony. I was busy most of the time telling people what to do and pursuing subs and materials. We set up a system to keep tract of the men that I was using from the unions such as carpenters and laborers as well. I was responsible for totaling everyone's hours for billing Mr. Gavin as well as the subcontractor invoices; to which we would add management fees and profit for ourselves. I signed and sent those invoices twice a month. Tony had been good to his word and I was getting paychecks that were at least twice what I used to make. The lawyers fixed it so that it looked like I was leasing my truck to the company. We were using company funds to pay me for the use of my truck, cell phone, and health insurance for my entire family. I had done some of the numbers from the invoices and what I knew the company was being paid for and thought that we should be making a large profit on this job. When I asked Tony one day about our financial standing, he said that we were just starting to make some money in our second quarter. I just thought that there had to have been some start up costs such as lawyers that I did not know about. About once a month, Bonnie and I would have dinner with Tony at the restaurant and it seemed as if he was trying to make sure he knew everything about what was going on in our home. He said that some of the personal questions were just fatherly but Bonnie and I decided that we would be careful what we said during one of these dinners. Tony owned enough of my soul at work that I did not want him to have some leverage over our private lives as well.

I remembered the day that Ryan had been born. Bonnie and I had done the Lamaze classes together and her mother had come along as a substitute coach if I was not around or could not be reached. We were in a class with six other women and their pair of coaches. We had waited for an opening to come available in our area so Bonnie was in her third trimester when we had begun the classes. Bonnie and the other women would listen to a lecture about the things that would happen during the birth and then they would all get on makeshift beds and start their labor. The classes went on for several weeks and we were on the last scheduled day when Bonnie suddenly felt a pain and some fluid ran down her leg. She was embarrassed at first and did not say anything until she had another pain. When the instructor came over to our table and began to talk to us, she witnessed the second pain sensation that Bonnie was having. She then asked us what hospital we had chosen for the delivery and told us we might want to notify them and do as they said because Bonnie's water had just broken and she was starting labor. I tried to remain calm but was not doing a very good job of it. We arrived at the hospital about one hour after the first labor pain. Bonnie was brought into an examining room and was told that she was already more than half way dilated. They then moved her into the delivery room and asked us to wait a few minutes so they could have the room to set up the monitors and such. I didn't think that babies were usually born this quickly and wondered if anything was wrong. Her mother assured me that everything seemed to be well with the baby and Bonnie and that she just appeared to be having a very easy delivery compared to most women.

I really didn't get to coach her much as Ryan was received into the world by the doctor. We both got to see him and then he was taken across the room for the measurements, clean-up, examined, and then placed into some warm baby blue blankets. We were asked if we had chosen a name for the boy and Bonnie told them to call him Ryan. We were both excitedly ecstatic as they brought Ryan over to us so we could take some pictures of everyone. Bonnie's father had arrived after the birth and was allowed to join us in her room. My parents lived out of town and would not be able to see their first grandson until tomorrow. I called a few of our close friends to tell of Ryan's arrival as Bonnie took a short nap. Life couldn't get much better than this.

We had waited just over two years before Bonnie would get pregnant for Tyler. We were ok with having two sons that would share more of the same interests together as they grew up. Ryan was almost too young to help with his brother until a year or so later. We had a good life going as I worked through the union most of the time and was making good money. I started the side jobs after Tyler was born because we had decided that Bonnie would stay at home for the first few years with the boys. While we were both working, we had bought the house and paid off both vehicles. We were starting to have a substantial nest egg even before going to work for Tony. We were not extravagant in the way that we lived. We did not eat out on a regular basis and created vacations and things from what we had or could use from friends and family. Our visits to my parents only required the gas to get to their house and we would barbecue as the weather allowed or picnic in one of the state parks in their area. We had been happy and strongly knit together. We were together so much that we only had a few friends outside of our family. The trip to Aruba around Christmas was going to be our first big splurge as a family. We thought that the boys were now old enough to enjoy some of the things we could try there like snorkeling. I was thinking that I would like to thank Tony for having ruined that part of our lives as well.

Bonnie had proven to be as good at raising a family as she had been as my friend and companion. Ryan was able to count to one hundred and say the alphabet before he had started school. Tyler wasn't very far behind because of the bond the two brothers had. It was wonderful to see the camaraderie that the time spent nurturing one another had produced. One did not have to look very far in the prison to see how families turned out that were at odds with one another. Many of the prisoners did not get visitors who had a true relationship with them but were mere friends. We did what we could to get our sons to interact with children their own ages when we took them to parks or other family oriented places. They had been taught to share toys and the likes with others and did not know what to make of a young boy in the park who took off with their ball. We had tried to explain some of the reasons a young boy could have had to do that and not to worry about it, but they both talked about the boy's action for a few days until we replaced the ball. I could see some of the same actions and attitudes in many of the inmates here. An attitude that said

I am the only one who is looking out for me and I do not want to be hurt or limited by others. It was an attitude that left them not trusting anyone of the human race. I wondered if I could ever become that calloused about life even in a place such as this. I hoped not.

Bonnie and I had been very proud to see the tenderness that our sons could display about life. Ryan was a little over five years of age and Tyler was an advanced two year old when we took them on a day trip into a natural wildlife preserve. It was one of those that had designated pathways and premade bridges to get across little rills and the like. We had not traveled very far when the boys started to pick some of the wild violets from the area near the pathway and giving them to Bonnie. She took them from the boys but told them that if they picked all the flowers no one else would get to see how lovely they were. We traveled a little further and a red squirrel began to bark at the boys from a nearby balsam limb. The boys laughed at how the entire squirrel seemed to vibrate with his barking. Bonnie reached into our backpack and brought out some trail mix we had brought for the walk. She showed the boys how to pick out some peanuts and toss them near the angry little squirrel. It took only a couple of minutes before it recognized the food that the boys had set out for him. They watched in amazement as the squirrel scurried over the ground and picked up several of the peanuts at once and ran off to hide them or eat them from a safer place. A little farther down the road the boys spotted a partridge on the ground and asked if they could try to catch it because if may be hurt. Bonnie and I just smiled as we told them to try and catch the wary bird. The partridge tolerated their pursuit for a few feet but then launched up with a loud thunder of its wings. The boys just came back to us and told us that they thought that the bird was ok after all. We continued into a valley and the woods became mixed hardwoods with their large green leaves and softwoods with their prickly short needles. We taught the boys that the trees that they saw in the autumn with all the colored leaves were the hardwoods and how nature had them go dormant during the winter. They both remembered that the green ones stayed green all year. We showed them the pastel green colored ends on the branches and taught them that that was how much the tree had grown so far this year. The boys were just taking this all in and loving it.

We sat the boys down at a vantage point in the small valley overlooking a narrow meadow and a meandering brook passing through it. We told the boys that if we sat there quietly for a little while we might see other animals that lived in the forest. Fortunately for us, a white tailed doe came across the meadow soon after we sat down. Ryan was the first one to see her and he pointed excitedly and said look. We had him be quiet so we could watch her for a little while before she ran off. She ambled out into the lush meadow and browsed as she went. After every bite she took, she would raise her head to look and listen. She would cock her ears in different directions as the calling of a blue jay or a crow could be heard. Her short white tail danced nervously on her rear. Suddenly she planted her feet sharply and galloped off away from the direction she had come with her tail straight up in the air. We signaled for the boys to be quiet and then we were treated to a shimmering red coat gliding along following the scent of the doe. The red fox did not have a chance of killing a healthy doe but he may have been looking for her fawn. When a rabbit suddenly broke from his cover in the field, the boys got to see how fast both the rabbit and the fox could be. About twenty seconds after they both went out of sight, there came a few piercing cries and then silence. The boys asked what the cries were and I told them that the fox had probably caught the rabbit and the screams were its getting killed by the fox. They were both upset at the thought of something getting killed but seemed to understand as we tried to tell them of the cycle of life where something had to die so that others could live. We talked to them about how even vegetables and grains had to die for us to enjoy them at our table.

The walk took on a little somberness as the boys walked along. Tyler did not make it very far before he was ready to get into the carrier I had brought in. He had to take nearly three steps to make up one of ours. He did have to ride backwards so Bonnie walked behind me and I held onto Ryan's hand. We stopped one more time to rest as we looked into the waters of a small brook at some trout. Bonnie told the boys to watch as she placed the tufts of a dried plant in the water near us. The trout would charge up from the deeper water to see if the tufts were edible but were never fooled into biting one. We soon left the stream and continued back toward the car. I saw a hawk that was circling above another meadow in search of food and I told the boys to watch it for a while. They were amazed to see it dive straight down and come back up from the ground with a snake in its talons. The hawk took it over to a tree and soon was pulling it apart to eat it. The boys said that they were glad that the hawk had killed the snake for its dinner. When we scared a rabbit by the trail, the boys told it to watch out for the fox that had caught its relative. A few song birds finished out the afternoon and we were soon on our way home. I barely had time to put Tyler in his car seat before he fell asleep as only exhausted hunters can. I too was glad that I did not have to carry the nearly thirty pound boy on my shoulders any farther.

# Five

The memories helped me pass the time in this unforgiving pile of concrete and steel. I wondered how long they would be able to sustain my mental stability before it started to fade into anger or some other emotion. The afternoon sun in the yard was really starting to be hot now as the sun climbed higher into the Southern sky and became more directly overhead. I don't know what started the fight on this particular Saturday but it became violent quickly and several inmates got in on the act. I wondered if it was like the time that I heard the two talking about the inmate they later broke the hand of in the yard when I first got here. There was a lot of kicking going on after one of the inmates fell to the ground unconscious. By the time the guards got to the inmate he was not moving at all. The other participants were led in shackles to the hole. Just to reinforce their authority, the guards imposed a lockdown for both cell blocks to give people time to think about the consequences. We heard later on in the cafeteria that the one inmate had been killed. All the inmates in both cell blocks were given a piece of paper to tell what they had seen in the yard. The paper was to keep it anonymous and definitely safer for anyone that had the courage to say anything or give up some names. It was not totally necessary because the cameras had been focused on the fight as soon as it began and the inmate delivering the death blow to the head of the down inmate was charged with murder and could now face death row. His accomplices would get added time to their existing sentence as well as a long time in the hole as they awaited a new trial. It became known later on that the fight started over someone cheating at a game in the yard. It seemed mindless to me and increased my level of fear about this place. It was almost an imposed time of safety with the lockdown for those two days.

We were finally going to get a chance to go back into the yard on Monday afternoon but I decided to stay in the common area until I met with my lawyer. My stomach was in complete knots as I tried to figure out what he might possibly need with me. One of the transport guards finally came to get me and we went to the same room where I had met with John Clark by the control center. He left me once the door opened and he could see my lawyer inside at the table. The formalities of saying hello and a couple of general questions about how my time was going here and then he got ready to be serious. I told him about witnessing the murder yesterday and told him it was a fun place to visit. He just looked at me before he brought out an entire notebook full of loose papers from his briefcase for me to look at. I looked at them quickly and noticed that they were mostly invoices Able Construction had received and those that I had created for our billing Mr. Gavin. He asked me if I was familiar with the documents that he had placed before me and asked if that was my signature on most of them. I told him that it was and asked him what difference it would make at this point of the game. He told me that he had been denied access to these papers by the prosecutors during my trial and that they were definitely critical to my defense. He asked me to explain the process that I used to give Tony the numbers on the invoices for Mr. Gavin. I went through it all as best as I could remember from my receiving the invoices of my subcontractors and the material handlers. I told him how I thought it strange that my subcontractors gave me two invoices for the same work with two names on them every time. He asked me if I had made any copies of the duplicate invoices anywhere in my office. I told him that I had kept a couple of the first ones to make sure I had done them correctly when I gave them to Tony in completed form. I told him that I had only charged one of the invoices from our subs to the invoices that we submitted but I gave both copies of all the invoices to Tony. I told him that I would submit one time charges from each of our subs as a line item that we would charge management and profit to on our invoices to Mr. Gavin. I would sign them as president of our company but that I never received the money from Mr. Gavin or made any deposits of money. He asked me if he could get the copies of the first few invoices that I had submitted for payment. I told him that they were in my safe at home and that Bonnie could supply them to him. I asked him if they were relevant to my case. He told me that I better sit down and listen to him for a minute. He made me promise that I would do nothing on my own and would only do what he asked me for. He also made me promise that I would not get angry enough to get into trouble here if he told me what he was working on. I agreed to both of the promises and then got ready to hear him out.

He told me that if I could supply him with the real invoices as I turned them in to Tony, he felt that he could get my case looked at again. He said that it could take a long time but if a judge found in our favor he might even be able to get me back out on bail awaiting my new trial. He told me that the second invoices were being paid by Mr. Gavin as a way to launder the money to himself and obviously Tony. I just sat there stunned at the thought of how stupid I really could be. Tony had not yet gone to trial because his lawyers were stretching out the legal system anticipating they could create a crack in the case. If I could produce the actual copies, he was sure that the federal prosecuting attorney would look favorably at my case and even consider dropping the case against me for testimony against Tony and Mr. Gavin. They were much bigger fish and had their hands in a lot of other illegal activity in the city. I asked him if Bonnie and the kids would remain safe while this was going on or if someone with Toni's given nature would try to force my silence. He assured me that the paper copies would mean that even if he could scare me that he was still going to prison for a long time. I'll bet that he did not know what you did to him in your rightful mistrust of him. I need you to write down the papers that you want Bonnie to make new copies of so you know that you can trust me and tell her to call me as soon as she has them ready. You will retain a copy in your possession and no one will really know where they came from until it is too late for them. He urged me to tell no one here in the prison and for Bonnie to do the same at home. We have to pull their teeth before we give them something to chew on. I wrote out where to find the folder in our safe for Bonnie and then we parted.

The next evening Bonnie sat on the other side of a glass wall as we spoke on the intercoms at each booth. She looked radiant to me as well as scared and concerned. She had worn a very conservative navy blue jacket over a white pullover shirt and black slacks that were not tight. I knew the hour glass figure that she had concealed from wandering eyes there in the visiting room. She told me how much that she wanted to bring the boys but had decided against even telling the boys where she was going tonight. She told me that she had not known that she could not bring them in until she read the sign on the visitor entrance near the parking lot. I asked her if she had heard from my attorney that day. She said that she had but he did not want to meet until I had a chance to tell her what to expect. I told Bonnie that I would not describe what I wanted her to do because I knew they could have bugged the intercoms to get information about anyone in the prison. I told her that she had written instructions that could change our entire situation with me in prison. I simply asked her to trust me and to not talk to anyone and I meant anyone outside about what was going on. My lawyer will tell you what is going on face to face so no one can hear. I do not trust anyone anymore I told her because of how far Tony could reach without our knowing about it. She then started to tell me how Ryan had brought home a toad that had been hurt and he wanted to make it better. Bonnie had to tell him that the best thing they could do was to take him behind the house and let him loose in the tall grass. He would be able to feed himself and heal from the minor wound that he had. I was again reminded of how tenderhearted our sons were. The hour was too quickly over and Bonnie was gone again.

The mat on my bunk seemed a little bit harder that night as I tried to keep all my emotions in check. There was the hope that my lawyer was right and I might be able to get my life back with my family. There was the very short hour of seeing my lovely wife that was dampened by the glass not allowing us to touch. I missed my sons and they were not going to be able to come to the prison and see me. There was the anticipation anxiety about Bonnie finding those papers in the safe and getting copies made for my lawyer. Then he would have to get a prosecuting attorney to look at all the new evidence in the light of truth. Would they believe it and bring it before a judge that could grant me a new trial or even trade my testimony for my freedom. That was almost too much to hope for as I tossed and turned in the darkness.

I must have finally fallen asleep because it was now time to go to breakfast with the rest of the guests. I realized as I roused from my sleep that I had been dreaming of playing with my sons in the city park. It had been a bright, sunny, and peaceful day of playing in the park as we wanted to and not where I was now. There was some interspersed spells of peace here in these confining walls and wire barricades but the danger that lurked about was far more prevalent. It was a world that prescribed danger by its own inception. The law of nature said that if you put enough violent men in the same place with minimal constraints, you could expect violence. There is nothing to deter a criminal with a life sentence from incurring more prison time for another crime even in a prison. When you got to listen to most of the men in here, they were not speaking about going home and picking up the pieces of their shattered lives but who they wanted to hurt during the short time they were going to be on the outside. The number of people in the prison where I was that expected to go home to a different life could probably be counted on your two hands. A federal prison was not where I had ever imagined that I would be.

# Six

I was not to know for a couple of weeks about how the meeting had gone with Bonnie and my lawyer. My lawyer had made a copy of the written instructions that I had given for Bonnie and mailed it so that she would have all the copies when they met for the first time. Bonnie had gone into our safe and gone down to the local drug store to make the copies rather than having to answer questions from anyone we knew. She had taken my advice that we could not trust anyone at this time except for a few people who were interjected into our lives before such as the babysitter. She had even placed the copies in the coloring book she had brought Tyler to keep him quiet so as to not look as if she was bringing anything to the office. She had not gotten dressed any differently than she would any day that she left our house to take the boys somewhere or go to a store. To have gotten dressed up could have aroused someone's suspicion if she was being watched. Bonnie began to take notice of the cars that remained in our neighborhood for any period of time that did not belong there. She would even look for piles of cigarette butts after the cars were gone to see if they might have been occupied for a while by someone who could be canvassing the neighborhood and our house in particular. She took out our binoculars that we carried on hikes to take down license plate numbers on questionable vehicles she could see from our windows during the day. She would draw all the shades to windows that could look in on their privacy during the nighttime. I had never known that Bonnie could take on the role of protector so well but I also knew better than play with a sow's cub. I also knew that Bonnie was a crack shot with a rifle.

Bonnie had left the house that day the way she would any day and brought Tyler with her. The lawyer's office was on the second floor of a building that had multiple types of business offices in it so it would not be obvious that she was going to my lawyers if she was being watched. She looked around one more time before walking up and entering into the reception area. A woman in a white blouse and lavender colored slacks sat behind a desk with dictation plugs in her ears stopped typing when Bonnie came in. She dropped the plugs down on her desk as she walked to the only other door in this room, knocked softly, and then went in without an answer from within. She appeared as suddenly as she had left and told Bonnie Mr. Segal will see you now and to go right in. Bonnie knew my lawyer from my trial but had never been the center of attention before. She sat Tyler on her knee as she took the chair being offered to her.

Bernie Segal asked her if she had received the instructions that he had mailed to her. She did not answer directly but handed over about twenty copies of duplicate invoices she had found in the safe where I told her they were. "Did you also get my warning about not talking about this to anyone you cannot trust explicitly. I even suggest now that the less people know about any of this, the less apt they are of becoming endangered by Tony or any of his people. I do not mean to imply that you are in any danger but the very nature of these people cannot be trusted."

Bonnie replied, "I have not spoken to anyone and I am now being more vigilant about the neighborhood and anywhere I go. I took in a special letter to the school that Ryan goes to and they said they would watch for any strangers who showed any interest in him at all."

Bernie said, "You can never be too cautious but I do not think that Tony believes he has any reason to fear any fallout from Sam while he is in prison already. I seriously think that when I present this to the federal prosecuting attorney that we will try to get Tony and Mr. Gavin imprisoned because of their being a flight risk. I am going to prepare all these invoices with the ones that they presented at the trial and prove that they were solely responsible for the money transactions that were illegal. I am going to try and get your husband's sentence reversed and while we are pursuing that in the court system, I hope to get him out on bail."

Bonnie said, "My head is spinning just about now and what you have told me that this information as evidence might do. Do you think that there is any real hope for that to happen?"

He assured her that there were all kinds of hope for that to happen. "The next time we get in front of a judge, I want to have pulled out all Toni's and Mr. Gavin's teeth and have the truth bite them into reality. The reality should become that they are going to prison for a long time instead of your husband."

Bonnie was almost beside herself by this time and just gave Tyler a hug as something to express her happiness at the news. Bonnie just sat there with Tyler on her lap continuing to hug him as Bernie looked at the duplicate invoices. "This is the proof that will set your husband free," he said again. Bonnie asked if there was anything else she could do to help.

Bernie assured her, "The only thing she should do now was to keep quiet about the information she had given him and do everything to remain safe and wait for the bomb to be dropped. By their using the subcontractors to help launder the money, they have committed racketeering as well as money laundering. We may even be able to bring in the falsified documents as perjury and jury tampering against your husband. Each document can be used as a charge of perjury and maximum sentence of three years for each count. The count of jury tampering with false evidence is good for fifteen years by itself."

Bonnie tenderly picked up Tyler and started for the door but she had to turn around and say thank you to Bernie before she left. Bonnie stopped in to one of the storefronts in the building and bought a shirt for each of the boys before going out to her car. She especially did not want anyone to know where she had gone now. As she walked out of the building, she noticed a man whom she had seen on the way in that was still sitting on a bench in view of the door and her car. She nervously went to her car and fastened Tyler into his car seat before getting into her seat and locking the doors. She pulled out of her parking space when she was able and went toward the entrance of the lot. She turned back in on another access and went back by where she had just been parked. The man was gone from the bench and she could not identify him in any of the vehicles that she could see. This time she went out of the lot and down the street away from their home. She decided that she would stop in a safe area and call to tell Bernie what she had possibly seen and she described the man to him.

Bernie told her," You should take any precautions you feel necessary and possibly get the police involved for protection. You should make a plan for a safe house to go to with people you can count on if you're in any danger or are being followed. I will hurry in getting this evidence to a federal prosecuting attorney."

Bonnie drove into our block from the opposite direction than was normal if you were coming from downtown. She did not see any strange cars or the man that she had seen before. She took Tyler out of his car seat and grabbed the two shirts as she continued on into the house. She decided that she was not going to endanger the boys by trying to keep them safe on her own. Once she had locked the doors and checked the surrounding areas she made two calls. She called the local police and asked them to send someone over to take a report on a suspicious stranger in the area. She then called her father and asked him to come over if he could that she needed him. Her father agreed to be over within the hour and then she tried to think of what else she might have to do to be safe. She started by making a mental sketch of what she could see from any window of her house during the day time and if there were any dangerous blind spots to avoid. She took several knives that we had for camping and placed them out of reach of the kids but in places she could get to. She taped one to the bottom of her grandmother's hutch near the hallway but was interrupted by a knock on her door. She put the other two knives in opposite desk drawers before answering the door.

The two policemen who came to the house were familiar with who I was and what other cases were involved with me. Bonnie was very careful to not make any mention of the new evidence but went into great detail about the man that she thought was following her around town and that she feared for her safety and that of the boys. She told them that there had been two cars hanging around the block at different times recently that did not belong there. She had not even told me so that so I would not worry any more than I already was. She gave the license plate numbers to the policemen as she gave them her report. They asked if Ryan went to a private or public school and if she felt he was safe there. Bonnie told the officers that she had given the school a formal letter of concern for her son and they were placing extra eyes on the playground during the times of highest risk. They took down all the information and the description of the man before they prepared to leave. They told her that 911 was still her best bet and that she should try to teach the boys when and how to use it. They were opening the door to go out again when her father came in to see why there was a police car out front. Bonnie thanked the officers and told her father that she would explain everything as soon as they had left.

Bonnie had to start by telling her father that there was nothing going on at this minute and if he would just calm down she would tell him why she had called him over. She assured her father that Ryan was at school and Tyler was in his room playing as she had directed him to do. They could both hear him playing an electronic game and making noises like explosions when he apparently scored a hit so he was convinced. She asked him if he wanted some coffee with her and he said yes so she took the time to get it for the two of them. When she put the two matching cups that belonged to Bonnie and myself down for the two of them, she said now I can begin. "Dad you know as well as any of us that Sam did not do any of the things that he was accused of."

He assured her that he knew that also but they had found some papers that stated differently.

Bonnie stated, "Yes, we all know about that but before I go any further I have to warn you that there may be some danger involved in my telling you what has come about. I believe that I have people following me around and watching the house and that is why I just had the police come and take a report. I do not want to see anyone get hurt especially any of my family but I do not know what these people want or what they are capable of doing. I just know that I do not have many people I can trust if there really is some danger involved. I need to find somewhere that I can go with the kids if we were in danger and it has to be somewhere that they would not look for us. That means that it can't be your house directly but I hoped that between us we could come up with a place that could be a safe haven until the police arrived. I also mean to discourage them from watching everything that we do on a regular basis and what routes we use to get there. I am even coming and going from our house here in different directions. If you feel that you want any part of this, I will tell you more but I won't tell you if you don't want me to. You can just help me find a safe haven and I will understand and respect your wishes from there."

He was very quick in deciding that he was willing to be in danger himself to help us out.

Bonnie started again, "We cannot talk about this outside of our own families she told her father. We found that Sam had put away copies of some of the invoices that had been manipulated by Tony and Mr. Gavin to make him look guilty. The lawyer is going to approach the same federal prosecuting attorney who brought the case to trial and give him the proof. He says that they could end up in jail for the rest of their lives so when the charges come down we do not know what they would be capable of. He is going to ask that they be remanded until they stand trial because they are a flight risk. The lawyer assures me that with hard copies of all the evidence that Tony and Mr. Gavin would gain nothing by trying to hurt us or even if they will know who turned on them. This information could come from any subcontractor that Sam was using on the jobs and that is why they will also face racketeering charges, falsifying evidence, and jury tampering. If our lawyer is right, he is going to get all the charges dropped eventually and meanwhile we anticipate being able to get Sam out on bail until his new trial."

Bonnie's father told her that he would do what he could and that he was glad to hear the good news. "I already have a safe haven picked out and I am sure that the owners will be totally agreeable."

Bonnie spoke up sharply, "Dad, do not tell me where it is! We cannot talk about this any more than is absolutely necessary and with people who can have no ties to Tony Gatzee or Frank Gavin."

# Seven

Bonnie and her father were just saying goodbye to each other when the telephone rang. Bonnie said hello and then her face turned ashen as she took a deep breath and sat down hard in a chair. Her father took the phone from her and asked who was on the line. This is the Carter School where Ryan attends came the reply and we just had an incident involving a stranger trying to lure him away from the school yard. Just tell me that he is all right her father said into the phone. The reply must have been affirmative because he simply said that they would be there immediately. They placed Tyler into his car seat and Bonnie's father drove hastily over to the school where there were two police cars in the school's parking lot and others could be seen down the street. An officer was walking a dog on a leash as they seemed to be checking the bushes along the street. Bonnie and her father parked near the police cars and walked up to the first officer that they found. They identified themselves and were directed to a Sergeant Benoit in the school principal's office without any of their questions being answered. Bonnie recognized the principal standing in the door and she was told that everything was ok and she told them that they had to speak to the Sergeant. As they walked in to the office, they could see Ryan speaking nonchalantly to the Sergeant. Ryan looked up and simply said hi to his mother, brother, and grandfather. The Sergeant asked them if he could speak to them privately in another room and asked Ryan to excuse him for a few minutes. They left Ryan and Tyler with one of the school secretaries in that room.

When the three of them got into the other office with the door closed, Sergeant Benoit asked, "Do you know who might have tried to lure Ryan away from the school grounds Mrs. Walker? The principal showed me a letter of concern for Ryan's safety from you as he directed his stare at Bonnie."

Bonnie looked at her father, took a deep sigh, and then sat down in a chair so as to calm herself. Bonnie started, "Sergeant Benoit, do you know who I am?"

He replied that he had some familiarity with Sam's being in prison for money laundering.

Bonnie then said to him, "Sam never laundered money for them and we intend to prove that in a court of law but Tony Gatzee and Mr. Gavin have not gone to trial yet for the same charges and a couple more. I have had reason to suspect that I have been followed as I do my errands in town and also observed by someone at our home. I called a couple of your officers out to my house earlier today to report having seen a man who was obviously trailing me and a couple of cars I have been observing near our house from the street. I just gave the description to them about an hour ago and gave them the two license plate numbers that I had copied. My father and I were just saying good bye from that meeting when the phone call came from the school. I am not sure if Tony Gatzee and Mr. Gavin are trying to attain my husband's silence by fear and intimidation or if it is just somebody trying to harass my family."

Sergeant Benoit said that everything that Bonnie had told him added up to more than just coinciding events. A light knock on the door startled Bonnie as she sat there. The officer told the Sergeant that the dog had picked up something near the last sighting but had lost the scent after crossing a couple of yards and reaching the curb to the next street. I believe that he got in a car there and left the area. Sergeant Benoit told the officers, "Get everyone back to the parking lot and I will meet with them there in five minutes." He looked back at Bonnie and her father and said, "I would like you two to go home and to keep a sharp eye on the area. I believe this close call will slow things down whether it was a sexual predator or one of Toni's men because they do not like to be the center of attention. I will pass this up the chain of command and I expect that a detective will want to speak to you tomorrow. Please do not do anything rash on your own unless you are in immediate danger and let us do the work we are trained to do."

Bonnie and her father stopped to get Ryan and Tyler from the other room on their way out the door. They thanked the principal for her help and went toward their car. Sergeant Benoit was with the other officers in the parking lot and waved to them as they left. Bonnie looked at her father and told him how glad she was that he was there when they got the call. I just don't think I could drive right now. They had buckled the two boys into their seats and pulled out of the parking lot. She looked over her shoulder as Ryan who was sitting in the back seat looking at a paper from school said, "Look mom, I got a hundred on this spelling paper today."

She took the paper from him and said, "Congratulations Ryan on your hard work. You are such a smart little man. You can teach Tyler some of the words that you had to learn."

When they arrived at the house, Bonnie had the boys come inside to play for today. She perused the street carefully from her window and also the back yard but did not see anyone or anything out of the ordinary. She then settled down in the living room with her father who seemed to be deep in thought.

Her father said, "I am trying to decide on the safest way to eliminate the most danger. If you and the boys are being watched and you move out after this incident, you may escalate their determination. If it was not Toni's men and was a sexual predator that was at the school, we could show our hand by moving you to what may be a safe haven in the case of an emergency. It might be best if your mother and I came here to stay for a few days as we see what the lawyer and Sergeant Benoit can unfold. Have you told Sam about any of this?"

Bonnie stated to her father, "The last time I went for a visit this was just speculation and I did not want to concern Sam with my imagination. To hear him speak about the prison he makes it sound dangerous in there." Bonnie stood nervously and moved to where she could hear the boys playing in their room. Something caught her eye in the back yard and she got the binoculars to have a better look. By the neighbors fence across their back yard was some movement in the afternoon shadows. She almost laughed at herself when she could see that it was a fat, red breasted Robin pursuing an afternoon snack. Bonnie told her father that the company might be a good idea so she could get some rest as they took turns canvassing the neighborhood. With that decided her father called her mother and gave her a brief account of the afternoon. He told her to pack enough for an overnight stay and that he was coming over to pick her up. He told Bonnie that he would pick up some Chinese food on the way back so no one had to cook tonight.

It was about an hour and a half later that they were all sitting around the dining room table sharing the Chinese food. Ryan was having fun trying to pronounce the Chinese words given on the fortune cookies. It was proving to be difficult for the adults to say what they had to say without alarming the boys. Bonnie knew that she had to let Ryan go to school in the morning but decided to at least drive him over. She wanted to thank the principal again for her diligence that may have saved her son's life. The thought brought a tear to her eyes at the possibility of having nearly lost her son and she stifled her sob in her napkin. Her father asked the boys if he could play a game with them after supper. The boys were both excited that their grandparents were going to stay the night. This usually did not happen because of how relatively close they lived.

Bonnie and her mother made quick work of cleaning off the table and putting the leftovers into the refrigerator. The three males were in the game room and being quite vocal about their accomplishments on the screen. The two women ended up on the porch swing so they could talk away from the boys. Her mother said, "Bonnie, I had not placed any danger in the equation with Tony and Mr. Gavin. I figured that after they had gotten Sam to take the fall for the money laundering that they would try to just coast out of the courtroom. I didn't even consider what they could do to assure Sam's silence even while he was in prison."

Bonnie took the opportunity to tell her mother about the new evidence that Sam had saved and hidden in their safe without Tony even knowing about it. "Mother, you should know what the lawyer said might be the real outcome of all the trials with this new evidence. Bernie Segal believes that when this evidence is produced to the federal prosecuting attorney that they will jail Tony and Mr. Gavin because of their flight risk. He also hopes to get Sam out on bail if he has to wait for a new trial or get all the charges dropped and have him released. We have been keeping this all secret so that the lawyer could pull all their teeth as he put it. The paper trail will be enough to land them in prison for a very long time without Sam testifying so they would not have any reason to attack or threaten us anymore. I do believe that I should call the lawyer or get him information about this episode at the school today."

Meanwhile, Sergeant Benoit had taken the information that had been given by Bonnie in the afternoon to the two officers. He had not given Bonnie any description of the man seen trying to lure Ryan away from the school yard as given in statements by two teachers. When he examined the two reports from the school yard and Bonnie's account of the man she saw on the bench, there were very many factors that were similar such as hair color and general build. He then asked the officers to find out the registered owners of the two cars that Bonnie had seen. The cars came back registered to the same company in the area. The company was owned by Tony Gatzee. Sergeant Benoit decided that it was absolutely imperative to get a detective involved and then to get some information to the federal prosecutor on this case. Meanwhile he made arrangements for Bonnie's street to get some visible patrols both day and night. He was sensing some real danger for this family. He made a call to Detective Flum from his precinct and gave him a synopsis of what was going on. "I believe that this family is in grave danger from Tony Gatzee and his friends. They do not want any of the money laundering charges to fall on them so they are trying to intimidate Sam through his family."

Detective Flum said, "Let me go over and talk to this family and look over the neighborhood. Meanwhile, get me a possible name for the operator of those cars."

# Eight

There had been another fight in the yard yesterday afternoon and we were on lockdown again in our cell. I was starting to believe that they were going to become a part of our life here in the prison. To this point I had not gotten drawn into one of them by chance or by provocation by another inmate. Bonnie had come for a visit the night before but had little to talk about except how the boys were doing. I apologized for leaving her to take care of the family, house, and everything else. I told her that I had let my pride get in the way of our family as I had never done before I had met Tony. They are out there laughing at how stupid Sam was and how easy it was to get over on him. Bonnie told me to not get down on myself because she still had faith in me as a father and provider. Bonnie said she believed with all her heart that things were not going to be as they are now for very long. At the very least, we will be seeing Tony and Mr. Gavin going to prison for a very long time.

I was lying there quietly when the door to our cell opened up. There was a guard at the door who told me to get all my belongings together because I was being moved to another cell block. I asked him what prompted the move and he simply said that I had asked for the cell block that did woodworking and that was where I was going. I got a chance to thank Don for what he had taught me and for the kindness he had shown me to date. He told me not to worry because our paths were bound to cross again before either of us got out of there. We were soon going through the maze of hallways to a section of the prison that I had never laid eyes upon yet. I followed the guard as he got the doors opened remotely by control and tried to figure out in what direction we were now moving. We had to go across an exercise yard that was not familiar but the layout was mirrored to what I was used to. We went back into a new set of hallways and stopped midway of the one that had gone to our left as we entered the building. I was brought into a new common area and then to my new cell where I met an inmate named Ray. I looked around after the guard had left and saw that Ray was using the bottom bunk and I would have to take the top one here. I took a few minutes and put my stuff on the top storage shelf before I settled in to my bunk. Ray simply told me what time we would be going to lunch and then went back to what he was doing in his magazine. Lunch was the same routine of going down the hall single file, around the control hub and into the cafeteria. The choices for lunch were equally as bad over here and we were soon on our way back to our cells. I asked Ray if he knew anything about when and where the woodworking was going on. He told me that we would be going in a short time because he was in the program also. I asked him the extent and quality of the work we would be doing. He told me that there were some of the people who only worked on production type stuff that became parts for another company outside of the prison. There were some who made the parts for some reproduction furniture manufacturer that was also outside of the prison. He stated that he often worked in that section because he did not like the scrutiny of the next level which was a furniture making group. They made different styles of furniture for state offices and some nonprofit groups like Habitat for Humanity when they needed kitchen cabinets. We were still talking about it when the doors all opened to go to the shop. We wound around through the halls until we came to an ell to the cell blocks. I found myself looking into the heart of the operation as I saw gluing racks, laser rip saws, CNC lathes, shapers, jointers, and every style of table saw imaginable. There was a box of hearing protectors by the door and most of the inmates were putting them on. I also notice that there were different colored hard hats being picked up by the inmates at the next station. Ray grabbed a red one and said that he would see me later as he walked on into the plant. I saw that the blue colored hard hats were the least in number and most of the inmates with them on also had a clipboard in their hands. I figured out that they must be a part of the system to oversee what was going on. I then noticed a sign that said all new entrants must go to the office with an arrow pointing to a set of stairs. I walked up the stairs and came to a door that said knock before entering. I knocked as the sign said and then waited to see if the door would open or if I was supposed to go in on my own. I was about to try the door knob when a blue hat started to climb the stairs. He stated that I must be new and I assured him that I was. He told me to follow him and we both went inside. The room we entered was not cluttered but was not clean either. The sawdust fines from all the saws left enough debris on tables to write your name on the tops. The tables were strategically laid out under fluorescent lamps with chairs enough for two people at every table. The room was much quieter than the general shop was so it was ok to remove the protective devices to hear speaking. There were pictures on the wall of what was probably being made now or had been made in the past by the shop. The blue hat walked over to a table and told me to sit down across from him.

"My name is Phil," the blue hat said as he took a sheet of paper from his desk. "Why don't you start by filling out this with your name and experience with wood working so we can start from somewhere you might be comfortable."

I took the paper from him and filled out the general information part. I then looked up at him and asked him, "What kind of history would be beneficial to your placing me?"

He simply asked me, "What was your last job before you came to the prison?" I started to write it down but he said, "Why don't you just tell me first and I can help you with what we need."

"Well," I said, "I had started up my own company with Tony Gatzee before I knew who he was."

Phil said, "You got involved with Tony Gatzee?"

"Yes, he came to me while I was working as a union carpenter and I believed his line of malarkey," I said. "I had been thinking of going on my own for a period of time and when the man I only knew as Mr. Jones wanted to be my silent partner I was too glad to join him. He already had some contracts for us to perform for Mr. Frank Gavin and we were soon in business. From the time we started, I was the one who got the permits and subcontractors with my name as president of the company so it was easy for them to have me take the fall for the money laundering they were doing. I did not see any of the actual checks except my own pay check which was substantial. They did have me prepare all the invoices that we gave to Mr. Gavin so my name was at the top of the list when the feds came to our door."

Phil then told me that they did very little actual framing as I probably was used to doing. I told him that I was a master carpenter and often had the jobs that involved intricate layouts and installations after we built the units. Phil asked me if I could build cabinets and things like that. I guaranteed him that he would be happy with any cabinets that I built for him. He told me, "I am not the one in charge of the cabinet shop but that he would take me down as soon as we finished. Why don't you just put master union carpenter on that paper for your records and we don't have to tell the whole story." Phil took the piece of paper and put it in a basket for filing. "Your case worker will know where you are in about twelve hours" he said. "Now let's get you down to meet Patrick Stearns in the cabinet shop."

I put the hearing protection back on as we went out of the door and went to the far corner of the shop. The pungent smell of the finishes was more evident in this portion of the shop. Phil pointed to furniture and other objects that were suspended on a track to dry out of the way from the work areas. We don't do copious amounts of work here but we do try to attain a quality above the normal standards. To our right as we walked along there appeared to be an area that was mass producing parts from maple and birch woods. There were several inmates sanding proportionally cut sections that appeared to be molds for the arm pieces to sofas. We continued along until I realized that we were approaching another blue hat that was near some elaborate cabinets. I stopped to admire one that stood out. The side posts had been fluted for a more colonial look to the piece. The cabinet was also stained dark as in the old colonial tradition pieces. It had curved legs that ended in a dainty looking foot for a moderately tall cabinet. The doors were window frame style and would be receiving glass inserts for the display area of the cabinet. The vintage reproduction brass hinges added to the overall appeal of the cabinet. Phil stated that an inmate might work alone on such a piece or have some of the parts made by others. We continued until the other blue hat noticed we were in his area. Phil introduced me to Patrick Stearns and gave him a two minute synopsis of who I was and my work history. Phil wished me good luck in the shop and said he had to go back to his own area.

Patrick Stearns was larger of stature than I was. He had a couple of scars on his arms that seemed to be matched in size and placement. His hard hat hid most of his salt and pepper hair and he seemed to be wearing prescription glasses and not only protective wear. His eyes seemed to be scanning the area around us when he finally spoke. "What would you describe as your greatest weakness with your work?"

I told him, "I am still trying to improve my staining and sealing techniques on the cabinets I have built."

He then asked me, "What I thought my strengths would be."

I told him, "I can build a strong, square, stylish cabinet with no trouble and I fancy myself at doing custom builds for preexisting spaces."

He took the information in with no real comments. He then told me that he would show me some of the equipment that we had at our disposal. We went around the shop and looked at all the saws, jointers, planers, and platform sanders in this area. He showed me the picture of what one of the inmates was doing and said, "We usually start a project from a picture. We can get all the normal hard woods such as mahogany, maple, birch, cherry, hickory, and some exotics as well to use in our projects. We can ask some other parts of the shop to prepare some of the wood that we will use including doing some glue-ups that we would finish in our section. You would get several hours to work in here for up to six days per week but we only require four days as mandatory. You can use two days discretionarily for rest or yard time. No one is in here all seven days. I share the oversight of this department with another inmate whom you will meet later. There are some basic rules about safety in the shop that is much different than outside. Hearing, head, and eye protection is mandatory at all time in the shop. If you find a machine that has a problem of any kind, it gets tagged off limits until repaired. Any kind of rough play will get you written up once. The second time you will be removed until the disciplinary team decides how serious and how dangerous it was. Being here is a privilege even though you are in a prison and as you probably already know; harming someone will get you extra time added to your current sentence. I am not a guard here but I have all their authority while I am wearing this blue hat. There is surveillance all around this shop but we are not usually bothered by the guards. I believe that a fellow like you will enjoy being busy while you are here versus lying on a bunk. When you enter the shop this afternoon, you will wear a white hard hat. There may be as many as fifty men in the entire shop at one time and the color of your hard hat is as mandatory as the hat itself to know if you are staying where you belong. I will teach you how to get wood and things from other inmates when the time comes. The other thing you should know is that most of these inmates take pride in their work over here. You will not disrespect their projects or their work stations. You will also find that some of the inmates will not speak to you until they get good and ready so don't take it personal. Now, I have two sets of cabinets that I need for the remodeling of some state offices that you can choose from and you can do a takeoff of materials, machines you will need to use, and approximate time it will take at six hours per day." He held up two pictures for me to look at. "The dimensions and wood to be used are on the bottom of the page. You look at them for a minute and I'll be right back."

I examined the pictures that Patrick had left with me. The cabinets had two different functions and required two totally opposite techniques for their building. One was a tall cabinet that would have file drawers within the doors on sliders with the top area getting cubicle shelving. That cabinet was going to attach on the right side and rear only. The other set was the infilling of a wall with cabinets that were built the same as most kitchens with upper and lower cabinets. They would also have drawers in the bottom set with adjustable shelving in the upper cabinets. I thought that the taller one piece would be the most difficult to build so I was favoring doing that project. The specifications called for maple wood to be used that was easy to work with and would get a golden maple stain and polyurethane sealer. I loved the practice of doing dovetailing in drawers and some mortised shelving would add a nice touch where the cabinet was too tall for anyone to look at the files within. I had made up my mind.

Patrick came back as I was looking around to see what equipment would do which parts of the project. He asked me to follow him so we went to an area where work was going on by an inmate on a raised platform. "This is going to be your assigned work station on this side of the platform. There are air lines and electrical outlets on both ends and there are some that can be swung over the middle of the bench while suspended to protect your work. This is Al on the other side and I believe that you two will get along just fine. Which project are you going to start with?"

I told Patrick, "I would like to do the tall cabinet because I favor the techniques needed and that helped me to decide." We went over a list of materials and how to get tools that were shared.

Patrick said, "We will try to get the basic set of tools such as a hammer, square, tapes, and straight edges accumulated for you to keep at your station. Even chisels are kept in the tool room so they are kept sharpened. We do not like for tools to walk around unless you are using them somewhere specific. You will have the wand passed over you and possibly patted down as you leave the area every day. If you simply forget to take something out of your pocket, it will only be forgiven a couple of times before you get written up. We have not had a directed attack between inmates in this shop for a long time because of the selection process and monitoring that happens here. I expect you to ask whatever you have to of me and not get into trouble. We are about to go for lunch and when you come back we will get you started."

# Nine

Sergeant Benoit called Bonnie early in the morning of the day after the school incident with Ryan. He asked her if they could meet and where it would be the easiest to do so. She told him that she intended to drop Ryan off at school around eight o'clock and could meet him at the diner down the street one half hour after that. Her father and mother said they would stay there with Tyler and keep a watchful eye on him. Bonnie had expected to have to do some more paperwork about the school so she was not nervous about meeting him.

There was a patrol car in the diner parking lot already when Bonnie got there. She went inside and found Sergeant Benoit sitting at a discreet table with another man. They had her sit with her back to the window for a little more privacy. Sergeant Benoit introduced her to Detective Flum once they were all seated. They were sipping on coffee and asked her if she would like a cup which she accepted. They offered her breakfast but she passed on the idea and said she had other errands to do today so could they get started. When asked, she told the men politely that she was trying to keep some sort of privacy to her life unless they needed to know. They told her that they would let her decide after they gave her some information. This brought a twinge of nausea to Bonnie as she let that statement sink in.

Bonnie asked," "Have you found something out that I should know about from the information I gave to your officers?"

They looked at each other and said, "Yes. To start with, the license plate numbers you gave us were from company cars that Tony Gatzee owned so you were correct in believing that you are being watched at home. We also compared the description that you gave of the man on the bench and the description of the man at the school by the teachers. It could have been the same man. We compared the description to known sexual predators in the city and it is no match but there is a chance that he is new in town or a beginner. We would like to know if you would sit down with a sketch artist and give us a sketch."

Bonnie told them, "Yes, but I have to do some errands first."

They told her, "We will wait for your call and also would you consider filing charges against an unknown stalker so we can bring a possible suspect in for questioning."

She told them, "I will if it might make my family safer."

Bonnie was soon on her way to the lawyer's office. She had told him that she needed an emergency meeting with him as soon as possible. The lawyer had told her to stop by when she could and he would stop what he was doing to speak to her. She took a zigzag pattern across town with an ever watchful eye on her rear view mirror. She was comfortable that she was alone when she pulled in to the rear parking lot of the office building and entered from a concealed side entrance. The same woman she had met the first time was on the phone when she entered. She motioned for Bonnie to have a seat as she wrapped up the phone call. She said hello as she jotted down a message on a form book and then went to the office door. Bonnie was asked to wait just a minute so the lawyer could put away some sensitive papers before she went in. He came out within a couple of minutes and apologized to Bonnie for the wait. She was soon sitting across from him in a large arm chair.

Bernie asked, "Are you comfortable and are you ready to talk about why you have called this urgent meeting? I have prepared most of the information to present to the federal prosecutor who is allowing me some time in two days.

Bonnie said, "There are things happening and changing very quickly around me and I am beginning to fear for myself and my family."

He asked her, "What do you mean by changing very quickly."

Bonnie started, "I had to go to the police because we are being watched at home as well as my being followed around town. Then someone tried to lure my son Ryan away from the school yard the other afternoon. Two teachers stopped it but I had to get the police involved again. I just left a Sergeant Benoit and a detective Flum who asked to meet with me this morning. They told me that the license plates I recorded on the two cars near my home are both registered to companies that Tony Gatzee owns. The man who followed me to this office building matches the description of the man who tried to lure my son away. My mother and father stayed with me last night but I am concerned about how far these men will go."

The lawyer just put his pencil down and looked at Bonnie. "Did you tell the police about the new evidence that we have against Tony and Mr. Gavin?"

Bonnie stated, "I didn't feel that I could because both you and Sam have told me to trust no one so I have not done that yet. I am supposed to do a sketch of the man who followed me at the station and to file charges against an unknown stalker so the police can question suspects once I leave the office."

Bernie said, "Tony will not like it if the police start to question or even arrest his people for stalking because that is just one step away from attempted murder. Let's just see what the detective can do once you give him the sketch. They may run it through a facial recognition program and get us a suspect. If one is found, they may be willing to sing rather than go to prison for attempted murder and kidnapping. A grand jury could easily bring these charges on someone who is also linked to a current federal investigation. I just want to keep you and your family safe so once you leave today I will call the federal prosecutor and see if he can move our time up because of the danger to you."

Bonnie simply asked him to do whatever he could quickly. Bonnie then went to the police station and worked with a sketch artist for a while. She had called home and told them why she was not home yet. She was not completely happy with the sketch but she was told that if the two people's description really came close that they would have both sets of witnesses compare thoughts. The detective did have her look at several pictures of men before she left but she did not recognize anyone. Bonnie was starting to get tired and realized that she had not had anything except the cup of coffee this morning so she went through the drive through window at a fast food restaurant on the way home.

When she reached out her window for her change from the cashier, she noticed the man who had followed her the other day watching her from across the parking lot. She nearly dropped her food but managed to control herself enough to pull out onto the street and start driving. How could she get herself some help? She was near her bank and she quickly decided to pull into the drive-up window. She sat in her car and asked the cashier whom she knew to call the police immediately because she was in danger. The cashier took one look at Bonnie and knew that it must be true. When the cashier came back to the window, she slid the transaction chute out with a note that asked what kind of danger. She simply wrote down that she was being followed by a stalker and that he was dangerous. Suddenly there were three police cars approaching from both directions of the drive through window. They missed seeing the man who had stopped on the street but Bonnie saw him leaving. She yelled out that he was getting away and pointed to the car going down the street. Two officers took after him and one stayed to talk to Bonnie.

Bonnie pulled across the lanes and parked out of the way of the normal bank traffic. She was trembling almost uncontrollably when she opened her window for the officer. She asked him if he could call for Sergeant Benoit or Detective Flum and he said he would see if either of them was available. Tell them Bonnie Walker is involved and that may help. She told the officer that she had just left their office from giving them a sketch of the man whom they were now chasing. The dispatcher came back on and said that Detective Flum would be there in just a few minutes. The officer asked Bonnie if she was hurt in any way and she told him she was only scared half to death. The officer asked if she wasn't the same woman from the incident at the school yesterday. Bonnie simply shook her head yes as she noticed Detective Flum pulling up beside her car.

"This guy is getting too brave," Detective Flum said to no one in particular. "Are you sure that it was the same man from the other day Bonnie?" he asked.

"Yes I am positive," she said, "but I didn't see him today until I went to get some food after I left your office. Do you think that he was watching me when I was there with you?"

Detective Flum said, "I am not sure but if he was there he is getting really cocky. The car was found empty just a few blocks from here after the man was seen getting out and running into a crowded store. We won't be able to make anything stick yet but they now know that we know about them. One of my officers will drive your car home and you can ride with me." Bonnie was still too shaken up to argue so she gave her keys to the officer who had stayed with her and gave him the street address.

Tyler came running out of the house yelling mommies home when Bonnie's car pulled into the driveway but he stopped dead in his tracks when the police officer climbed out of the car instead of his mommy. Bonnie was just pulling up to the curb with Detective Flum when she called to Tyler that she was not in her own car. He still did not know what to do so he just stood there until Bonnie came over and picked him up. Mommies ok Tyler. I just got a ride home that is all. Her father was out on the porch by then but he did not ask any questions while they were still outside. Detective Flum waved to them all and said he would speak to them later as they drove away.

Bonnie went into the house with her family and played with Tyler for a few minutes in the living room. She asked him, "Have you had lunch yet?"

Tyler said, "Grandma made me a peanut butter sandwich.

"Well," Bonnie said, "I haven't eaten yet so I am going to get my bag of food which is still in the car and we can reheat it and share."

Her father told her that he would go out and get it as he left the room. He promptly returned and said, "You must have a story to tell us."

"I do" she said, "but it is not for all ears and I haven't had anything to eat all day." They placed the bean and cheese burritos in the microwave and waited for the buzzer to sound. Tyler decided that he would like to have one so he shared his mother's lunch at the table. Bonnie asked him if he wanted to go and play in his room while she talked to grandpa. He was totally content with the idea and was gone as soon as he had placed his dish and glass into the dishwasher. Both of her parents waited in the living room for her to finish and come to sit down. Bonnie could not help but look out the windows toward the street and the back yard before she would sit down.

She did a replay of the morning for her parents starting with the diner. "I met Detective Flum while I was at the diner and he is who just brought me home. I left them and saw Bernie who told about the time he was scheduled with the federal prosecutor. I asked him to hurry after she had told him about the episode at the school and how the cars in the neighborhood belonged to Tony. Then I went back to the police station to work with a sketch artist and filed a complaint about an unknown stalker around our house. I was feeling nauseous from not eating all day by that time and so I had stopped to buy some lunch on the way home. That was when I spotted the man who had been tailing me the other day as I was leaving with my food. I decided to drive into our bank and got the teller to call the police from the drive through window. They came so close to catching him. That is how my morning went and why I got an escort home."

Her father just stood up and took a look around the back yard and the street without saying a word. Her mother said, "I believe that Tony is getting nervous and scared people will take dangerous chances to get away from whatever is scaring them."

Bonnie said, "I do not know how they were finding me every time I leave the house. It's like they have a monitoring device on me or my car somehow."

Her father said, "I believe that you are absolutely right and that they must have planted a gps device on your car. With one of them, they do not have to be near you all the time. They can monitor you by computer and relay the information by cell phone on where to intercept you."

Bonnie said, "If you are right, Tony knows that I have been to the lawyers twice recently."

Everyone in the room jumped when someone knocked on the door. They were not watching outside as much as they had been before the conversation started. It was Detective Flum standing at the door when they looked out and they let him in. He had some pictures for Bonnie to look at again.

Bonnie got all excited when she saw the picture of the man who had been stalking her in the group of pictures. "I'm positive that this is the man who has been following me."

Detective Flum said, "The teachers have also identified the man as the one who tried to abduct Ryan. I now have a warrant for his arrest in place and my men are trying to locate him."

Bonnie asked, "Detective Flum will you speak to Sam's lawyer, Bernie Segal, if I can get him on the phone?"

He assured her, "Of course I will but I'm not sure why you want me talking to Sam's lawyer about this?"

Bonnie said, "There are some very special circumstances he may choose to tell you once you give him your information." Bonnie was able to get the lawyer on the phone and told him whom she was going to have him speak to. He said ok and Bonnie let Detective Flum and the lawyer talk.

# Ten

Sam had eaten lunch with the group from the shop and then returned for the afternoon shift. He put on a white hard hat as he had been told by Patrick and went to where his work station was. Patrick came over to him and brought him over to the tool crib. He was given a set of basic tools and then taken to meet the material supplier. Patrick introduced him to Chris who was also a blue hat. Patrick gave him the order number that I had chosen and was soon leaving the two of us to decide on what materials to get first.

Chris said, "I suggest using some maple finished veneer rather than a glued partition for the tall cabinet because it is going to be mostly free standing. You can give it a solid front and we can decide how you want to do the doors. That might be where you can glue and shape solid wood panels. We may have to suggest four doors for something this tall to keep it all straight. Have you been showed who and how to get help when you need it here in the shop? The inmates in the red hard hats are helpers and trainees. They could tail a table saw or maybe just help you move material to where you need it. You will notice that there are multiple places in the shop where you can turn on a red light to summon some help. You can also arrange to have a red hat for an entire period of time without needing to use the red lights by going through Patrick. There are at least five red hats in the shop at all times and sometimes more if there are enough requests for steadies as they are called. I think that I will get you a red hat and we can bring two sheets of maple veneer to your work station."

The afternoon passed quickly after I had the veneer to work with. The red hat and I cut two sheets in half and laid them onto my table. I was just about to mark out the shelving and drawers when a loud whistle went through the shop. I looked around and asked Al what that was all about. He said that the whistle meant that we had fifteen minutes to return tools to the crib and get ready to go back to our cells. It seemed that I had just started. It raised my hopes that it would allow time to go by more quickly while here in prison. I did not have any tools to return so I just started to walk to the exit area. I placed the white hard hat and other protective gear on the racks on the way out to where we would be patted down. I had soon returned to my new cell and found that Ray was not in the cell at this time and the door was open. I asked the guard what the status was and he told me that it was yard time but I would have to settle for the common area or my own bunk. He told me that if I had gone to the yard from the shop that I could have stayed out there for about thirty minutes but now I had to remain there. I knew that the routine would be easy enough to learn if I just got a chance to talk to people for a couple of days and watch. If there was one thing this prison had it was a routine for everything.

I tried to get a message to my case worker, John Clark, so I could get a message to Bonnie on where she would have to go for a visit. There were specific visiting areas for each of the cell blocks and I was now on the opposite side of the prison. She would even have to use a different gate and parking area when she came the next time. I did not want to miss the hour we got to see each other for any reason. I did not know at the time that the things happening at home were not going to allow her to come this week.

I started to settle in to a routine that was not as difficult or unnerving as the first cell block had been. The project that I had started went along very well and I had the case all assembled within two days and started on the shelves and drawers that would go in it. The solid wood frame and doors would be the last thing I would build. The pace was mediocre throughout the shop so there was no pressure to perform by the clock. Patrick stopped by on occasion to see if I needed anything. I did ask him one day if I would be putting the panels together or if I could have them made prior. I went ahead and ordered the panels for the four doors and I received them on the fourth day after I ordered them. I had trouble with a belt sander one day but only had to return it to the crib to get another one for use. This shop for all practicality was a well oiled machine.

I made the drawers from veneer and dove-tailed the four corners for strength and gave them a stylish solid front that attached with blind screws. I scalloped hand grips in the fronts so they could be pulled out easily without losing any space for handles. I ordered some drawer glides that were rated for up to seventy five pounds and attached them. Once I had the drawers done, I decided to see what I needed to finish them while they were not in the cabinet. I found out that you could have your work finished by a crew that did nothing else so I opted to do that with the drawers. My project was coming along very nicely.

I was working on my project one day when a pulsating alarm went off in the shop. I looked at Al who told me that there was a medical emergency and we would have to leave the area just as if it was quitting time if the normal whistle was sounded. He said otherwise we are to quit working and just stay at our station unless directed by a guard to help. I noticed two guards headed into the area with all the saws and they came back by in a couple of minutes with a red hat inmate holding a bloody bandaged arm over his head as he walked with them. Al said that we would get the all clear buzzer once the guards had the inmate all the way out of the shop. At least it wasn't a brawl I thought to myself.

John Clark sent a message back to me that there was a cell block change letter sent to the primary person on the visitor list whenever any of the inmates had a transfer. He also told me that my lawyer was coming in on Friday to see me. I did not let my hopes get too high and was only expecting a status report from him. Bonnie had not come to visit this week so I had no way of knowing what was going on with my family. I just allowed the routine to keep me calm because it was easier than fighting the system.

In the quiet of my cell, I would often consider what my sons were doing at home. It was still common to find myself dreaming about them if I dozed off or daydreaming some of my fondest memories. Every camping trip took on new meaning in my heart when the thought that I could not be going with them for some time to come ran through my mind. The missing intimate companionship of my wife brought anguish to my dismal soul. That inner most part of me that can only be reached and filled by the certain deep part and heartfelt emotions of one other person. The one you can bare yourself totally to. Bonnie had always been my soul mate and I yearned to be a part of her life again. The thoughts were enough to start a hatred for Tony Gatzee and Mr. Gavin growing within me. At the worst times, I wanted to lash out at them if only in my mind. I had never had these kinds of thoughts before and when I regained my rational I knew that I would never do the things I was thinking of doing to any human.

My project was coming along well as the week progressed. I had the three lower drawers built for the files and was doing the top shelves as the pattern called for them. I had decided that the three drawers and the shelves were not requiring equal distances but I was going to separate the doors by height to match each section with a visible style in the middle. I would be able to fasten the solid wood front all the way around the cabinet with blind screws and at the middle style making it very stout. Patrick was pleased at how the project was coming and my skills at creating a fine piece of furniture. I had to request a red hat for the days that I was shaping the raised panel doors. Besides making the work easier, it was nice to get to speak to someone who didn't feel threatened by me or the work. I could see after a couple days at my station that my work was of a higher quality than Al's and he felt intimidated by me. I tried to show him a woodworking technique for his door mounting one day and he was not short in telling me to leave him and his work alone. I tried to calm him down but he had not spoken to me in two days since. The red hat knew that he could learn here in the shop if he tried to. He even hinted about an option where he could become my apprentice as well as my red hat. I didn't know about the training so I told him that I would ask Patrick when I had a chance.

I had started to go back out into the yard on some days. It was at least some fresh air compared to the cell block and the shop with all its smells. I did find that while I was in this yard there seemed to be less aggression between the inmates. I even found that the guards would speak to you on this side of the compound. Ray even tried to find out about me and was willing to tell me some of his life including having left behind a family. He had been in for two years so far and they had only come for two visits because of the distance to the prison. He was quite certain that he was going to get divorce papers any day from his wife or a lawyer. The price that anyone paid to be in prison was multi faceted when you took into account families, employers, and how you would be treated once you got out. It was much more than the time and the mental cruelty that we faced every day while in the prison.

# Eleven

Detective Flum waited until he was back at the station before calling Sam's lawyer back. They had spoken for a few minutes while he was still at Bonnie's home but he soon realized that some of what they had to say to each other should be done away from the family. He told Bonnie and her family that he had to go to the police station to fax the lawyer some stuff rather than stay and possibly expose them to more of this turmoil and danger. It was very clear to him that they were dealing with men who were looking to save themselves by any means. They were feeling the noose get tighter around their necks every minute now. He was told that the man had been arrested in one of Tony Gatzee's restaurants for the stalking and the kidnap attempt. The other officers were bringing him into the station for questioning and arraigning for the crimes. He might be willing to tell who sent him out to kidnap Ryan and stalk Bonnie. This information he had for the lawyer but he did not know yet what the lawyer could tell him about this case.

When the two started to talk on the phone, it was the lawyer who asked the first question. He asked Detective Flum if the stalker could definitely be tied to Tony Gatzee. The detective told him yes and they were considering making the charges attempted kidnapping and attempted murder for the stalking. The detective said that they could make a case for attempted murder because of the ties back to the money laundering charges. Well, the lawyer told the detective how they had the real evidence of Sam's innocence on paper and how they were trying to silence Sam by intimidation of his family. I made a call to the federal prosecutor after you called me and he wants us both in his office at nine o'clock in the morning. Do you think that you have enough to bring Tony in today and diminish the danger that Bonnie and her family are in.

Detective Flum answered, "Not unless this guy sings can I touch him tonight but if he is willing to make a statement tonight I will pick him up tonight. I will put someone in the home tonight for their safety but I do not think that Tony will want to buy any more time in prison by endangering them anymore. We took this guy right out of Toni's restaurant so he knows we're at his door again. My concern is that he makes it out of the country tonight."

Bonnie received a telephone call from Detective Flum, "I know the police are sending a plain clothes female officer to be at your home tonight. I would like to arrest Tony tonight but I am not sure yet as to whether or not I will be able to. I need for this stalker to give us Tony as his boss for this crime. I am not sure that having everyone in your family staying in one home is a good idea tonight when Tony knows where you live. Could your parents take the boys to a safe house for the night and a female officer will stay with you. I am ninety-nine percent positive that we will have Tony and Mr. Gavin in prison within twenty-four hours."

Bonnie told him, "We will do whatever will keep us all safe from Tony."

Detective Flum told her, "Do not let your father use your car because I think that there must be some kind of locator such as a gps on it allowing them to know where the car is at all times. Regretfully some of these crooks with enough money have better equipment than the police and they don't have to wait for a court order to use it."

When they finished their conversation, Bonnie told her parents what was going on and what the detective had asked them to do. Her parents quickly threw their stuff back into a suitcase as Bonnie got the boys a couple of days of clothes plus what was on their back ready to go. She simply told the boys that they were going to their grandparents for the night and that she would pick them up tomorrow. They didn't seem to question why and everyone was soon on their way. Bonnie had checked the street and the back yard for anyone suspicious before opening the door. As they were pulling away from her home, she watched a woman pull up in front and wave to her on the porch. She quickly flashed a hidden badge and proceeded up to the house and suggested they both go inside. She said, "You may call me Donna and I assure you Bonnie that everything is going to be ok. I am here to see that no one gets hurt. Did your parents go to a safe house?"

Bonnie told her, "I do not know where they went Donna because we were told to keep it a secret for added security. For all I know they will check into a motel off the beaten path. We have lived in this area all my life so they know the safest places and where to be concealed."

Donna said, "I need to know the complete layout of the house and the back yard as well as I can see it at this time of day. The house doesn't have many hidden corners so that will help. I will be able to see both sides of the house if I place a seat right over there she said pointing to a spot in the dining room."

"We can move whatever you want," said Bonnie, "and if we need to we can place some stuff in the way for obstruction.

Donna asked, "Bonnie do you have any weapons in the house?"

She told her, "I have Sam's shotgun that is loaded and hidden behind my bedroom door. I taped a hunting knife under the hutch out of sight. I have put two others in the desk drawers on opposite sides. None of the knives are in sheaths any more. Donna, I know I am not afraid to use them if there ever was a need."

Donna looked her in the eyes and told her she believed her but let's hope it doesn't come to that. Bonnie asked her if she had eaten yet because she had not. Donna said no but she would fix and eat a sandwich later. Bonnie told her that she would fix two sandwiches now and put hers on a plate and put it in the refrigerator. Donna told her that she had to walk around the house and become as familiar with it as possible. Donna was on the side of the house when a car rolled by very slowly. Donna leaned against the house so the people in the car could not see her there but when it passed under a street light she recognized Detective Flum's car. It continued down the street but Donna expected her co-worker to come back around as soon as he had checked the surrounding streets. She went back inside from the back yard so as to not be seen from the street. Bonnie had drawn all the curtains towards the street and they got a bed sheet to cover the big window in the living room. They turned off all the overhead lights and placed lamps near the windows so they were not casting shadows. The telephone rang and startled both of the women. It was Detective Flum announcing that he was about to knock on the door.

Detective Flum commented, "I like how well strategized the house looks and how he could not see movement in the house through the curtains. I have to let you know Bonnie that the man we arrested tonight would not give us the name of who was having you followed. We have a meeting with the federal prosecutor at nine o'clock to go over the evidence that Sam's lawyer has. We will have Tony Gatzee behind bars by tomorrow. Try to get some rest because I will need you tomorrow to go with us if you can. I will pick you up right around eight so we have a few minutes to go over what the prosecutor will have to hear. Good night to both of you. By the way, there will be patrol cars in the area all night long and they will be regular squad cars so our presence will be known."

As Bonnie lay on her bed, she wondered what Sam would think if he knew the dangers he had caused her and the boys. She knew that it wasn't pleasant for Sam in prison and she also knew that Sam had no idea what kind of man Tony was when this all began. Sam had his ego stroked by a master who needed another puppet to command. He had even lied about his name for obvious reasons. She wondered if they would be able to be together again after this was settled in court. What would life in prison have done to her husband and the father of their children? She had already seen the backlash of their friends believing the worst about Sam. Friends who used to call her for coffee so their children could all play together had found lots of excuses to not come around anymore. The formidable loneliness was the worst when she would go to an empty bedroom with a double bed. She at least had the boys to preoccupy her mind when she was lonely. She cursed Tony as she thought of him having tried to abduct Ryan. A sudden rustle in the living room made her jump to attention by the bed. She was starting for the rifle but slowed down when she remembered that Donna was out there and that there was no other noise. She listened at the door and heard footsteps going to the kitchen. She cracked open the bedroom door as quietly as she could until she could see Donna looking in the refrigerator. She coughed to get Donnas' attention so as to not startle her.

When Donna looked at Bonnie she simply said, "I am sorry for having to make noise but I had become hungry when I had time to settle down for the long night ahead."

Bonnie told her, "I am having trouble getting my emotions to settle down for the night and I was not sleeping."

Donna told her, "Please try and get some sleep because the federal prosecutor will need your input on this stalking and attempted kidnapping. I called in to the office a few minutes ago and they report that it is very quiet around Toni's places of business tonight and there are squad cars going around your house at least once an hour. I think you should try to get some rest while I am here."

There was a lot of turmoil in and around the office of the federal prosecutor once everyone had gotten there. Sergeant Benoit, Detective Flum, Donna, and a couple of officers she had seen at the school were on one side of the table. Sam's lawyer and Bonnie were seated near an empty seat that had a microphone for recording depositions on the other side of the table. The federal prosecutor and his assistant sat at the head of the table. He started by telling Sam's lawyer, "I have examined the new evidence and found it quite compelling in Sam's defense. When we prosecuted the case the first time we only had the invoices that had been inflated by Tony to cover the laundering money. We did not have any of these that Sam prepared for Tony. We have found that the numbers on Sam's invoices were doubled by the amounts of the subcontractors duplicate invoices. That would bring in the charge of racketeering as well as a couple of others I won't bore you with as time does not allow me to. Now Detective Flum, I have only had a few minutes to look at the charges against this Mr. Smith, if that is his name that you arrested last night. You have arrested him for attempted murder and attempted kidnapping of Sam's family."

The detective answered him in the affirmative and told him that Bonnie was here to attest to the charges.

"Thank you, we will get to Bonnie's testimony in a little while," said the prosecutor. "You say that you have proof that this Mr. Smith works for Tony at one of his businesses."

Again the detective answered to the affirmative and added that he was arrested while working for Tony at this place of business and was being held in prison.

The prosecutor said, "Well, I have already made a petition before a federal judge and we have a warrant for the arrest of Tony Gatzee and Mr. Gavin both. I have work to do right now with another case but someone needs to find both of these men and bring them in and place them in prison. The judge has already got the information on the attempted murder and attempted kidnapping and they will be held without bail on these new charges combined with the prior charges at the arraignment. I am going to leave my assistant to take the statement from Bonnie and we will need you detective to bring in the two school teachers to meet with my assistant also. Please excuse me ladies and gentlemen but this is shaping up to being a very long day for me. Good bye."

# Twelve

I had planned on working in the shop until lunch and then waiting in my cell for my lawyer to show up. My project was ready for final assembly before shipping it off. I was going to finish it this morning and present it to Patrick for final inspection. It had turned out better than anyone had expected by giving it the four raised panel doors. I was attaching the doors with my technique and did not notice that Al was watching me from across the table.

"Now I see what you were trying to tell me that other day," said Al. "That really does make it easy for one person to hold his doors true to the style."

"Well, I'm glad that you can appreciate it more now," I said. "I had that taught to me by an old cabinet maker and I have never forgotten it. I have one small run of polyurethane on the inside of my door panel but it is small enough that I am not going to try to sand it out. I think that this thing is ready for final inspection."

Al said, "It looks better than anything I have ever done."

"Thanks Al," I said as I started to look for Patrick. "The first ones I did were not as good as this either. I had to watch and listen to the people who were teaching me. I got mad at some of them myself. Your work is not all that bad compared to others and you will continue to improve. I think that I will put this power drill back in the crib and see if I can't find Patrick before lunch."

Patrick was pleased with the way my project had come out and he had some red hats come with a dolly to move it to the shipping area.

I said, "Patrick, I am going to take the afternoon off because I have a scheduled appointment with Bernie Segal, my lawyer shortly after lunch. I will probably see you in the morning for a new project."

Patrick said, "After seeing the quality of your work, I am not going to let you get an easy one." We both laughed as the lunch buzzer sounded.

I had gotten to the point where I did not lie around my cell very much anymore. I was lying there now enjoying the thought of a well done project behind me and knowing that I had gained the respect of my supervisor. The problem with having this much time alone was the fact that I could miss my family with no diversion for my mind. I could ache for the touch of my wife and to hear my sons vying for my attention. I never had done anything to lose these things but they were out of my life now. I wanted them back!

I could tell that it was getting to be later than the time I expected Bernie to have come. Ray had come back to the cell and it was getting near time for us to go to the evening meal. Finally, there was a guard at my cell door. I got up from the bunk when he came in. I was not expecting what happened next. He told me to gather up bag and baggage and to follow him. I tried to ask him what was going on but he would only say that I had to bring all my belongings and follow him.

We left my cell and made our way through the maze of mechanical doors to an area that I had never seen yet. We went by command central and continued through yet another three doors. We came to a room that was near a bunch of offices and went into the last available door. In the room was a gentleman that was not in a uniform sitting at a desk. He asked me my name and my social security number which I recited to him.

"May I know what is going on?" I asked the gentleman. "I really would like to know what happened to the appointment I had with my lawyer today and why I have been brought here with bag and baggage."

The man said, "I am here to process you out of here. You have been released on bail awaiting a new trial. If you will cooperate, we will be done here in about twenty minutes and you may go with your wife who is in the next room behind that door."

I simply said, "Yes Sir." I don't remember what he asked me or what I signed because my head was reeling from what was going on. I simply knew that I wanted to be on the other side of that door before I woke up from this dream.

When we were done the man said, "Young man, I wish you the best of luck at your new trial and that I never see you in here again. You're free to go out that door."

I did not want to find out that this was really a dream but I got up from my chair and went out that door. I looked at where I was and I was in a room with my wife running towards me. As we embraced for the first time in what seemed like forever, I just started to cry with joy. I didn't want to talk where we were so I picked up my stuff and we made our way out of the prison.

"What has happened?" I asked Bonnie once I knew we were out of the prison. "I was expecting Bernie's visit today and not this miracle."

Bonnie simply said, "Come on. Let's get out of here and we can talk about it on the way home. There are two boys who do not know that you are going to be walking into our home with me. I will tell you this right off and that is that Tony Gatzee and Frank Gavin are on the inside of the prison right now and you are not. With the evidence that you provided Bernie and what else has happened to the boys and I, you are out on bail until your next court date or forever if the charges are dropped."

I was just turning onto the highway from the prison when the words that Bonnie had said sunk in enough to raise an alarming fear in me. "What do you mean by what has happened to you and the boys? Is everybody ok? Did someone try to hurt you while I was in the prison?"

"We don't have to talk about all of this on the way home," Bonnie said. "We are all ok but Tony did try to intimidate you by intimidating me. With help from Bernie, Detective Flum, and the federal prosecutor' we are going to be fine for a long time because you and I will be old and grey when Tony and Frank die in prison."

I drove the rest of the way home with just a sense of thankfulness, wonder, and pure joy at being free to hold my wife and soon my boys. We made small talk about the awe of how quickly things can change.

I looked at my beautiful wife and said, "Have I told you lately how much I love you!"

When we arrived at our home, Bonnie's parent's car was in the driveway. She went in the door first and got the boys into the living room while I stood outside the door. She asked the boys if they liked surprises and of course they answered yes. "Well," she said, "I hope you like this one."

I walked into the room on her cue and the look on my sons' faces was one of sheer joy and surprise. The ensuing attack to get to me was fantastic to see and be a part of. We all kissed and hugged until we were all tired and needed a minutes rest. I got a handshake from Fred and a hug from Paula as soon as the boys backed away for a minute. "We are both glad that you are home," Fred said. "We have been praying for this and have kept you on our prayer list at the church for months."

"I don't know how much prayer had to do with it," I said, "but thank you and all the people of your church. I would like to think that my being innocent to be a factor in this and that someone was finally able to figure it out."

Paula said, "The bible says to put our trust in the Lord and he will be our defense against our enemies and our accusers. The Lord promises that the days of the evil ones are numbered and that vengeance will come by His hand for us."

I said, "Paula, I am just too glad to be out to argue with you about how I got here. I am very thankful that I am not going to be lying on a three inch thick mat on a steel bunk tonight and the company will be better. Boys, what time do you have to go to bed?"

That comment started a friendly chaos from the boys about not wanting to go to bed until we had talked a little more. Fred and Paula made a comment about how it would be nice to sleep in their own bed tonight also. I asked them what that meant and Bonnie interrupted me by telling me that I did not need to know everything within the first hour of being home. Her parents said goodnight and soon it was just the four of us trying to calm down enough to just go to bed for the night.

As Bonnie and I walked toward our bedroom I asked, "Why is all the furniture moved and the lamps by the windows?"

Bonnie simply replied, "Tomorrow! Right now you and I are going into our room and having a welcome home party."

# Thirteen

After Bonnie and I had our welcome home party, I got up to take a shower. The familiarity of our relationship and being in our home was exhilarating after months of being told when I could shower. We had closed our bedroom door when we had come into the room but it did not slam into a steel frame and go thud. It also had a knob on it and not just a locking mechanism that could only be worked from the outside of the cell and I could walk out of it at any time. I did not have to wait on my bunk until the electric mechanism was triggered by the control center.

The bathroom was filled with exotic smells as I entered it. I smelled the smell of toothpaste near the sink. The bathtub had a variety of smells from the moisturizing oils, body wash, and shampoos that were on a shelf at the end of the tub. I found a partial can of shaving cream on my shelf and a razor that I could use while standing in front of a clear glass mirror. After the shave and shower, I was able to reach in and get a freshly laundered bath towel from the linen closet. I had to admit to myself that they had not held such an intriguing fascination to me before the incarceration. Now they represented a freedom that I did not want to lose again.

Sleeping next to my wife was almost too much to believe. I laid there in bed fascinated with the silence of our bedroom. I could hear something like a garbage truck in the distance echoing the sound of metal on metal. The words to the Christmas song came to mind as I remembered the lines that said Peace on earth, good will toward man. I was feeling that as the rhythmic sound of breathing beside me heightened my peace of mind. I was thinking that would I or could I lose this again to the likes of Tony Gatzee. I did not want to think about that as I gave way to sleep.

The sun shining into our bedroom window in spite of the blanketing curtains was enough to wake me with a start. I was expecting a guard to have come in my cell to do a random urine test for drugs so I feigned sleeping. I had not had a cell with a window to daylight while I was in prison. Not hearing any voices or hearing any footsteps I opened my eyes slightly to look around. I realized then that this was a pleasant dream and not the usual nightmare that accompanied me in my sleep on a regular basis. I lay there and remembered the dream that would have me running from something that was scaring me on a repetitive basis. Some nights I would see dangers that resembled Tony and some nights I could look over my shoulder and see some of the inmates that I had learned to fear in the yard. During those dreams I never found peace until I woke up. I knew today that I was waking up in a place of peace with people that I loved.

I turned on my side enough to see the clock by my bed. It read only seven- ten a.m. so I tried to just lie there quietly and not wake anyone else up. It was actually more than an hour later than I could sleep in the prison so I was quite rested. I had only been awake about five minutes when Bonnie's alarm went off to get Ryan ready for a ball game. I rolled over and gave her a kiss good morning before she got up and put on her robe to go and wake Ryan. She looked back as she walked away and jokingly said, "You don't want to think that you are going to lie in that bed and bother me all day just because you're home. Some of us have work to do just like any other day. Why don't you get up and speak to Ryan before he goes to the ball field with his friends who are picking him up."

The house was soon bustling with two boys that wanted to play with me as Bonnie was making eggs and toast for the lot of us. Ryan had on his uniform and had gathered up a duffle bag that he carried the rest of his stuff in. Tyler was just wound up because I was home kept asking what we could do together. I found it unusual that Bonnie had not raised all the shades or opened the curtains as she used to do first thing in the morning. It was even more unusual when she would peek out a window to the back yard and also toward the streets in front and still not open them. We were just finishing up our breakfasts when a car horn honked outside and Ryan told us good bye.

The phone rang as we were picking up the dishes and I let Bonnie answer it. She said, "Hello. Oh hello Detective Flum. Yes Sam is home and as far as I know we are not going anywhere this morning. Okay, we will see you when you get here." Once she hung up the phone, she said, "That was Detective Flum and he is coming over to meet you and we may have to do some paper work for him now that you are home."

"Did he have a part in getting me out of prison?" I asked.

"There were a lot of people who were a part of getting you out of prison and keeping the boys and me safe," she said. "I will give you a very short part of the story before he gets here. I would appreciate it if you would let Tyler go play in his room and we can talk." I sent Tyler to his room and she started, "Tony Gatzee was having me stalked by one of his people. I don't know why I noticed the man but I did and he would follow me around town as well as other things. They would sit in front of the house for hours if we were home but I got their license plate numbers and turned them in. We nearly caught him when he followed me to the bank but he got away again. It was the same man who tried to lure Ryan away from the school one afternoon but two teachers stopped him. With the help of Detective Flum, Bernie Segal, and the federal prosecutor, Tony Gatzee is in prison for attempted murder of me and attempted kidnapping of Ryan as well as the original money laundering, racketeering, and falsifying evidence. They are being held without bail by the federal judge who let you out on minimal bail until you have a new court date or the charges are dropped."

I knew as I sat there that Bonnie could read the shock on my face. "You and the boys have gone through all this while I was in prison?" I asked.

"Most of it has happened in the last three weeks," Bonnie said. "There are several police officers who know me by name now as well as you."

The knock on the door got both of our attentions. Once inside Detective Flum shook hands with me and said hello to Bonnie. We were still at the table and offered him a cup of coffee.

"I really didn't come over for coffee," the detective said. "First off, I wanted to make sure that you were all safe and if there was anything that you needed from me over the weekend."

Bonnie answered first, "I have had no indication that there has been anyone on this street who does not belong here. We spent a relatively quiet night with my parents going home and the boys going to bed at their usual time. Do you have anything to tell us that we don't already know? I just gave Sam a quick glimpse of our last three weeks but we have not had time to discuss it and probably won't in front of the boys."

The detective started again, "I don't know any more of the charges that Tony and Frank face but they were safely tucked away in the federal prison last night where you have been Sam. The man, Mr. Smith, who we arrested for the actual attempts on your family, has decided he can sing a new song now that they are both in prison already. His real name is Mike Piccalo according to his finger prints on file and he has written out a confession stating that Tony was the man who hired him. He has been promised a different spa to visit for his testimony. He also went on the record and stated that Tony was trying to keep your silence in the courtroom because you were to be the patsy in the money laundering charges. You may get a free ride Sam by the time this is all done."

I said, "I was too naïve to know that I was being played for a sucker. I only kept the copies to make sure that I did not get cheated out of what I supposed was honest profit. I didn't know I was holding all the aces in the deck against Tony and Frank with those copies. I do know that I could have ended up in prison for something else if I had known what they were doing to my family. I would like to thank you for all you've done for my family."

Detective Flum said, "You have to give a lot of credit to your wife for how this all turned out. I don't know what made her so vigilant as to notice her being followed in her car and being watched here at home but she made our job much easier. She gave a letter to the school that made them aware of a possible threat to your family and they listened well enough to stop the kidnapping attempt. She had the sense to go into the bank drive up window to get help when she did recognize the man following her again. Most of the credit is due to her and you should be very proud of her. You might not have had a family to come home to if it wasn't for her."

I said, "I didn't know I had such a savvy wife but I've always known what would happen if anyone tried to hurt her kids. You might be interested in knowing that she is a crack shot with a gun in her hands."

The detective said, "I didn't know that but I will keep it in mind. When Donna got back to the station yesterday, she told us she had no doubt that Bonnie would kill someone to protect her family. I think that I am going to leave you now because I usually don't do these kinds of home visits so soon but I want you to know that we are just a phone call away if you ever feel in danger. Goodbye now."

I said, "Thanks again and Good bye to you."

When the detective opened the door, he almost got knocked down by Ryan as he got home from his practice. Neither one said a word as the detective left and the door was closed.

# Fourteen

The weather outside was beautiful with only high cirrus clouds dancing in the jet streams. The boys came out of their rooms and asked us if we could go to the lake for a while. We told them that we did not have time to make it a camping trip but we could pack a lunch for the afternoon. We were soon in the car and on our way out of town.

The hike out to the lake was as picturesque as I had ever seen it. There were wild flowers of every color along the path and as usual it wasn't long before Bonnie had a small arrangement from the boys. We met a white tailed doe and her fawn using the same trail as we were but they did not want to stay around when the boys tried to get too close. There was a stream that came from the lake and traveled along on the side of the trail. I got to show the boys where a beaver was chewing off a tree to fall it near the brook. They were fascinated that a beaver would try to cut down and move an eight inch tree to build its home or its dam.

As we crested the last little rise to the lake, we were treated to a glimmering display of light dancing on the minute, windblown waves near the shore. There were some rolling hills on the far side of the lake that were still heavy and dark green from the summer foliage of its resident trees. There were a couple of small kayaks traveling together breaking up the glassy surface of the lake as they went along. The vee-shaped ripples that they were causing were traveling out and disappearing shortly after they passed. I just stood there mesmerized at the scene and was thinking about what a difference just one day

could make. I found myself thinking that in a moment of time most of
the people that were in prison had given away the opportunity to see
what I was seeing. I wondered how many families would like to trade
places with me right now.

Bonnie had the boys round up a few dry sticks from nearby so we
could build a fire. The park rangers had a little fire pit that was there
for people to enjoy. We had brought our open fire toaster from our
camping gear and had told the boys they could toast their sandwiches
before we ate them. It was a wire mesh screen that was hinged to
wrap around a sandwich and had a long handle to hold it over a flame.
It worked well if there were not too many people trying to eat at the
same time. Bonnie took out some bottled water and some Gatorade
from the backpack we had carried in and set it out for us to share. She
then came over to see why I was being as quiet as I stared at the lake.

"I was thinking of what a difference a day makes," I said.
"Yesterday I was one of eight hundred men who had very little hope
to see days and times like this and now look. I have you and the boys
sitting around me at a beautiful lake with no assault rifles in a tower
overlooking our actions. I don't have to be done my meal in less than
twenty minutes nor be quiet in the halls. I just want you to know how
much I love you."

We embraced each other on the shore of that lake and watched
our sons go after more wood for the fire. We helped the boys toast
their sandwiches and then let them take off their clothing to play near
shore. By late afternoon we had two boys that were ready for the walk
out to the car and go home.

On the ride home Bonnie asked, "Do you think that the prayers of
my parent's church had anything to do with your being out of prison
and my being safe after being stalked for almost three weeks."

I answered, "Honey, I believe that we are good people and that
the truth has set me free from the walls of that prison. I believe that
your vigilance over your family got you to ask for help from the
police officers who finally arrested Tony Gatzee and Frank Gavin. I
have never believed in anything else such as a God or Jesus like your
parents. You also knew when you married me that I did not want that
for myself but I have never stopped you from going to church when
you wanted to such as Christmas."

Bonnie softly said, "I have to believe in times like this that there is more to our lives than our being good people. I have known a lot of other good people who were murdered, raped, or assaulted during similar times in their lives. I really believe that there is a God who hears our prayers and keeps us safe in times like this. There was a voice that told me to notice the cars sitting outside our house and the man who I kept seeing wherever I went. I believe that the hand of God was protecting me and our sons. Didn't you tell me that there was always danger around you there in the prison?"

I answered, "For the first couple of weeks I was terrified in the prison. I learned to savor the quiet and safety of a locked cell. In the yard you could be reached by one hundred-sixty people who were there for violent crimes. I witnessed one man getting beat to death by a group of men and it meant nothing to them except some more time added to their life sentence. I overheard two prisoners planning an assault on another inmate in the cafeteria and then witnessed them stomping on his hand as if it was an accident while they were in the yard. I learned to trust no one until I was moved into the wood working shop. For the weeks that I was in the shop I only saw one accident to a man who got hit by a piece of flying wood from a saw."

Bonnie started again in a soft voice, "Do you believe that you are safely home because you are a nice person or maybe the prayers that went up for us did some good? I have never pushed my belief on to you about the Savior of the world known as Jesus Christ but I have to tell you that I turned to prayer more than once while you were gone. I also saw how Jesus answered my prayer for safety and wisdom for our family over and over again. Do you think that your being a nice person will protect you from Tony? What if the judge in your case doesn't see you as a good person but as a money launderer in cahoots with Tony?"

"I believe that the truth will provide the means for me to stay out of prison from now on," I said. "Bernie has the evidence in the copies of the invoices that I turned in. He has presented it to the prosecutor who presented it to a federal judge and now I am out of prison and intend to stay out. I can't say that your prayers helped or if they didn't."

Bonnie said, "All I know is that Tony and his lawyer twisted the truth and you went to prison. I am convinced that the Lord had his angels watching over us and I thank Him for that. There is a weak voice in the back of my mind that is saying that they could twist the truth again if God does not intervene for us. I continue to pray for us with a fervency caused by the fear of man and I would like you to learn how to join me in prayer."

We were pulling into our driveway so the conversation came to a natural stop as we got the boys out of their car seats and into the house. Bonnie said in a quiet voice as we both had our heads in the car that we had to get to the safety of our house because there was someone watching us again. I wanted to look around but resisted and simply led the boys into the house. Bonnie ran around the house and closed curtains and blinds as I got the boys into their room. Bonnie said she was going to try to get a plate number on the car and told me to call 911. She cracked a curtain enough to get the binoculars where she could see when she saw two men getting out of the car. She yelled at me that they were coming from the side of the house. She said, "Your gun is loaded behind the bedroom door. Are the police on the way yet?"

"Yes they are responding," I said as I made my way into the bedroom. I checked the shotgun before I left the room and went to the living room. Bonnie was holding a knife that she had gotten from somewhere and she told me to get to a spot in the room where I could see both doors without moving. Bonnie went into the room with the boys and closed the door behind her. I didn't know that she had them get under their beds while she guarded the door.

I got down on one knee where I could see both doors but I studied the back door because Bonnie had said they had gone to the side of the house. I could not see anyone but I saw the knob turn on the back door and leveled the shotgun in that direction. The two men came in as they shoved the door out of their way. I let the first round go as soon as I had a target. I pumped the action and let another round go as they both stumbled back from the first round. I did it one more time as they fell backwards outside the back door. I held the gun ready but they were not moving so I walked toward them as sirens started to come into hearing. I yelled at Bonnie to come out of the room and bring the boys out with her. I told her to take the boys out the front door to a neighbor and to send the police to the back door.

The police came from both sides of the house with their guns drawn. I had gone far enough to see that neither one was going to cause any more trouble on this earth. The police rounded up all the guns including mine for safety and then asked me what had happened.

"Is Detective Flum available?" I asked in response to his question. "I shot these two men as they broke into my house with intentions of killing us. If you can find Detective Flum, this incident will make more sense and be much easier to explain. I have to make a phone call now to get my family to safety"

I went inside the house and called Fred and Paula. I gave them a quick account of what had just happened and asked them to come and pick up Bonnie and the boys for the night. They said that they would be right over. It was then that Detective Flum walked into my living room.

"I was afraid it wasn't all done yet," he said. "Is everyone okay?"

"Everyone except those two at the back door," I said. "I shot twice as they came through the door with their guns drawn. I don't think they are going to answer any of our questions though. I know that they worked for Tony but when are they going to quit their attempts on our lives?"

The detective said, "I think that they will now know that you don't intend to go down without a fight. We can have the prison shut down all communications to and from Tony. We will pick up the trail in the morning as to who they are and where they came from. Do you and your family have somewhere to go for the night? I will post someone here at the house to protect the scene and your belongings until we can clean up the mess even if it takes two days with tomorrow being Sunday."

"Bonnie's parents have been called," I said. "We can all go there for the night and I will give you their phone number. We might all have been killed if Bonnie hadn't seen them when we got home."

# Fifteen

When Fred came over to our house, he had to park on the next street. He found Bonnie and the boys in a police car and sent Bonnie back to his car with his keys. A policeman escorted them to help with a sleepy Tyler. Fred went over to where Detective Flum and Sam were talking and asked Sam if he was coming with them. The detective answered for him and told him to go along and someone would come and get him tomorrow if they needed one of the cars. Fred told them that he could do that tomorrow and he had to tug on Sam's arm to get him started. They were half way to the car when Sam finally spoke.

"I just killed two men who were going to kill all of us," Sam said. "I knew as they came in the door that it was them or me and I want this to be over so it is over for them forever."

Fred said, "You only did what had to be done. I am sorry that it came to this but I am not totally surprised either. Let's not talk about it in front of the boys and we can start to pick up the pieces in the morning."

We were soon all in bed and Bonnie knew that I did not want to talk about the shootings tonight. "I would like it if we all went to church with my parents in the morning," she said. "There are some good councilors who can talk to us and help us with our feelings. They even have people who can evaluate what the boys are thinking about this traumatic event."

I told her that I would consider it. I then turned away from her without even asking her how she felt. The shock of the whole episode was starting to get to me now the adrenalin was wearing off. I woke up in the middle of the night in a cold sweat just terrified to go back to sleep. I tried to lie there quietly as Bonnie's rhythmic breathing calmed me back from the fear. I had not been able to speak to anyone in my family since I pulled the trigger until I was leaving the scene with Fred. Maybe there was some credence having the councilors at the church for all of us to speak to.

We ended up using Fred and Paula's two cars as we divided up to all go to the church. None of our family had clean clothes but we didn't let that stop us. Fred continued to be my guide while the boys and Bonnie went with Paula. Fred said as we drove, "I will get the people we need to speak to us in private and not make this a spectacle before the entire congregation. We would not be able to protect the boys from the entire congregation's remarks and questions. Are you ready for the questions that you will inevitably have to answer?"

"I only know that I have done nothing wrong," I answered. "I am not proud of what I did and I hope that I am never in that situation again but I would do it exactly the same way if I had to. I imagine that there will be some who might think that I could have done it differently but they were not in my shoes looking back at two guns. I have been in such a shock that I have not even asked my family how they are doing. First being sent to prison and leaving them and now separated by the shootings is starting to create a chasm of emotions that I do not want to fall into. I do not want to hate Tony or his people but it would be an easy path to take."

Fred said, "You would do well to stay off that path. I have made arrangement by phone for all of us to go to the board room rather than the sanctuary. We will all be in the sanctuary while the main service is conducted by Pastor Mike Murray and back to the board room after. You are in a safe place here with people who care about you and your family."

Once we were in the board room, we were greeted by several of the people in the church. Two women took Paula and the boys to yet another room in which to speak privately. Bonnie and I met two couples who were to be speaking to us. One couple took Bonnie and the other took me to separate corners within the room. It turned out to be just a way to introduce them and get us talking as if there had never been a problem in the world. They did not raise one question about what happened but started us thinking about the feelings of our mate and sons. We were soon all being led to the sanctuary for the service.

The sanctuary seemed capable of holding three hundred parishioners but was about one hundred seats short of a full house. There was a lively worship song sung to begin with by a group that was up on a stage and that was a cue for the congregation to come to order and find a seat. The six of us sat together in an area just to the minister's right as he faced us. One of the women who had gone with Paula and the boys chose to sit near us and occasionally speak softly to Tyler. As the music was winding down, a man rose up from the front row that was wearing a matching set of trousers and suit coat. He walked up to the dais and turned to face us. He adjusted his collar just a little as he waited for the music to subside. He seemed to be a man in his early forties with a friendly smile. When the music ended, he said, "Good morning everyone! Why don't we take a minute and say hello to someone sitting near you and especially to anyone you might not have seen before. If you are a visitor, we welcome you to the house of the Lord as a brother or sister we haven't met before."

When the noise seemed to be abating, he got everyone to listen to some dates of interest and tell of a few people he knew who needed to be kept in prayer for differing reasons. He then brought back the worship team as he called them to lead us in some more singing. I was surprised to hear Bonnie singing some of the songs as she stood next to me. While we were all singing, people would walk up and place what appeared to be offering envelopes into a basket at the foot of the dais. After they had sung a few songs, the pastor went back to the dais and everyone who had been on the stage put down their instruments and took a seat with the rest of us.

The pastor started, "Good morning everyone and for those of you whom I have not met yet, my name is Pastor Mike Murray. I am glad that you have all come to worship our Lord and savior Jesus Christ and to hear the words of truth by which we are all to live."

The message that continued was on how wonderful it is to walk a life of faith and to know when someone hears from God. He told of how the bible was the most basic way to know how God wanted us to live. He expounded on that with how someone who had a personal relationship with the Lord could count on Jesus to speak directly to our hearts and minds. He then brought it to the point of how brothers and sisters in the Lord could live as examples to others around them and be a living gospel. He then finished with a remark about how this might not be important if a person did not know Jesus as their savior. He told us all that if anyone wanted to know more about this Jesus they could come up and speak to him on the stage and the rest could go home.

Most of the congregation started to leave the building while a few people went up on the stage. We all knew that we were supposed to go back to the board room for some more discussions. When we were all with the same people again, I had to ask them a question.

"What did the pastor mean when he said that the Lord would speak directly to your heart and mind," I asked. "Why I am asking is because of something my wife was telling me the other day. She said that she heard someone in her head telling her about the man who was stalking her. She said that she took directions from the voice and that led to the man being caught and imprisoned. She was also the one who saw those two men in their car when we got home last night. Her actions saved our lives as well as what I did."

The man said, "It is as literal as he spoke about. God is able to speak to us in many ways such as reading the bible, dreams, visions, softly spoken words only your mind hears, and at times audible voices that you hear with your ears. God is truly concerned about our well being while we are on this earth so he thwarts the devil's attempt to harm us. If your wife said she heard this, I would be very quick to believe her."

"I don't believe that I have ever had such an experience," I said.

"Do you know the Lord Jesus Christ as your personal savior?" the man said. "That is where it all begins when we put our lives into His hands like those of a loving father. The bible is rich with promises of what God will do for us if we repent of our sins and believe in Jesus as our Lord and savior."

"This is one of the first times that I have come to church when it wasn't Christmas or Easter," I said. "In the past, I have never felt the need for help but I have to admit that I have been intimidated lately. I thought that I had the world by the tail and it couldn't hurt me but I now know that I believed a lie. I haven't had much time to be afraid but I woke up in the middle of the night last night in a cold sweat paralyzed in fear. I'm just very glad that no one saw what I had to do really and they didn't see the aftermath. All this came about because of my pride and ego and it nearly cost me my family not once but twice."

"I think that it is time to bring Bonnie into our conversation," the man said. He beckoned the other group to come and join us. "I believe that you two need to hear what the other is thinking about last night and maybe since you were separated. It is very important that you find your emotions as early as possible, reveal them one to the other, and find a means to not succumb to emotions that will damage your relationship together. Sam you have already been speaking about your fears and it will be our goal to find out if there are any grounds for you to be afraid. We will be doing that to all of them that we can have exposed in a safe and loving way."

We had been conversing for about twenty minutes when Pastor Mike came into the room. He just pulled up a chair with us and did not say a word. The man whom I was with was laying out some ground rules for our discussions and telling us how we should write down emotions we were feeling. That we should try to commit to at least one hour with them during the week and to have their telephone numbers should we find ourselves in turmoil. We decided to meet with them for an hour on Tuesday afternoons until I went back to work. That was when Pastor Mike decided that it was his turn.

"I have to ask you what is important to you at this juncture in your life," he said. "I know from talking to Fred and Paula Lang that Bonnie was very close to the Lord when she was younger but has gone to relying on herself in the years that you two have been together. I also know Sam that you do not have a relationship with our heavenly Father. It is something that you should consider when the devil has had such a field day with your lives. We have an advocate in Jesus Christ that will stop the attacks of the devil and will give us peace in our hearts. The one thing that you were allowing to set the parameters of your meeting times was going back to work. It tells me that you are trying to deny how the devil has had you in prison and now has gotten you to kill two men. The effects that these two things will have on your life are of phenomenal proportion and will get preeminence for the near future. Do you still feel adequate to handle all of this on your own whether you are guilty or not?"

"The only thing I know for sure is that my pride is what I am guilty of. I did not do the money laundering and I shot those two men as they attacked us with guns," I said.

Pastor Mike said, "Pride is what made the devil get banished from heaven by God. Why don't you go home and try to get settled as well as you can and I will try to join you on Tuesday."

# Sixteen

When we left the church, we drove by our home to get everyone some clothes and to get both of our cars. I was the only one that went into the house. The police officer that was there at the time asked me to stay away from the back door if I could as he let me under the tape depicting the crime scene. I asked him when he thought I could put a new door on and he told me that it would probably be afternoon the next day at the earliest. I asked him if the department had the technology to examine Bonnie's car for tracking devices. He said no but that our cars were both new enough to have devices installed at the factory that a lot of new equipment could track.

Bonnie had taken both of the boys and put them into their seats in her car. She came to the door long enough to take one of the suitcases I had filled and then told me she would meet me in a little while. I asked her if she wanted me to bring in some fast food but she said her mother had made a stew in her crock pot while we were at church. I finished getting what I thought we would need for a couple of days and then followed her to her parents' house.

The meal was easily prepared and soon we were all lying about in the living room. Fred asked me if I would take a ride with him to go and see something. I looked at Bonnie to see if she was okay with the idea and she said that she was going to take the boys down to a local playground so the boys could let off some pent up energy. We were soon on our way to another subdivision near her parents' house. We pulled into the driveway of a large home with what appeared to be an attached garage. Fred led us to the door and let us in with a key.

The house inside was neatly laid out with a modern kitchen including a double wide refrigerator, dishwasher, larger than normal range with six burners, inset microwave and inset oven. The living room was well lit by natural lighting from windows. There was a bathroom in the hall that led from the living room to a master bedroom with two walk-in closets and its own bathroom with both a tub and shower. There was a back entrance in the kitchen and also stairs to the second floor. On the second floor were two bedrooms with their own closets, a bathroom, and a den style room with book shelves and another large window for natural light. The entire upstairs was carpeted in a beige sculpted carpet. The stairs had some nicely finished newel posts and balusters done in a dark cherry stain. At the end of the living room downstairs, there was a room that served as a laundry room and mud room as it led directly into the garage. The garage was oversized and had some wood working tools toward the back. There was a door to the rear of the garage at the adjoining side. It led to a large fenced in back yard with a swing set and monkey bars with a slide attached.

The entire time that we had walked through the house Fred had only told me about the amenities of the house and nothing more. When we were back in the living room, I asked him, "Why are we here?"

He looked at me and said, "This house belongs to some of my best friends in the world. They raised their family in this house from about the time their kids were teens. The kids grew up and married and started to have children of their own. They would come here to visit so my friend Tom had the back yard fenced in and the playground put in. He got kind of bored and that is when he put in the woodworking shop. A couple of years ago Tom dropped in his tracks after only two years of retirement. Mary was just devastated. She had the house painted throughout and has been trying to sell it. She is living with a daughter until this sells and she can buy her own place. I watch over the house for her and keep the grounds tidied up. I made a call this morning and spoke to Mary. You can buy this house as you see it for a much discounted price because of who I am. You have permission to move right in so you can repair your current home and sell it. With the equity in your current home, you could own this one for about the same payment. The shop is licensed in the city so you can make a living from here if you want to. I brought you out here alone first because I did not want to disappoint my daughter if you do not want to leave your current house. I think it would be helpful at starting the healing process for both of you."

"It is definitely a beautiful house," I said. "I am interested enough to have her and the boys see it. I know personally that I would remember last night every day that I was in our current house. This house would allow for our sons to have individual rooms in the near future as well as a place where it would be difficult for anyone to get near them without our knowing. You say we could move right in?"

Fred brought me back to their home but Bonnie had already left with the boys. I decided that I would speak to Mary before I brought Bonnie over to see the house. We spoke for a few minutes and I told her how much I had liked the house and what it would mean to me and my family. She said that she was excited that friends that she knew would be buying their house. We did discuss the amount that she wanted and it was well below market price. I told her that I did not want to cheat her and she said that the satisfaction of having the house go to such wonderful people was worth the difference in the money. She also told me that she was not in a position of need. I thanked her and said that we would take it. She told me to go ahead and move in as soon as possible and we would talk soon.

I hung up the phone and said to Fred, "I hope Bonnie likes it because I just bought that house."

Fred said, "Congratulations! I know this is the first step of many that will be needed to heal. We will let you show it to Bonnie and the boys when they come back and you can surprise her with the news while you are there."

Bonnie came back in about an hour and I went to meet her in the driveway. I said, "I want to show you something down the street before you all get out of the car. It will only take a few minutes and then we will be right back. If you will just go down this street and I'll show you where to turn left up here. Now if you will just pull into this driveway right here."

I got everyone out of the car and Bonnie said, "I know this place. It belonged to Tom and Mary who were good friends of my parents.

What are we doing here? I know that Tom died a couple of years ago but I do not know what happened to Mary."

I did not answer any of her questions but walked up to the door and unlocked it for the second time today. We all walked in and I just stood in the living room and asked, "do you want to see your new home?'

Bonnie just stood there with a dumbfounded look on her face.

I said again, "Do you want to look at your new home? I know that I have not even asked you what or how you are feeling since yesterday. I have been barely able to breathe for myself and I do not have a grip on my emotions yet, but I do know this. I could not stay in our current home without reliving what happened last night over and over again. Your father brought me over here to see it alone because he did not want to disappoint you if I could not move from the other house but I want to. I spoke to Mary on the phone and if you want to be with me, we can move in tomorrow."

"Of course I want to be with you!" Bonnie said. She kissed me passionately before she started to walk around. "You better show me my new home Mr. Walker."

We all walked through the house, garage, and large back yard. The boys ran over and tried the slide before we went back inside. I said, "I even get all the tools with the house and the workshop is licensed by the city so I can work from here. Do you like the house Mrs. Walker?"

"No! I love the house, Mr. Walker," Bonnie said, "and I believe that the boys approve also as we watched them running around. Are you serious about moving in tomorrow? That would mean that we would not have to spend another night in our current house."

"We would have to check with Detective Flum before moving anything," I said, "but I don't see why they would not let us. I can then clean up the mess, repair the door, and get that house ready for sale. I will check with Bernie and see if he can help us with the sale or who he would recommend for us. I know that your parents do not mind us being there but it is a little crowded in their home."

We spent a little over an hour in the house as Bonnie planned how she wanted to arrange our furniture in this bigger house. She jokingly said that most of our furniture could be put in the closets here at the new house. I told her that I was glad to see her smiling in anticipation. When we pulled up to her parents' house, she ran in to tell her mother who tried to act at least a little surprised. The rest of the day was a little lighter hearted.

We made a call to Detective Flum in the morning and gave him a synopsis of what we intended to do. He said he would call us within the hour as he had to speak to the district attorney about any possible charges against Sam as a procedural thing. He said, "I will have to get with you sometime today or tomorrow to have you write out what happened the other night for the file. I hope that by the time we meet I will have some other information for you about who they were and what they wanted. There is very little question that they waited for you for quite a while by the cigarette butts that were retrieved by their car. Why don't you guys put together a plan of action for your move and I will get the house released as far as a crime scene. I'll be talking to you soon."

We made a couple of calls to people who did moving about their availability and their rates. There were two companies who could help us today but one of them wanted an exorbitant fee for short notice so we were left with one choice. We made some calls to have the electricity placed in our names as well as the water department with the city. We checked out the option of getting cell phones instead of the land line and we soon had some cell phones in our pockets or handbag. We had a new insurance policy written for the new address when we called to see if our homeowners policy would help pay for the damage done by the gunmen. I was surprised to find out that it would pay for all the damages that had incurred.

Detective Flum called back as he had promised within the hour. "When I told the prosecutor who you were and the story about last week, he said that he would not pursue any charges against you. I can now officially release your house from being a crime scene and you can do what you have to. I will be sending over our clean up specialist for the blood and stuff but I also have to remove the police officer who had been on duty at the scene. I have the information that I told you I would get but I want to go over that in person. Were you able to find a mover for today?"

I told him yes and I also gave him our new cell phone numbers that we would be using. I asked him if I could come down to the precinct around ten tomorrow and he said he would be ready for us.

# Seventeen

The mover arrived at the old house around eleven in the morning while we were trying to decide the most important things to go in the one load we had hired them to do. They made quick work of the kitchen, living room furniture, and the three beds. They were able to load the bureaus that we had in our room and then box up some of the linens, towels, blankets, and a few toys for the boys before the truck was full. While they were loading that stuff, I made a makeshift lock to secure the back door. A crime scene cleaner had come earlier in the morning and was gone before the movers came so we did not have to explain to them. I put some of the food from the refrigerator into a cooler and put that in my truck along with strapping the television in the back seat.

The truck was unloaded by three thirty in the afternoon with the beds assembled in the appropriate rooms as well as the rest of the furniture dispersed throughout. Bonnie then went over and got the boys from her parents. I made one more trip to get the rest of the food from the refrigerator and some items we had forgotten to pack like toothbrushes and extra toilet paper. We had cold cuts for supper and then tried to find enough linen to make the beds. We made bedtime an adventure like camping so the boys would sleep away from us for the first time in their lives. It had proven to be a long day and both Bonnie and I were glad to get to bed early ourselves.

In the morning we made two lists while we were eating. Bonnie was going to the grocery store with her list and I was going to the old house with mine after I had gone to the precinct to see Detective

Flum. The boys were very adamant that they needed their electronic games as soon as possible. I was going to get some of my tools moved because of their value to me as a source of income. Bonnie reminded me that we had an appointment with the people at the church this afternoon as I was about to leave.

I arrived at the precinct a few minutes early and made my way back to the detective's office. He was on the phone when I knocked softly on his door. He waved me in and I stood near the door until he was finished looking at some of the commendations he had on his wall. They were an indication that he was proficient at his work which we had come to know firsthand. As he hung up the phone he said, "Come in and sit down Sam. You may want to when I tell you some of the information that we have now."

"I did not like the tone of that," I said as I sat down. "I don't believe that a tornado could have made much worse an impact on my life than having met Tony Gatzee."

"I would like to hear how you and Bonnie are doing first," the detective said. "What you two have been through would probably feel like a tornado. You seem to be taking this rather well compared to a lot of other people I have had in my office. I hope the move to a new home will prove to be a positive step."

I replied calmly, "I do not know if I am even over the first shock from the other night but we are taking steps together as a family to come out on the other side of this in a good way and not just another statistic. The new home was an answer to prayer before I could get it out of my lips. I know that I would have relived the other night over and over again if we had stayed there. You might stop by in the near future to see our new outpost against the enemy."

The detective laughed and said, "I am glad to see that you can still see some humor in this turmoil. I would love to stop by soon when I did not have to be there. Let me give you some more good news before business. The two men that you shot were brought in by someone and have a serious reputation. I will give you the names if you want but they were professional hit men and they had a bounty on their heads. You are going to be able to put twenty thousand dollars for one and thirty five thousand dollars for the other down on your new house."

"I am going to get paid for killing those two men?" I asked. "I don't know if that will stop the nightmares but that is unbelievable. Now the important question is can you tie them to Tony? I want the rest of this nightmare to be over and start getting on with our lives. I want to know for sure that I am not going back to prison because I am not guilty and can go back to work."

"Our prosecutor has gotten in touch with the federal prosecutor in your case to catch him up on what is going on out here," the detective said. "I have a written statement from what you told me to look at and sign for the record about the other night. We have not tied the two men to Tony but let's face it; we don't have too many other choices in the pot. They are now monitoring every communication in or out of Toni's concern and are not allowing visitors at this time. I believe that you may have to testify in court about the validity of your copies but you will be given a pardon of any wrong doing and your history will be cleared from your name. You will have no record of any charges that were not dropped. If they accept some kind of plea agreement, you will probably never see Tony or Frank again. A couple of FBI agents have paid a visit to the rest of Toni's family and they were given a few words of advice in your behalf. We told them of having paper trail enough to send Tony away for life and if he didn't want to face the death penalty for murder it would be wise to leave you and your family alone. We also told them where to find the two men that they had sent to your house. I think they have a clear picture now."

I read the detective's document about the other night and signed it. "I would like to imagine a life without Tony and prison," I said. "I believe I have had my pride put into perspective for me. I would like to thank you for all you have done for us so far and please do come over when it is not a 911 call from us. Good bye!"

"You're welcome Sam," Detective Flum said. "I may use the excuse of bringing over those two checks to see your new home. I'm sorry for all you have been through and I hope the nightmare is really over."

I went to our old house and got a quick load of items that were on the list and then just picked up what else I could fit into the truck. When I got back to the new house, Bonnie and her parents were inside working. I told them that I was going to unload the truck but I had something to tell all of them when we were done. Fred helped me unload and Bonnie and Paula got some lunch ready for everyone. On one trip to the garage I saw that the boys were building a new highway in the back yard. When the four of us were all at the table, I took Bonnie by the hand and I started my story.

"I met with Detective Flum this morning to sign a statement about the other night," I started. "He told me that I was cleared of that shooting but he went on to tell me who I had shot and more. They were professional hit men from out of town and there was a bounty on both of them. I am going to get paid for having defended my family against two armed men a total of fifty-five thousand dollars of bounty money and there is more. I am going to get a clean slate from the felony charges and I am free from prison permanently. The FBI went to Toni's family and told them to leave us alone and where to pick up the two men that they had sent. I believe that a big part of the nightmare is over."

Bonnie, the boys, and I cleaned ourselves up and put on some clean clothes to go to the church this time. We all started separately with the same people again and then had a time of being together. Pastor Mike came in quietly again as we were talking as a group. One of the men asked me, "Have you been able to focus since the shooting or is there an overriding emotion driving you and your actions?"

"I feel as if I am on a roller coaster and I cannot take time to feel anything yet, I answered. "I have been troubled by fears of the unknown but in the two days since we first met I have a new life. We bought a new house and moved in partially enough to not have to spend much time in the old house. I haven't felt guilty for killing those men and now that they are paying me for having killed them I probably never will. I have been assured that I will not be going back to prison and that my record will be cleared completely. I have a new life with my family and that is a good thing. Things are changing so completely and so rapidly that I do not have time to get emotional."

Pastor Mike asked, "Do you think that everything in your life is going to go as well as these two days have gone or might there be a down side? You have changed everything in your life but have you resolved anything? Do you feel that you have done all this by yourself or is there possibly an advocate speaking to His father in your behalf?

Bonnie I would like to hear some of your thoughts about who may be at least partly in control of what is going on in your lives."

Bonnie started, "Pastor Mike, I have to admit that several times since Sam had gone to prison I have been in serious prayer for him. I knew the Lord as my savior a long time before I got married but I let my love for Sam take the dominating role in my life. I know that I had my parents keep Sam on your prayer list here in this church. I needed a reminder that my life is not my own but it needed realignment with the word of God. As Paul writes in his epistle that a husband is to treat his wife as the weaker vessel became my motto and I left off the second half of that verse where the husband is to love his wife as Christ loves His church. A Godly woman is supposed to bring her husband to the Lord by example but it won't work if it is in total silence of her love for God. I know that God's mercy has been to our favor in the last few months to say nothing about His phenomenal care in the last two days. I know that if Sam had been killed the other night, he would not have gone to heaven."

I jumped in about then, "I have always been a good person! I may not know the scriptures the way Bonnie does obviously but I am not a bad man."

Pastor Mike said, "There are no good men in heaven Sam, only the righteous shall see the glory of God and spend eternity with Him. We are made white as snow before God when we accept what Jesus did for us on the cross at Calvary. God the father had Jesus his son die on a cross for the forgiveness of our sins. When we now believe that Jesus is the Son of God, ask Him to forgive us our sins, and repent; that is to turn away from our sins and commit to stop doing them anymore, He is faithful and true to His word and forgives our sins. From then on we have the right as adopted righteous sons of God to spend our eternity with Him in heaven. Do you understand what I just said?"

I answered, "I understand what you just said but I know a lot of people who have done what you said and they continue to do unrighteous things in their lives."

Pastor Mike said, "You are right but God can see our hearts. He can see if we love Him and actually are trying to stop our sinning. Jesus knew on that cross that He not only died for the sins until I said the sinner's prayer and asked Him to come reside in my heart that He was going to have to forgive the sins that I have committed since. I often have to go to Him and ask His forgiveness anew and He is always willing and able to do that. I do not sin as much as I used to so it is getting easier. You also need to know that Bonnie or I cannot ask the forgiveness of God for your sins. It is an individual who goes to the Father for forgiveness and that is why He is called your personal savior."

I said, "I need to think about this some more I guess. Where do you go to find Jesus so I can ask Him myself?"

Pastor Mike smiled, "You don't go anywhere. God is everywhere and you can speak to Him from anywhere. When you accept Jesus into your heart, you will come to know a peace that your mind can not conjure up. He will make Himself real in your life the way you need Him and that may not be the way I sense His presence but that's okay. You will know that He is with you wherever you are. Would you like to do that now and I will pray with you."

With those words I just began to cry for no other reason than I could not stop myself. I was feeling emotions and reliving parts of my life in my mind that seemed to be releasing into the atmosphere. The most recent events like killing those two men and working my way back through the time in prison appeared in my mind and then seem to disappear. I do not know how long this went on but when I was finally able to stop, take a breath, and look around I found that Bonnie was still crying and some of the other people were crying with us.

Pastor Mike said, "I think you have found your savior."

I said, "I haven't said anything. All I did was cry."

Pastor Mike said, "There are no rules about how Jesus comes to let us know that we have had our sins forgiven. He knows our hearts and he bestows His grace in the manner He chooses. I think that you will be able to resolve some of the things in your lives now."

# Eighteen

The house was starting to take shape with our furniture in it. Fred had volunteered to help me clean up the other house and to be around if I had some new questions about knowing Jesus better. I had gotten a hold of our home owner insurance and found out that I could not do the work on my own house so they sent someone over to fix the door at the other house. When that work was done, I did some cosmetic stuff to get the house more sellable. I went with Bonnie to see a real estate agent that was a friend from school. We used her guidance to set a price on our old house and listed it with her agency. She told us that we had to disclose any problems we knew about the house but we did not have to say anything about having to kill those two men there. We used the quick sale of our house as a place to start using our new found faith together in prayer.

I was starting to organize the garage the way I would like it to work from. I added a work station similar to the one I had had in the prison and moved a table saw to align with the top of the station. By placing a small roller stand between the saw and the table I could rip plywood by myself. I was working with the garage door open one day when we had a surprise visitor.

"Is this the Walker homestead or is it Fort Walker," Detective Flum said as he entered the garage. "Today I was looking for the Walker residence because I have some business to discuss with them."

"I'll see if they are home," I answered him as I walked up and shook his hand. "What do you think of my work shop?"

We spent the next few minutes looking around the shop and the back yard where Tyler was playing. Ryan was in school for a little while yet. I went in the door to the house and called Bonnie to come greet our guest. We showed the detective around the house before we sat down at the kitchen table for some coffee. "Were you serious about having some business to speak to us about?" I asked him.

He put an envelope on the table and said, "I told you I would bring these two items to you and here they are. The other thing I came by to see you about came from a very strange source. I guess you made a cabinet while you were in prison and it must have been a beauty because someone hunted you down because of it. The warden of the prison is a friend of mine. He was so impressed by your work that he wanted to have you do some work for him. He cannot use anything that the prisoners make because of the possibility of someone seeing it as conflict of interest or favoritism. When he found out that you had been released and all the charges have been dropped, he can now hire you to do work on his house. I told him that I would ask you before I divulged your phone number in light of what happened recently. Are you interested in the work?"

"Of course I am," I said. "We have decided that most of what you just put on the table is going to be around for our children to choose a college if they want to so I have to go back to work very soon. The only thing I want to add to this set of tools I have now is a thirty-two inch belt sander but I will have to leave my truck in the driveway if I do that. If I can market enough work I will not have to go back to paying those union dues. Instead I will be paying an accountant."

We laughed together and then finished our time together in general small talk. Once he was gone Bonnie asked, "Are you serious about trying to work out of our garage instead of the union?"

I told her, "Yes I am and this time I am not doing it because of pride but by the provision of the Lord along with this house. I have everything I need to build quality cabinets and furniture and install them if people want me to. I do not know why we have found such favor with the Lord but I have an idea that it is not over yet. I have always had the dream to build fine furniture for kitchens and bedrooms."

Bonnie answered, "I can see what you mean by the provision of the Lord. I have known the day when I would have panicked to hear you say those words but I am at complete peace that we are enjoying God's favor and I will support you if that is what you decide. At what time did you tell Bernie that we were coming by today?"

I told her, "We have to get Tyler cleaned up and get going right away so we can take him to your mother before we go."

We walked into Bernie's office a little later than I had arranged but it did not seem to offend him too much. Once we were seated we questioned him about doing our real estate transactions or if not who he would recommend. We got to tell him how we got the new house and even about the work that was starting to come in. He gave us the name of an associate who he trusted to do our work. He had me sign a paper for release of bond by the judge while I was there and that is when we both realized that this would probably be the last formal meeting between us. I thanked him profusely and started to get up from my chair when he asked me, "Do you want to work off part of your bill at my house?"

We ended up setting a time to go to his home in the evening so we could see the work needed and to meet his family. We then made our way over to the office that Bernie had sent us to for our real estate deals. We then spoke to Jim Simonds' secretary about our needs. She set an appointment for us to meet with Jim in two days in the afternoon and if we could to find out whom Mary wanted to use for a lawyer. We thanked her and took the card with the phone numbers and the time to meet. We had also asked Bernie for the name of a good CPA that we could use. She was next on our list of people to find today but she was only two doors down in the professional building.

We walked into the office of Sarah Carter and were greeted by a woman who was doing data entry at her desk. The woman used the phone to speak to someone and then hung up. "Mrs. Carter can give you about ten minutes," she said, "It is the door at the end of the hall."

We were greeted at the door by a woman who held out her hand and said, "Hello, I am Sarah Carter."

I started as we were seated, "Bernie Segal gave us your name for our needs. I have two of them that I can identify and you may know of more. We need to know how to handle a possible tax burden on some bounty money and I am going to start a woodworking shop."

Sarah said, "The first one is easy. There are no taxes due on federally paid bounties so that money is yours. As far as setting up a business, I would use two rates for my charges. We get a lesser fee for general bookkeeping services than what I charge for my time. You can make it even less expensive if you are willing to set up a computer program at home, do most of the entries yourself, and sending me the information by internet. We would prepare any sales tax reports from here and income taxes would be done the same way. Is that what you wanted to know and if so do you want an appointment to get started?"

We took an appointment along with the list of information that she would need to establish us as a company. She emphasized a legal name that would meet current and future needs that we would file papers for with the city. She said that she could apply for the state id and federal id. She also asked if we were going to incorporate for safety in legal matters especially if we were working out of our home. I told her that I would pose the question to Bernie when we saw him later this week. As she was leaving, she gave us the name of an independent financial advisor that we should probably speak to.

When we picked up Tyler, we had time to speak to Fred and Paula about some of the things we had on our mind so they could pray for our wisdom in the choices we would be making. When we got to the part about the financial planner and told them the name, Fred let out a little chuckle.

"What is suddenly so funny?" I asked. "I'm trying to not get overwhelmed and you think something is funny."

"Who did you say that the CPA recommended for a financial advisor?" Fred asked.

"She recommended Samuel Pickens," I said.

"Now what is the name of the couple who have been meeting with you at the church?" Fred said. "Didn't you know that Sam and

Celine's last name was Pickens? Sarah Carter and her husband, William, go to our church also."

Now it was my turn to chuckle. "I think God is trying to set me up the way Tony did but I think He means it for good," I said. "I am amazed at how He takes care of us and threads us together."

We called Mary that evening and asked her if she had a lawyer that she wanted to use that was local. She gave us his name and said that she would call him and tell him Tim Simonds' name on our behalf. She asked us if we liked the house so far and we told her how much it meant to us. She said that she would leave the exchange of money up to her lawyer when we closed on our old house. I asked her, "I thought that you needed the money to buy a smaller house and move out of your daughter's house."

Mary said, "I have always had the money to buy another house but I have been able to help my daughter while I have enjoyed my grandchildren. It was easier to tell her that than to admit how lonely I had become after Tom passed on. The pain of my loss is becoming more bearable and I am sure that I will be able to find my own house soon. What with the survivorship clause of Tom's retirement and the life insurance payoff, I have no needs. Actually, I want you to not send any money until I check with my accountant on how to best avoid giving all the money to the government in taxes on the sale of the house. I may need to receive the money over a period of a few years to help in that department. I will get back to you soon okay. Also, I have been told that you are a new brother in the Lord and I will end with a great big God bless you. Bye now!"

"Wow!" I said, "Another blessing from God from another sister in the Lord."

As Bonnie and I lay in bed that night I asked, "What do you think would be an appropriate name for our new business? I tried to come up with an acronym with the use of our initials but that is too awkward. The neatest name I have come up with is Walker Enterprises to use when all of us are involved in the coming years. I believe that the word enterprise is more functional if we diversify in the future than to use something like cabinet shop in the name. Do you have any ideas?"

Bonnie said, "I like the name Walker Enterprises and I also like my sleep. Good night!"

# Nineteen

I had spent about one hour with the warden of the prison discussing everything from my visit there for a period of time to what I had come for. His wife wanted a closed cabinet with some partitioned shelving to place in her laundry room. I had drawn a simple sketch with the dimensions she wanted it to be built and discussed what kind of finish she wanted. She had wanted it in raw wood that she could paint to match the rest of her laundry room. The warden wanted a cabinet for his library in which he could conceal a safe for weapons. He wanted functioning drawers in front of the safe and a few shelves similar to what I had done in the prison. There would be a false back behind the drawers so no one could see the weapons in the rear.

He said, "I guess I am speaking to a man who can appreciate the ability to get to a gun quickly. I have never had to do what you did Sam and I never want to be in a similar situation but it comes with the territory."

I said, "I never in my life dreamed that I would be in the situation that I found myself but I would do it again to protect my family. I already had some apprehension about possibly having to return to prison but the one thing that kept me sane there were thoughts and memories of my family. I was not willing to lose them again and certainly not that way."

Then the warden asked me a question that I never expected, "Sam, do you have any suggestions for me about the system I run?"

"I don't know if you have the ability to sort the men more," I said. "You are mixing everyone in there to where it is not possible to maintain any emotional hope within yourself. The dangerous lifers are mixed throughout the system and are completely capable of intimidating any inmate that they want to. I heard and saw inmates plan assaults on others and even witnessed the killing of an inmate with the wisdom to not say a word about what I knew to be true. The first ray of hope that I had in there had been when I was able to go back to what I am good at rather than the thought of merely abiding in a place where I had no hope."

"I got to see the kind of work that you did in that environment so I know that you will do an excellent job for us," the warden said. "By the way, I would like you to use cherry as the solid front and I will finish it myself as I did the other woodwork in my office."

"I have a question for you sir if I may ask it," I said. "I met some men in that shop that had a lot of potential from the red hats to the blue. How could I find out the status of some of those inmates and find out if they are getting to be released soon."

"I can get the information on any one from my computer here or at my office," he said. "If you give me a couple of names, I can tell you all about their dates and if they were violent offenders. Why?"

"I am creating a new business and I could offer some of them some work for me if it would help them keep from re-offending," I said. "I have been blessed more than I have been cursed and I have a new desire to help someone other than myself if I could."

We finished our business and as I was about to leave the warden said, "I believe you were telling me the truth about wanting to help some of the others when they get out. You write down their names and I will call you if I think you could help them. Good night!"

On the ride home I took the time to thank Jesus for His provision and the strange way that it came about. We were going to the church tomorrow afternoon for our continuing meetings with Sam and Celine Pickens and now I intended to give him some business as an extra thank you. I thanked God for having made all these connections to bless us with. By the time I got home I was tired but exuberant about our future with these first orders for custom furniture. We were also meeting with Sarah Carter to establish the Walker Enterprise LLC accounts. I wasn't making any sawdust yet but we were making headway.

We were just finishing up some blueberry pancakes I had made for the boys' breakfast when the phone rang. Bonnie answered it and was soon speaking louder and she told the person on the other end that she could tell me. I took the phone and it was Bonnie's friend from the real estate office. She had a young couple who had made an offer on our house that was within three thousand dollars of our asking price. They were preapproved for at least that amount of money so this sale could move forward very quickly if we accepted the offer. We agreed to meet later in the morning to sign the sales agreement and I hung up. I just turned to Bonnie and said, "I guess God isn't done blessing us yet! Get ready Ryan, I am taking you to school today."

I went by a lumber wholesaler on the way home from the school to find out how to set up an account with them and how much volume I would have to handle to get their best pricing. They told me that my business license would be enough to get wholesale prices but if I wanted large quantities in the future where I would take entire skids of random lengths and widths, they would negotiate prices by type of lumber. I told them I would be back with my license and speak to them further.

I went home to get Bonnie so we could go and sign the sales agreement on the old house. Once we had done that, we went by Tim Simonds' office and gave him a copy of the sales agreement. He said they would let us know when the papers would be ready. I asked him if it was legal to use the name Walker Enterprises, LLC yet. He said that everything was approved by the state and we would receive the paperwork directly from them.

We made a quick stop at our insurance agency to see if we had to amend our policy to run a business out of the garage. They assured us that they could take care of our needs but yes we had to change our homeowners and get a business liability policy also. They made it very clear that if and when I wanted to hire someone even if it was part-time basis that I would have to amend it again with a worker's compensation rider. They said that when we were ready to do that we could just call them and it would become active.

We were finally on our way to meet with Sam and Celine at the church when Bonnie said, "I think the first piece of furniture you build will have to be a filing cabinet to keep all this stuff sorted out. We haven't even got the state or federal id yet or how Sarah wants our information kept and I am out of shoe boxes to file in. You are going to have to go to work soon or we will be out of money from starting our business."

I told her, "You have to spend money to make money. I know it is complicated but I know you will listen to Sarah and get it all right. She told us not to pick a bank or open an account until after our meeting tomorrow so there is more to learn still. Sarah said that if we listened to her advice it would all flow from then on. God is letting us use the wisdom of brothers and sisters in the Lord to help us make our decisions."

We were just pulling into the church parking lot so the subject was changed for a little while. We spent our hour doing a lot of thanking God for what He was doing in our lives. I had to admit to having a brief nightmare about the shooting one night but it had not initiated the usual fear response that I used to have about that night. Bonnie told of having memories of when she first held our sons. She told of all the joyful emotions related to those days and how she still had to fight being angry at Tony and how he had tried to take Ryan from us. She said she would take those thoughts and seemingly overcome the thoughts of the potential loss by looking at her sons today in our new home and know that we were blessed by God. Sam and Celine both told us how remarkably well we were healing.

When we had closed our meeting with prayer, I asked Sam if he had time to talk to us on a personal matter. They both said they were not on a time table so we could take some of their time. I asked him if he would be interested in being our financial advisor and planner. We had not openly discussed the bounty money with anyone in the church so we had to tell them about it. He was fascinated to know that our CPA had said that there were no taxes due. We also told him of having placed our house in a sales contract that morning and how we were waiting to know how Mary would want to be paid for our new house. Sam said to us, "You sure know how to complicate a story don't you? I will take some of the information that you have given me and start to run some scenarios for you. I may have to speak to your CPA also."

"Thanks for giving us your time twice today," I said. "Please call us when you want to meet if it is different than just on Tuesdays."

We were soon on our way home to try and get some down time. I played a game with the boys on their game boy before we all settled down for the night.

Sarah Carter had done most of the work needed to open our accounts by the time we were in her office. We had made it clear to her that she needed to train Bonnie on most of the bookkeeping stuff. She had us sign the applications for the state and federal ids and then was telling us what computer program would work best with her system. She told us that we could use a particular bank that was compatible to having our computer print our checks and file them in the proper categories all at once. She gave us a quick rundown of how important it was for the government to see a complete paper trail in regards to the company. When we had all the preliminary information settled, we told her that she might hear from Sam Pickens in regards to our financial planning and if what she was doing would keep all our requirements up to date in regards to personal taxes as well. She said that she could do a wrap around package if we wanted and we assured her that we needed her complete help. We took an extra minute of her time as we were preparing to leave to tell of my recent conversion and how God was intertwining us with so many Christians all of a sudden. When we told her Bonnie's maiden name, she got all excited. "You were on the prayer chain while you were in prison," she said, "and now I know the rest of the story."

We decided to stop by the bank that Sarah had suggested on the way home. We were sent to the office of the business accounts manager on the second floor. We used Sarah's name and told them what she had suggested as our needs. I was surprised when the manager told us that there was a computer program for the business public that was much less expensive to purchase and maintain than what they could offer. The bank could still offer the checking account management of deposits and checks that they provide or your computer prints. The manager said he could give us some signature cards to fill out and when we came back he would want to take a copy of our business license for the files. The brochure that I am putting the card in will tell you what we offer and Sarah can guide you also.

We took all the information home to study. I went to the lumber wholesalers to get my first order of lumber for the warden's project and by the middle of the afternoon I was making sawdust and thinking that it was great to be at work and at home too.

# Twenty

We had bought a nice bottle of red wine to give to Bernie and his wife on the way to meet with them. Bernie greeted us at the door and invited us in to meet his wife Cherie. We presented them the gift as we went in to the living room to get acquainted. Their home was in a favorable part of the city but seemed to have a little aging to it. The woodwork was a trifle dark for the size of the room so all the furniture was light earthy colors. The small talk went on long enough to be polite and had a genuine tone to it when Bernie offered to show me the work they wanted to have done.

Bernie said, "We love the location of our home but as we go through the rooms and decorate we try to do away with some of the dark décor. I wanted to have you look at redoing the entire set of kitchen cabinets and we want to add a new window to move the sink and to build a pass-through to the dining room. I have determined that the wall from the kitchen to the dining room is a bearing wall so we would have to head it off and shape the opening under the header. You can do all the work including the window or I can farm it out to someone else."

"I believe that I would like to do it all for the ease of coordinating everything except your plumber and electrician. You may have to eat out of a can for two weeks or so. Is Cherie okay with that?"

Cherie piped in, "If I get my new kitchen done in a light maple or birch, I would chew the cans open for him."

We shared some laughter with them over that and then we discussed more of the details that Cherie wanted in her kitchen. It was obvious that she had put a lot of thought into what she wanted and had some desires that she did not want to compromise about. I tweaked the layout on a sketch pad, measured all the dimensions I would need to build and install the cabinets. I asked them to select their kitchen sink and window as soon as possible so I could have those dimensions. I asked her what type of counter tops she was going to have put on after the cabinets were in so she could consider what type of sinks would work. We ended the evening knowing that we had gone from lawyer and client status to a foursome of friends.

The garage did not turn out to be as convenient as it could have as far as working room was concerned. I did not have the first two orders anywhere near completed when I started hearing from people who also wanted things built or remodeled. The warden gave my name to two of his friends who wanted some quality furniture built. Bonnie had gone out and bought a new computer program and a separate printer so we could do our end of the bookkeeping in conjunction with Sarah's tutelage. Fred had come over a couple of times when I needed a couple of extra hands with the work but he did not want me to count on him.

I never got tired of God's timing in our lives. He had supplied people to help us or we were able to do everything in a timely manner so far. I had just decided that I needed to try to find someone to help on a more permanent basis when the warden called. One of the two men's names that I had given him was able to get out in the very near future and he asked if I wanted to come to the prison and speak to him about his future plans. I decided that I really wanted to try to give an inmate from that prison his hope back. I set the date to go and see the man the next day.

As I approached the prison the next day, I nearly turned around as my stomach churned and my jaw tensed at the idea of going back into those walls and being behind some locked doors again. The warden had made arrangements for one of the office people to take me to a conference room and wait for Al to be brought out. Al had not been told why he was being singled out from the work shop to come to the office. When he saw me in the room he let out a gasp.

I said, "Hello Al! It's nice to see you. I bet that right about now you are wondering what is going on. I came to speak to you about things in general and find out if you had any plans for when you are to be released next week. I might have a proposition of interest for you."

Al said, "I don't know what kind of pull you have around here but we can talk if that is what you want. I have been in here long enough that I do not have anything to go back to. Everything I had of any value my brother sold so I could have some money for commissary in here. My wife divorced me and moved away while I was in here so I don't have much to talk about. I got notice along with my release date that I had a small amount for an apartment from the years of working in the shop but I really don't have any plans."

"A great deal of my life has changed also since I was here," I said. "I accepted the Lord Jesus Christ as my personal savior and that was the catalyst for a lot of other changes for me. One of the things I have done is to start my own furniture and cabinet building shop at my new home. I have gotten so many orders already that I am about four months behind and I get new calls every week it seems. I am now a friend of the warden and he is the one who told me that you are getting out. I liked what I saw in you while we worked across from each other and you seem teachable. I am offering you a job working for me in my business if you are interested. We have a friend who is in real estate and we can start looking for an apartment for you. I have to tell you that I was losing hope while I was in here and I want to help you find some hope again. I want to be one of your supporters when you get out but I want you to know up front that I would fire you at the first sign that you were doing anything illegal. Is that clear?"

Al said, "I don't know why you really want to do this but I don't have many options available. I will accept your offer for help and you will never be sorry that you did this for me."

I was rejoicing about how the meeting had gone. I was true to my word and went by the real estate office on the way home. While I was there talking to the agency rental manager, Bonnie's friend Terry called me to her office, "I wanted to remind you that the closing on your house is next week at Tim Simonds' office. I also have a new listing that you might be interested in. I have a client who wants to retire and sell his woodworking factory. It is not very far from your house in a commercial area that is easily available by big trucks. It includes his current contracts, inventory, machinery, buildings, and office. He did several hundred thousand dollars of business last year. This is not the kind of sale where you put a sign on the front door and let all your employees know what you are doing. I will be making some calls for him to specific targeted persons of interest. Would you like to meet him and see what is there?"

I said, "I am just trying to get my business off the ground and you want me to consider something of this magnitude."

She looked me in the eye and said, "Sam, I know that God wants me to show you this property. I usually don't have the nerve to say something like that to anyone but I think God will strike me dead if I don't do this."

"Well," I said, "We don't want Him striking you dead until at least next week. Give me a call tomorrow after you have set an appointment. I need to break this to Bonnie gently."

Bonnie was not home when I got back so I went to the garage and started to work on the last touches of the laundry room cabinet for the warden. I also had a good portion of the library piece cut out and ready to start the rough assembly. I was finding that I would not be able to do any finish work on the days that I was working. The garage was so small that the fines that got away from the sawdust catcher got onto everything while I was working. I would have to prepare pieces on certain days and do the finishing when I was not making sawdust. That was going to create a great deal of dead time and if I was thinking of hiring some help I would need to find a solution.

I went in to see Bonnie when I heard the boys in the back yard. She was in the middle of folding some clothes and I told her I needed to speak to her. "I had a talk with your friend Terry at the real estate office today. She has a new listing that she wants me to look at to possibly buy."

Bonnie interrupted, "I thought that you loved this house as much as I do and you know we got it by the grace of God."

I said, "I know that we got this house by the grace of God. I know that we have received blessings on blessing. The listing she has is a wood working factory with everything there as a complete business. I wasn't going to look at it until she said that God had told her to show it to ME. I want your support before I do anything but I told her that I would look at the business with her. I do know that I am having some problems trying to do the complete process with a piece of furniture in the garage. I cannot work and do the finishing at the same time. At the rate I am getting orders, I will have to turn them down because of timing and room. The other thing is that I want to help people like Al who is probably getting out of prison and coming to work for me. I just don't know if I am able to take on an entire group of families to help at one time."

Bonnie said, "I knew what she had spoken to you about because she had called me after you left to go and see Al. I wanted to know how you were going to approach me this time compared to the time you went into business with Tony Gatzee. I told her that I would have you call her and I wasn't going to tell you about it myself. I didn't know if God had healed you enough that you would even consider doing this again. I hear a humble man instead of the prideful man asking me for support after you had made up your mind already. I would like to go and see what a wood working shop looks like. I think that I will get some of our friends praying that we have the wisdom of God in this."

I said, "Call me in around six if you have supper ready. I have to work on the orders that I have on the tables and get them out of here. I need to be working on Bernie's kitchen by the first of the week."

I delivered the warden's laundry furniture the next afternoon and secured it in place. The warden had come home to help me get it inside and place it. I asked him if he wanted me to bring him the big piece on Friday or Saturday. We agreed on ten o'clock on Saturday morning and he would have a neighbor there to help if we needed it. He asked me how the hidden compartment was working out and I told him he would have to see it to believe it.

I had a couple of long days getting everything fit the way I wanted it in the locking mechanism of the safe but it was a thing of beauty with a cold secret when I got done. I got to the warden's house a little after ten but it was not a problem for them. I had bought a little material dolly to use once we got it into the door. The cabinet was only two inches shorter than the door was high so we had to be careful. I had removed the drawers and put them in the cab of the truck for the transport and to lighten the cabinet. There was a lot of wood that went into making this. The cabinet was not to be attached to the walls so we had to remove the baseboard from the wall where it was going. Once we finally had it in place, the warden wanted to see the safe right away. When he looked in the back, he could see that I had grooved a receiver plate of wood to accept up to five guns and not let them turn. I had done a similar receiver plate at what should have been mid-way up the barrel of most rifles or shotguns. I then got the false back out of the cab and placed it against the bottom receiver and some stops I had made at the top. I had cut out a hand grip at the top of the false back near the two sides. The sides had blocks and receivers one inch in on both sides so the drawer slides would not interfere with the removal of the back. I had applied some simple slip locks to hold the entire thing in place. I then got the drawers from the cab and installed them. They were made to hold legal size folders and that would be all you could see when you opened the doors. I then brought in the two doors and hung them on the hidden style hinges that I had selected to use.

The warden said, "I am so impressed with your work and your ingenuity. It is everything that I could have hoped for. You will have to come back and see it after I have done the finishing of it. My wife has already had me prime the laundry room."

I said, "Remember to finish the back out of its position so it will not get sealed in place. I am glad you like it."

We spent a few more minutes talking as the warden wrote out the first check to be paid to Walker Enterprises, LLC. I was just about to get in my truck and leave when the neighbor asked if I wanted some more work. I told him I would look at it if he did not have a deadline because I already had one that had a deadline for completion. I went with him to his house and took a sketch pad with me. When we got to the door of his house he said that I would not need the sketch pad because he had a picture he could copy. He had a picture of a colonial style replica china cabinet that he wanted to get to surprise his wife. It required window style doors with nine lights per door. The copy of the picture had the dimensions all written out and included a suggestion for the finish. It also had a suggested price if you ordered it from the company in the magazine. He asked me if I could do it for the suggested price and I was sure that I could so he wrote me out a deposit check. Before I took the check I asked him if I could modify the doors to two less lights and increase the strength of the cabinet. He said he would be happy if I could keep it looking balanced with a lot of visibility behind the doors.

On the way home I was thanking God for his favor. I then took a mental assessment of all the work I had recently taken and decided I had to stop taking orders for a while.

# Twenty-One

Bonnie and I were on our way to tour the woodworking factory while it was operating. The owner said he did not want anyone to think that it had not been a good endeavor for him over the years so he wanted to show it with the people doing their work. We prayed all the way together for the wisdom of God and to know His will about how we were to be living our lives. We were directed to the office where we met Dan Billingsly. His office was as plain looking as he was acting. He was in a casual shirt and blue jeans shorts that went to his knees. It was easy to see that he had spent his life as a working man. We introduced ourselves and then sat across from this man.

Dan said, "I believe I was like Daniel in the bible when I started this shop. I had a vision but I knew that only God had the answer. In the beginning I was working beside my wife who had to do the bookkeeping because we could not afford to hire it done. It wasn't as complicated as it is now. We started with having six men working for us at the end of the first year and we still had only the most basic tools. The computer operated saws we have now did not come along for a long time after that. We would get bigger contracts and would improve certain parts of the process that we needed to do the contracts. We did not become serious about finishing some of our products until about fifteen years ago. Now you will see the most modern vapor recovery system available to man as well as airless sprayers for the application. We have conveyor systems for moving items at certain speeds or simply from department to department. We actually had this metal building built right over our original shop and then removed the original. I had people looking at us when I did that. God has been faithful in bringing in good contracts for parts or total items and giving us the ingenuity to do it in a cost efficient and profitable way. I now employ more than seventy men and women if you include the shift splitters. Those are the people we try to accommodate by pairing them with people who can finish or start an eight hour shift such as students. You will find that I pay above average for the industry to my employees but I have a very low turnover rate. All of our employees can qualify for incentive bonuses in several ways. I believe that a man is worthy of his wages and God continues to bless us with a profit when we do right by them. I have financial records that you could have your bank look at if things get serious between us. I'll bet that you two would like to see what is behind that door."

We donned hard hats and followed Dan into the factory. Once you opened the door you got a feel for the immensity of the building. There appeared to be a circular flow of materials as it went through the shop. We started out at the unloading and sorting dock for incoming lumber that was bought only by entire skids by species. It could then be placed through a series of saws that shaped and sized the lumber for projects. Dan said, "We use every part of the lumber that comes into these doors including the sawdust. We burn the marginal cut offs to operate the finishing dryers all year round but we use it to heat this shop during the cold months. I had metal ventilating vents manufactured and installed in the three cupolas you can see in the roof. The successful exchange of the air in this building during the summer months is vital. Most companies do not do anything at night but I find the comfort level can be changed drastically by ventilating the building during the cool of the night. The entire cupolas are blocked off to the outside air by insulated covers during the cold months."

We continued to where we could see several people organizing species of wood into sizes that would combine to make glued panels. The bundles were placed onto a rack where the sides were glued and then pressed together by hydraulic presses. The racks were always turning so that the panels would spend a little over an hour in the hydraulic presses and then could be removed and were ready to become furniture. The panels then traveled to the area where they were planed and sanded to the desired thickness. They then moved into the areas where they were cut to the ordered sizes. Again the cut offs were sent by a belt to the burning area or to the assembly area. As the pieces became the finished product, they were sent to the finishing room. Each piece would receive its stain and then go onto this conveyor chain that was suspended above several working areas from the rafters. This was timed so that it came back beside where it had started and got a sealing finish and went by timed conveyor to the shipping department. The entire plant efficiency was fascinating to me but I didn't know what Bonnie was thinking. Dan had us go back to his office as we completed our circle.

Dan said, "Do you have any questions before we go on?"

I said, "I am genuinely impressed with what you have now but I wondered how specific you could be with filling orders."

Dan answered, "I used to take a great deal of specific orders that required customizing especially in the assembly room. I turned this factory away from the custom stuff and have become more of a production company and I have done well most years. I want to slow down and actually want to eliminate my having to be here altogether so I have not spent the money to become more custom by order. I know the factory can produce custom as well as production in the way we have it organized now. It was just easier to produce several hundred or thousand of one item than piece by piece. Custom also has to be marketed differently and often involves delivery problems as well. I know these things can be overcome with a little effort but I want to pass that job on to someone younger."

I said, "Do you have some numbers for my wife and I to consider before we go further?"

Dan said, "I have given this much thought and have run some numbers by my CPA as well as my wife. The number I am going to give you is for a turn-key situation. In other words you are buying land, building, inventory, machinery, current contracts, non-competition clause, and I am willing to stay up to six months as advisor and advocate of the new ownership. I also have been told by my CPA to hold the mortgage at a reasonable rate of interest with amortization over a five year period so that I do not give it all to the government and can't afford to go fishing. The number that I have come up with is seven hundred-eighty thousand dollars. I would hold the mortgage for five hundred thousand and would require payments of one hundred-twenty thousand dollars per year for five years and that would include all the interest that I would ask. I also want you to know that I know what you have been through in the last year including your recent conversion and your troubles. I actually chose you from several others who have shown interest in buying me out over the years. In a way I have manipulated you to coming here today and meeting with us."

I caught on to the word us and suddenly realized the woman pictured on the wall with him was the woman who had met us at the door and was now listening to the conversation from behind us. At that point she came over and stood beside her husband.

She said, "Yes Dan and I have selected you because God has told us that as Saul was anointed King, you have been anointed by Him to take over for us. We could not have a family so our lineage ends at our death but God's blessings are forever for those who follow hard after Him. We believe you are that man."

I was dumbfounded after these comments and turned to look at Bonnie. She was teary eyed when she looked back at me but did not say a word. I said, "How did you find out about me?"

Dan replied, "I know you haven't met many of the people at the church yet but we have several mutual brothers and sisters in Christ who have become intertwined with you. We have the same CPA and financial advisor at this time as well as my being one of Pastor Mike's Elders at the church. We know a lot more about you than you do us. We also have to admit that we have not officially listed this business with anyone but we thought that you would not question a short story being told by your real estate agent."

I said, "If this is a con job by God, He is even better at it than Tony Gatzee. I know that I can't rule out being very interested in this venture but I told my wife that I would never entertain a project without her support again."

Bonnie finally spoke and said, "I know the hand of God when I see it and I am not the one who will withhold my support when I can see so clearly. I believe that God wanted you to see how well He can supply when you were willing to run a business in our garage so you would be willing to put your hand on His plow for our lives with this factory."

We actually closed our meeting with a word of prayer and then went home. I was quiet on the way home so Bonnie said, "Now Sam Walker, if you are trying to think how to make this work you better stop right now. God has a complete plan for our lives and we just need to obey. So you just go home and work on what you can in the garage until God shows us the next step. I believe that it will become clear after we close on our old house tomorrow."

I said, "I agree but I did not think that I would owe over a million dollars by the end of the week either and I need to pray for the faith to do this. I wanted to help some of the people with no hope in that prison and now I will be working with seventy men and women the same week that I said that I would help one.

# Twenty-Two

We spent the next few days looking at the logistics of what it would take to make purchasing the factory viable. I don't think that either Bonnie or I had any doubt about buying it but it would have to involve multiple lawyers, an investment team, and a management team. Neither one of us had business degrees so we might have to hire an advisor or position someone in the factory. We got Sarah Carter and Samuel Pickens deeply involved with where we knew God was taking us and relied on their wisdom immensely. I made several trips back to the factory to see what could be done to add a custom assembly area. There was a small area that could be used for now but it turned out that there was enough land involved to add the custom department as an addition and join the two entities.

We needed to know what part of our lives the purchasing of Mary's house was going to effect. We made a call to her lawyer to see if Mary had decided how much money she wanted now if not all of it and how she wanted us to pay back the difference. It turned out that Mary had been advised to not take much money from the sale of the house for at least one more year and then to disperse it over a period of ten years in payments. She asked for minimal interest and wanted to close the deal as soon as we were ready. We offered her twenty thousand dollars toward the house at closing and told the lawyer we would close as soon as the papers were ready.

Now we knew what to expect from the sale of our house as far as reserve funds for the purchase of the factory. We were still reluctant to spend the bounty money at this time but we would have to see what

Samuel Pickens had to say. We went by Tim Simonds office to ask him to get with Mary's lawyer and finish that up if he could. We then asked him what we would have to do with Walker Enterprises LLC if we bought the factory. He said that we would simply have Walker Enterprises LLC become the owners of the factory and we would remain the owners of Walker Enterprises. He said that if we had to use another investor that we could limit his ownership to a proportion of the factory. He said that it was all the use of a legal paper trail. We then asked him if he would lead up the purchase of the factory and he said that it would be no problem.

We then went back to Samuel Pickens office and discussed where we were with the negotiations on the house and the terms to buy it. We then tried to understand how much more we would have to borrow to make the purchase and what we would have to look at for terms on that money. We knew what Mary expected of us and we knew what Dan Billingsly wanted of us but we needed to have the rest of the asking price and some working capital to work the factory. We had gotten the operating expenses and income information from Dan and we could need as much as one hundred thousand dollars to operate for a quarter without income as a reserve fund. Samuel took the information and was putting it into a computer as we spoke. Samuel said, "If you work with the factory numbers first, you are telling me that you need three hundred-eighty to four hundred thousand to make this a reality. You know what you have from the sale of your house if you are going to consider it for the purchase. Now what would you say if I told you that I had an investor who wanted to lend you up to a quarter million dollars as a pure loan and they want to remain anonymous. They want a reasonable interest payment for the first four years and then a balloon payment return of their money on the fifth year. They do not want to take part ownership of the company but it would look like a second mortgage to protect their investment and make the money payable by the company. In other words, you would have four years of operation to set aside the balloon payment and you would have enough from the sale of your house to use as a reserve."

Bonnie and I just sat there with tears in our eyes. The entire road had been paved for us by the Lord and all we had to do was walk on it. When we picked up the boys at Fred and Paula's we told them of what God had done. We all rejoiced together before we went home. As we pulled into our driveway I said to Bonnie, "This surely could have been a different story to tell if God had not protected us from those two gunmen and started us down the road we are on. I am no longer afraid of owing in excess of one million dollars but I am really praying that I stay on the road set before me."

Bonnie just said, "We will just walk this road together. You, I and the Lord are now on the road of righteousness and His blessings are ours if we continue to do His will."

I had found time to have made a good start on building Bernie and Cherie's cabinets. I was spending so much time in meetings that it had not been a problem doing the finishing and not cutting on the same day.

Dan had told us that we should get to meet his sales staff and a few others of his technical staff as we were preparing for our takeover of the factory. That was set for the first of the month which also was a Friday and the lawyers were franticly trying to get the wording of the final contracts in order. Tim Simonds had set our LLC in order to become the parent company of Things of Wood as the factory was called so that part was in order. The funds were on deposit in the Walker Enterprise accounts to pay Dan and his wife at the closing. Sarah Carter had been bookkeeper for Dan so the rolling of the payroll into our accounts was going to be simple on her end. Dan had decided that all accounts payable and receivable would be examined and if the balance was within reason we would merely accept them both with the turnover. The last thing we had to do was to announce the transfer to his people so they could meet their new boss.

It was the afternoon of the third day before the closing and we had assembled all the workers after shutting down the entire mill early. Dan was first to address his people and his wife stood beside him as he spoke.

"I would like to thank all of you for being here today and allowing us to speak to you. I have been thinking about this day for over a year now and it has finally come. In three days I will no longer be the owner of the factory I started nearly three decades ago. I have been blessed beyond measure to have had each and every one of you working for me. I thank God that in all that time we have not had the loss of a life here. We have beaten the odds in that category. I don't know how many of you have seen the man that I am about to introduce to you walking around the factory lately but I want you to know that I handpicked him for the job along with the leading of God. He is a man with a vision the same as I was when I started and he will take you and this company to new places. I won't steal his thunder but will let him tell you what you can expect from him. Yes he will have to prove to you as much as you will have to prove to him how you need each other. I am not done speaking to you but I am going to be around for a while to have my goodbyes with some of you who have been here for years. However, at this time I would like to introduce Sam Walker and his wife Bonnie to you."

Bonnie and I joined Dan and his wife on the make shift platform from which we could look out at the people. I started, "Hello everyone. It is an extreme honor to be standing by these people who pioneered this business. Dan's visionary leadership has made this a factory to be proud of and an outstanding place for you to work. I do have a vision for where we will expand this business and make it bigger. I do not want to lose one employee during this time of transition but I am sure that I cannot totally fill the shoes of the man you have been working for. That does not mean that I don't expect you all to stay under my leadership at least until we can discuss any nuances that I may bring. I bring the hope that we can add some custom work to our production line as well as designing furniture that can be ordered on line or from a future catalog. You will see no real changes in any facet of what you have come to expect here as employees. You may see a new account number from my bank but the name will remain the same as well as the products you have been making. Dan has offered to stay for six months before he gets his fishing pole out for good so that may help your comfort level. I would like to give you all a chance to speak to Dan and his wife one more time so this Friday's work will stop around one in the afternoon and my wife and I would like to sponsor a barbecue near the loading dock for all employees to meet us and to wish Dan and Gina farewell. I hope that you will all stay for that meal and the time is on us as well. At this time I will let you meet my wife Bonnie."

Bonnie looked around the room before she spoke. "I see several women who work here in the crowd. I am glad that you can find this a place to earn for your families. They are the reasons we all go to work. You will not see me here very much because I am raising our two sons at this time. I do intend however to give you ways to get in touch with me for any reason you would like to. If there is one thing that I positively know, it is that communication is the beginning of friendships and I look forward to meeting all of you as we spend time here together. Thank you all and I look forward to knowing your names very soon starting with the barbecue."

Dan finished the meeting with this, "I want to repeat the fact that I handpicked these two people for you to work with. My last official day as owner is Friday and I look forward to helping Sam and Bonnie get off on the right foot and I pray that you will support them as well. For those of you who want to go home now your day is complete. For those who want to say hello to Sam and Bonnie we will all be here for about an hour. Thank you again."

# Twenty-Three

Bonnie and I had gotten an apartment for Al to come to when he was released in the morning. We had gone to a consignment shop and gotten some reasonable furniture and bed to put in it. We got a variety of drinks and a few choices of cold cuts and bread and put them in the refrigerator. We put in a chair that we had replaced at the new house and a couple sets of linen and bath accessories with toiletries. It wasn't a mansion but I knew from experience that it was more comfortable than where he was coming from. I was hoping that he would be comfortable here and find a way to live on his own again. I didn't know whether his being alone would be pleasant or if he would mind the silence. These were all things that affected my emotions while I had been in prison but I was blessed with going back to what should have been ordinary. Al had lost all of that while he was in prison.

I went to the prison at the set time to pick up Al and his belongings. I was a couple of minutes late so Al was already outside of the main gate and looking around when I stopped to pick him up. I asked him, "Are you excited about getting out?"

Al said, "I thought that I would be very excited but it has turned to apprehension if not all out fear. I am two presidents behind on news to say nothing about knowing how people are to act any more. My closest link to sanity or insanity is you and I don't know why you are doing this."

I said, "Al, I met some of the most hopeless men I have ever met in that prison. I wasn't there all that long and emotionally I was having trouble keeping it all together. I was able to remember my sons and wife out here and that was my most stabilizing force. I now rely on the Lord Jesus to keep me safe and in His will at all times. You wouldn't believe how He has changed our lives since I last spoke to you about coming to work for me. In two days I will own a complete woodworking factory that has seventy employees in it and growing. I believe that God has softened my heart for people who are as close to despair as you can get and not commit suicide or reoffend to go back in. I have a place for you there because I want to increase the custom furniture side of the company. I want to help people find hope again both in a savior and life in general. My wife and I sought council in our church after I killed those two men and..."

Al interrupted me, "You killed two men and you are not in jail. I got to here this story for sure."

I said, "It is nothing that I am proud of Al. My former business partner was trying to keep me from testifying at his trial. He had one man stalk my wife and family for three weeks before they got him arrested. That is the time I got out of prison. I had been home less than twenty four hours and we were all coming home from the lake when my wife noticed two men watching us. We made it to the house where we hid the boys under a bed and I got a shotgun from our bedroom. I did have time to call 911 before they broke into our back door intending to kill all of us and instead I killed them both. I would do it again but it was not pleasant to deal with after I had first done it. I was in shock for a few days until our councilors helped me back to reality. It was ruled self defense and there were no charges filed against me."

Al said, "I can see the self defense part. Did they manage to hurt anyone in your family?"

I said, "No, I got them both before they got off a shot. We bought a new house so I would not have to relive the attack every day. There was a wood shop in the garage and that is when I asked you to work for me. We will start in my garage but we will end up at the factory. I am still getting custom orders every week and right now I can only take their names. I am in hopes of building a custom order assembly building attached to the current factory. Would you like to see your new apartment? We are here."

I gave Al his keys and we went in and had a look at what was there. "I know that you will still need a few things but I didn't want to not let you decide some of the things for yourself. I will take you down the block now and let you open an account at the bank we use so you can get that check cashed. We then can go to a consignment shop and finish getting you some things."

Al said, "I still don't know why you are doing this but I can say thank you with an honest heart. I can also say that I have never met anyone like you."

We ended up the day in the garage assembling some of Bernie's cabinets. I was working on a tall pantry cabinet and I had Al working on some of the basic boxes for the lower cabinets. We were building the boxes out of maple plywood and doing the fronts in solid maple and attaching them together with blind screws. We were gaining quickly with two people versus one.

Bonnie called us in to clean up for supper around six fifteen. I had not brought Al into the house before that so I introduced my family to him. He didn't seem comfortable around the boys at first but they started pulling him into their room to show him their games. We had them wait until after the meal which they reluctantly did.

Bonnie had set the food on the table and was waiting for me to say grace. I prayed over our food and then passed the first vegetable dish to Al. I said, "It took me a while after I got home to not eat my meals and look at my watch at the same time. I can also tell Bonnie that I do not care for something and not be concerned about going hungry because I can have extra of something else. The boys will pester you now until you play some kind of game with them or watch them play."

Al said, "I think my tongue is going to rebel with having to taste good food again. I have not been around children since I went in. I am not used to all that energy and fast motions but it is not their fault and I do not mean to offend them."

We finished the meal with small talk and then Al went in to watch the boys with their games for a few minutes. Al thanked Bonnie for the meal as we left to take him home. I told him that I would pick him up around seven in the morning so that we could make a day of it.

We started early the next morning after having a cup of coffee. I said, "I want to get you to a point that I can go to the factory for a while and you can stay busy. I have one wall of the upper cabinets cut out and you can go onto that when you finish the three boxes you have started. We will start to cut out the fronts when I get back. If you have time or get stuck you could start to plane the maple down to the right thickness that is piled right here."

Al said, "I will keep busy with no problems. You go and do what you have to do and I will see you when you get back."

My goal at the factory this morning was to meet some of the key people now that everyone was on the same page. I wanted to meet the one salesman other than Dan and meet the receptionist. They both were dressed in clean but casual clothing and the receptionist was dressed very modestly. I then went out to the plant and met the two maintenance people. They told me that the factory kept a service contract with the manufacturer for some of the very technical saws and the likes. I asked them if there was any equipment that was giving them a lot of grief and they replied no. I then found two rooms that I had not noticed before. I asked what they were and I was told that one was the elaborate electrical panel for the four hundred-eighty volts of electricity coming in to run the three phase motors. The other was a room that was cooled or heated and had hepa air cleaners to maintain the pc's for the entire company.

I then went to meet the people in the finishing department. I asked them if they were currently busy all the time or if they could finish some custom work as well. They showed me some of the baskets or hangers that we could use to dry the products and they were confident that they could keep up with all the work at this time. I went to see the shipping department to see if we had room to put a set of kitchen cabinets or the likes. They showed me the racks for material waiting to be shipped and there was capacity for more than was being used currently. I asked them if there was something that would make things better in their area and they said the truck dock needed to be lowered on the outside of the plant.

I just went around the plant meeting a few more people as they did their jobs. Some were doing work where they could not stop and I told them I would meet them on Friday. I ended up in Dan's office to go over the accounts receivable and accounts payable before the closing in the morning. It appeared that the accounts receivable were a few thousand dollars more than the accounts payable. Dan said, "I had our lawyers prepare a sheet for us to sign that you assume both tomorrow and had a clause put in for one of us to collect a difference if there is one. I do not want to pursue trying to find that number beyond what I have here. I am ready to just have you assume both as they are before us now with no exchange of money. We have up to six months as gentlemen to find a severe imbalance but I am fairly certain that our books are up to date."

I said, "I am okay with that. I will see you at Tim Simonds office at ten in the morning."

I went back home to see how Al was doing and he had all his lower boxes assembled. I asked him if he had eaten yet and he said no so I went and asked Bonnie to get us some lunch and I had Al come in. I told Al that we could have this work finished in the factory and that would allow us to keep working the saws. I would like to have these boxes ready to go to the factory by this week end.

Al said, "That should be easy. You didn't tell me what style door we are going to use on the fronts so I did not know what widths to cut the maple after I got them dressed to three quarters of an inch."

I said, "I was going to have some panels glued up at the factory to do a raised panel door. I will call Cherie after dinner and verify that one more time. They will have to be square or I will have to buy a jig for the shaper. I do not think that I will offer her anything but square to expedite this order. I have never asked you if you have done any construction such as replace windows or head off some existing walls."

Al said, "It has been a while but I still know the basics well enough to do it. I am guessing that you have some construction to do at a house."

"This kitchen set is a complete remodel and we are adding a window for the sink area and a pass through to the dining room," I said. "I have to admit that I wasn't as busy when I took this order but it is for my lawyer as part of my bill and I wanted to do a good job for him."

Al said, "Well we will just have to do the best job ever for him."

I asked Bonnie, "Do we have the meat and rolls for the meal tomorrow or are the people making the salads bringing it?"

Bonnie answered, "You take care of the factory and I will take care of the meal."

# Twenty-Four

I was amazingly calm at the closing considering the amount of money that we would now owe. The two lawyers had done a spectacular job of preparing the papers and there was nothing that needed touch up or modifying during the process. Tim assured me that we had met all of Dan's requests for the factory and the property transfers were in order. All we had to do was sign where we had to and write the biggest check I had ever written.

As we left, Dan and his wife Gina said that they had to go to their bank on the way back to the factory but would come as soon as time allowed joining in as guests of honor for the meal.

The nervousness really started as we went to get the boys and Al and bring them to the factory. We were now responsible for the well being of an extra seventy people and a major factory. Bonnie just said, "All you have to do is leave it in God's hands because we are following him."

We had asked the people on the receiving dock to make room for the tables and chairs that the caterers were bringing and to help them set up. I could see different departments getting ready for the weekend shutdown. The people in the factory were used to getting their paychecks on Wednesday so that was out of the way. We had actually accepted the payroll from that day and we would be paying them on the coming Wednesday. The caterers were starting to cause the odor of food to waft through the factory and I went and gave some of the departments the signal to wrap up what they were doing.

Dan and Gina came into the factory just at one o'clock and it was easy to see that Gina had been crying. She had composed herself before she came in but she was soon crying again as a cheer went up from the employees in their honor. The caterers appeared to be ready at the serving tables so I began, "I want to thank you all for coming and if you will be so kind to allow me to bless the food and this couple we can begin."

I blessed the food in a loud voice but even I noticed that my voice faltered as I blessed Dan and Gina for the years to come. We allowed them to go first and get seated at a table we intended to share with them at their side. We expected people to come to the other side of the table to speak to them or us. I was amazed to see that Bernie and Cherie Segal had accepted my invitation to join us today. Tim Simonds and Sarah Carter also came for a short visit and the meal. I tried to encourage the youngest employees that they were special to us and how we hoped that they would remain with the factory. I believe that the dinner was a good ice breaker for the days to come.

I was pleased to see several of the employees give Dan and Gina card envelopes or small packages as they came to wish them the best. As I watched their mannerisms with the employees, I was able to get a feel for the ones who had taken the time to know their employers. The closer they were to Dan and Gina, the harder it would be to get the same loyalty without the help of time.

We had some of the lingering employees help the caterers break down the tables and load up their equipment. We distributed the last of the food to some of the workers and we took some of the leftover meat that wasn't prepared today to take home. Al had taken a walk around the factory as we finished the meal so he might know how some of it worked. As we drove home, he said he saw the potential of a custom assembly area near the shipping department. I agreed with him and told him I had a partial layout in my mind but we could toss it around at the first of the week. I dropped him off at his apartment and the rest of us went to get some down time.

Sunday morning found us in church as a family. As I looked around the sanctuary area, I found that I could recognize several of the families around us now. Pastor Murray was diligent in trying to greet as many of the congregation as possible whether it was before the service or after. I told him that we should all get together some time so our families could meet. He only said soon would be good. We were about to sit for the service when I noticed a younger woman being prayed for to the right of the altar. We were sitting near Samuel and Celine and I asked them if there was a problem we should be praying for. Samuel said that she was a single mother of two children and had just gotten laid off from work because her employers had sold the business. I asked them what she had done at her place of employment and they said she was a receptionist/bookkeeper.

I made my way down to where Pastor Mike was just getting done with the woman. I said, "I hear tell that you are looking for work?"

She said, "Yes, I cannot raise my children on unemployment."

I said, "I do not want to interfere with the service, but would you please speak to my wife and I before you leave today. We will wait for you after the service."

When I went back to my seat, I told Bonnie that I just might have found the person to take Gina's place at the factory. We enjoyed the services at our church and today it was no exception. We lingered in our seats for the woman to find us afterwards. I had whispered to Samuel that I might hire the woman and he just said that I would not regret it.

Bonnie and I took the woman outside to speak to her because there were four boys who really didn't like to sit much longer than necessary. We took them to a grassy area to the side of the building and away from the traffic. I said, "I am Sam Walker and this is my wife Bonnie. We bought a wood working factory on Friday and the former owner's wife was the receptionist. You would be asked to direct calls or take messages as well as greet anyone who came in the door. I am in hopes that you might do miscellaneous filing or bookkeeping prep for our CPA as well. Is this in line with what you used to do and were you looking for full time employment?"

She said, "My name is Diana Williams. I have done what you are looking for with my last company for ten years. My husband left us when he went to prison about three years ago and won't be out for six more months. Most of the people at this church do not know that I am still married. I would like to get a full time position if the money is right and if you want to try me. I was on salary with the other company and made six hundred dollars per week. The other company had a place where I could take my kids to where they would get on the school bus in the morning and get off in the afternoon until I was done work."

I said, "I do not know how long you have been coming to church here but you might know Dan and Gina Billingsly who attend here and until Friday morning owned Things of Wood factory. I did not see them here today but I need someone to do what Gina has been doing. I would have to ask my wife directly but you might be able to drop your kids at our house until we can find something better and more permanent. I believe that I could match your old salary to start with. Would you be able to start right away if you had a solution for your children?"

Diana said, "I only knew them by name and did not know they had a factory but I have not been coming here for very long. I could start tomorrow if I had a place to take the kids. I don't have the money to take them to a care center at this time."

I said, "Let my wife and I speak for just a moment and we will get right back to you. I know that God had me buy this factory to help people just like you and your family. I'll be right back."

Bonnie was very agreeable to having the children for a few days while we looked for something better. We gave Diana our address and told her to come by around seven and she could go to the factory. It felt good to be the answer to someone's prayer for work.

# Twenty-Five

Al had figured out the bus schedule enough by Monday morning to be at my house before seven. We went out to the garage and started back up on Bernie's cabinets. I told him that I would be by around noon so we could have lunch and take some of the work to the factory for finishing. Diana came just before seven and she followed me to the factory once the boys were in the house with Bonnie. The factory was going full tilt when we got there. Some of the department heads had keys to get into the building and one of the maintenance people had the job of getting several of the machines up and running. I had only been there a few minutes when Dan and Gina came in. I introduced them to Diana and everyone seemed to know each other in a limited way. I asked Gina to show Diana how the intercoms worked so she would be more comfortable. I then asked Dan if we could have a couple of minutes together alone.

I said, "Dan, I have to get a feel of how much product is ordered currently and how we pursue the sale of more. The other thing is when do we order material for the shop for inventory?"

Dan answered, "I will take some time today to check with the shipping department to find out at what stage any and all orders are at in completion. I have a way in the system here of knowing how much material I will need for any kind of order. I then translate that into desired numbers of bunks and try to make sure I have them here on time. Most of the time, I get a call from a lumber broker at the docks. If he has room on a truck to send me some bunks or if they have a special price on something I might want I can have it put on that truck for delivery. I also can call and place an order for the next time he has room on a truck for my needs. The material will get here in less than a week no matter how we order it. When we sell product, we may do it by specifications sent as a trial run or they may bring us some of their prior samples for us to duplicate. Once an item is on our inventory list we never have to experiment again unless they want to try another type of material or combination of materials. If we are making the hidden components of some furniture or something like that we can sometimes mix materials to decrease our costs. You have met some of the people who sell our products that I have already priced and produced and they are very attentive to our customers. It will all come to you quickly."

I said, "I need to know how much of the production time I can use to start doing some of the custom orders that I already have. I need some door panels glued and I have some cabinet boxes that I need finished. I would also like to know if you have any recommendations from the people I have here now that would be suited for the custom work. I also need to know if the person who did this big factory is still in business and able to do one for me."

The morning went by too quickly. I checked with Diana and told her that I had to leave and get some materials but would be back right after lunch. She did not seem to have any questions and told me that the phone system was very adequate at making her job simple. I got my truck and went over to the house. I spoke to Al as we had our lunch and then we loaded all the base cabinets that my truck could hold. Al had written down the sizes for all the door panels that we would need so I could have them made. I was soon on the way back to the factory.

I had some people unload the cabinets and take them to the finishing area for me. I gave them their directions for the clear natural finish and then went to the shipping department. I asked them to crate and hold the cabinets in the racks and I would tell them when I brought more. I went down to the gluing department and asked them how they wanted my orders written. They said to just write them down and they would keep them on a pallet for moving. I was then able to go back to the office and see how that was going.

Once I was back at my desk Dan asked, "Do you want the good news or the bad news first? The bad news is that we need to order some more birch and maple this week. The good news is that one of our customers just added three thousand pieces to be produced. I took the liberty to order the materials from the broker for the order. I also took the liberty to tell the customer how they could expect the delivery as far as timing in conjunction with what I could gather from the work I did this morning. It will take up to three months to have that order run along with some of our continuing orders. I have tried to pay the people enough that we do not have to work a sixth day during the week. I believe that they all need one day of rest and one day for their families. I tried running a period of six day weeks one time and my production fell off instead of climbing so I push delivery dates if I have to. I also have a good faith policy with all my customers no matter how long I have done business with them. I require twenty-five percent of the current order before I will cut one stick of wood. I learned that lesson the hard way."

I told Dan, "I want to organize the people so that I can tell by looking at them where they belong. It will help me know whom I can move to do some of the changes I have to do and also train some people in ways I can promote them. I don't know if the term floaters will work but I need to know expertise as well as trainees. In the prison shop we had a group of people who wore red hats and were the ones that leaders assigned to help the people with expertise. I will need this to better create my custom shop."

Dan said, "I understand what you mean. I never thought of the hat color but that is one way of doing it. It is an idea we can bring to the employees when we give out their checks. I often had a note to add in each envelope after Sarah sent their checks over. I will have Gina show Diana how we used to do it. Speaking of Diana, I wanted to thank you for hiring her. I also want to know how much power you want her to have as far as speaking for you because it was different for Gina and I to know how everything was going."

I said, "I believe that the role will shape itself because I am not rigid in how a job gets done as long as it is done appropriately and timely. I want all my people to know that performing a job well and consistently well will be noticed by me. Would you have time to meet with the head of maintenance and myself this afternoon? I want him on board with the new custom shop from the startup."

When I had given my ideas to the head of maintenance and Dan about where I was going to start assembling the custom area, we all went out to see the actual space and how it would tie back in from the new building. They agreed to give me the pros and cons as they saw them right away. I then had the panels loaded into my truck to take to Al. I then made another round trip to my house and brought back some more cabinet boxes to be finished. I ended the day with some conversation with Diana and Dan about what parts of finance I wanted people to know as far as their roles were concerned. Dan reminded me that the pay checks would have to be picked up in the morning at Sarah Carter's and it had to be me so I could sign some papers.

I left the office around nine-thirty to go to Sarah's office. I had to give her my signature to install on her computer and sign a release so that she could print it out electronically. As we waited for the payroll checks to be printed, she gave me the written copy as a report for our records. We also discussed the forms she wanted me to use for new employees so the checks would be correct and then they could go on direct deposit. She told me that Dan had everyone go on direct deposit so they had to think about removing money. She told me that Samuel Pickens taught a personal financial freedom class for companies that was a great educational asset for their employees. If people take his class, he will advise them free for a year in their finances. I told her I would check that out if it meant I could have better employees longer.

When I got back to the factory, I had to wait for a delivery to finish so I could park. I took a mental note to see if we could change that for the better when I had the new building built. I noticed when I spoke to Diana on the way in that she was quite distraught. I asked Gina if she would mind taking the phones for a few minutes so I could speak to Diana about hiring forms. I went into my office and waited with Dan for her to come. I asked her to close the door behind her and asked her to sit at the desk.

I said, "I would like to know what happened since yesterday that has you so upset."

Dan looked up from what he was doing as Diana started to weep softly and then sobbed. I didn't force the issue but started again, "I really want to know if there is something I can do,"

Diana started to compose herself and answered, "I may have to leave town immediately. I got a call from the prison where my husband Frank has been that he is getting released as early as Monday and wants to come home to me and the kids. I don't know if I can deal with him again. He never beat me or the kids but he is an angry man that has had problems at work in the past. The kids are old enough now that he could influence them in a negative way. I really don't know what I can do."

I said, "Why don't you give me the information about where he is and I have friends who can get us information about him. Just write it down and I will spend some time on it today. We have a couple of days to make a plan."

We finished our talk and I showed her the forms. Dan brought out a policy letter for new employees about grounds for discipline including immediate termination for illegal drug use and the right to have random samples drawn for a lab without cause. I told him he was a tough man to work for and chuckled. I dismissed Diana before I called Detective Flum. I hung up from our call and Dan said, "Why do you care?"

I answered, "I lived with men like him for several months while I was falsely accused but I got to see the reasons for the despair. I didn't know Jesus at the time so I didn't even have the hope of salvation during that time. God intervened for me and gave me a heart to intervene for others in similar situations. When I hired Diana, I was thrilled to help someone out of the grips of a troubled life. I didn't see it then but I think God set me on a path to intercede for their entire family as well. This factory is just a gathering ground for those whom God wants to help including myself. You say God handpicked me to buy this place and to bring forth its new blessings for others and I'm trying to be obedient to His will."

We both just drifted back to the work at hand and I said, "I suppose I have to learn how to pay for what you just bought." We both chuckled and then he showed me how to have an invoice go through the inventory first and then on to get paid within ten days of our receiving it. It turned out that Sarah was the one who did almost all the check writing and managed the petty cash account also.

I made several calls during the rest of the day and had an appointment to meet with Frank Williams at ten in the morning at the regional prison. The report that I got was that Frank was a changed man from the time he arrived. I chose not to tell Diana anything until I was back. Dan said he would be sure to be here to cover but he was going fishing with some kids from the church on Friday and would not be in.

The ride out to the prison required prayer against the memories that were still able to put a sweat on my brow. Bonnie had told me that I should get someone involved with some of these interviews for prayer coverage and two more ears to hear the truth. I had agreed to give that a chance to becoming real for the next time. I pulled into the prison and went through all the security points and was led to a small visiting conference room. I met with Frank's case manager for a few minutes before Frank was brought out. We all introduced each other but I only gave them my name and not why I was there.

I started, "Frank, I have come out here today to see who you are and not who you were. I work a program with ex-offenders that incorporate but is not limited to age, family history and current expectations, work history and abilities, church, and especially current needs to make any part of this feasible. I see a man before me who looks docile but anxious. You appear to be on the early side of forty years of age and have known physical work. You have on a band that says you have hope. How am I doing so far?"

Frank said, "I am a thirty-nine year old man who is a very good carpenter. I used to be a very angry man but I have much better self control than I used to. I have been shown in many ways that I need other peoples help and have changed a great deal in how I treat people. I have not seen my children in nearly three years but I long to see them and my wife Diana. I hope to live with them when I leave here but I have not heard from them."

I interrupted him, "I want to know if you are interested in committing to my program. You would work for me with other people and you would have a place to live. You would be agreeing to have intense counseling from people in my church who do this

professionally to restore you and your family. You would receive
some spending money but your expenses would be drawn out first.
This would take at least one month of intense treatment followed by
maintenance counseling. I will give you some time to think about it."

Frank said, "I don't have to think about it. I am ready to commit
to you and your church right now. I don't know who you are or why
you want to bother with me but I have seen enough of what you can
do in the last few hours to know that you care."

I said, "Okay! I will give my office number to your case worker
after you leave and I will pick you up when they tell me I can. I'll be
seeing you very soon."

Frank stood and shook my hand on the way back to his cell. I
gave the case worker my number and told him to leave the message
with Diana if you have to. He did a double take and asked if I had just
said Diana. I told him yes but he could not say a word because of the
safety net we would have around his family could be jeopardized. I
then hurried home to the office. I needed to get Samuel and Celine
ready for the kickoff.

# Twenty-Six

I had to leave Al alone for long periods of time but he was doing fantastic work. We decided that he would come over in the morning to the factory and see how it would be to mount the doors there. The last of the boxes were ready and some of the doors were made. This would give us an even better idea on how to create the layout for the custom work. I had two names from existing employees that I was going to meet with and find out about them.

We met at my house in the morning and loaded more boxes and some of the specialty tools needed to mount hinges and then the doors to the cabinets. I had a platform moved the day before to the new custom area. I unloaded the boxes we brought on this load and had them taken to the finishing area. I then had some of the finished work come back for the assembly from the shipping area. It did not take long to realize this was very labor intensive. I left Al with a helper for a few minutes so I could meet with Samuel and Celine in my office.

I said, "Good morning you two. As I told you yesterday on the phone, I have a new project for all of us. Before we go there I need to know if I can hire you to teach a money management class to my employees in the near future. You can think on that but I believe you both know Diana whom I hired last week. Her husband is getting out next week and wants to come live with her and the kids and she is scared of the man. I met with him yesterday and asked him to commit to counseling, work, and general restoration with no mention that I knew Diana. I found him docile and seemed repentant about what he had done to his family. The case manager says that he has calmed down immensely while he has been there. I need you to help me evaluate whether Diana can give Frank a chance with supervision or if I need to find new living quarters for him to come out to. I have asked Diana to stop long enough for me to speak to her when she picks up her kids from our house tonight. I have to ask you if you can be there for me please."

Samuel said, "We will make a point of being there for as long as we are needed. Why don't we plan some pizza so the kids will be okay together? We will bring the pizza and join you at five tonight."

A little more small talk and a check with Dan allowed me to go back out to the assembly area with Al. I had stopped by and got one of the two men I was considering for the area and had him follow me. Al was already on his second door and seemed to now have a pattern in his mind. I said to the new man, "I am considering you for the work in the new assembly area. You and one other so far are being considered. This is Al and he knows what he is doing or he comes to me. That is rule number one. This is going to be high end stuff such as the cabinets we are building here or some furniture which is already on order. I am very serious about this and will be adding a new building right over there that will adjunct the equipment we have. I need to know if you are interested number one and then your skill level and aptitude will be assessed. I need you to finish the day helping Al and you will go back to the floor tomorrow. Do you have any questions?"

I spent the rest of the day going over Dan's evaluation of orders we had on the books. I also had to become involved because a customer wanted to add a new material and finish color to modify their lines. We arranged for one of their company officers to see the new samples at the factory next week. We had to give some of the new material to be put through the process for our evaluation as well as their tastes and expectations. This was quite common in our industry as flavors of décor changed in our society as well as some other parts of the world. As I left for the day, I asked Dan if I could expect to be eating fish this weekend. He simply told me I could order anything I wanted at my favorite restaurant.

I had called Bonnie and she was up to speed when I got home with Diana right behind me. I was glad that the summer heat was starting to get here and the children were all outside. We made small talk and I told Diana we had pizza coming so we set up the table in the back yard. I had not let her know who was bringing the pizza so she was a little startled to see Samuel and Celine walk in. I simply told her the truth that I was still learning how to counsel people so I had asked someone we all trusted to join us. We fed all the kids and had them go back to playing while we talked.

Samuel opened us up with a word of prayer and then we asked Diana what Frank coming home meant to her. She started, "I have been married for a total of twelve years to Frank. He has been in prison for over three years of our kid's primary years. I won't say that it was a bad marriage but it has not been what I had envisioned. I came from a peaceful family who could face down tribulations of life and not be totally defeated in the process. Frank just never seemed to ever get back up and not be angry. He also does not have the same background of faith in our Lord and Savior Jesus as I do. I want to run away as much from my personal fears as fear of Frank. What if I no longer can respond to him in love after three years? What will his embrace mean to me or our kids?"

Celine said, "Do you think Frank may have some of these same fears? Do you remember a self serving man or a downtrodden man? They have to be addressed differently in our lives."

Diana said, "I see what you mean. I have the choice right now of kicking him while he is down or considering helping him up."

Celine said, "You have the God given chance to show him and teach him what love is in your life. You have the chance to be as vulnerable as he is whether he knows he is vulnerable or not. You can define love to him as Christ would have us do. Of course you don't have to do any of this and let the rest of your life collapse around you and your children."

I said, "I went out to see him at the prison yesterday. I saw a broken man with very little hope that wasn't founded on you. I believe Frank needs to meet Christ as Savior and both of your worlds can meet in love. I told him that I would hire him and find him a place to live if he would submit to the counseling required. He was totally willing immediately to that plan. I need to know if I have to find him an apartment or if he will be joining you with supervision. I believe that it would be easier on the kids if you worked this out in your home."

Diana said, "I never wanted to run away but I felt alone and did not know I could have so much support from people I barely know. I promise to go to the counseling with Frank and the kids. I haven't even told them that he is coming home yet. Could you help me with that tonight?"

Samuel said, "We would be glad to. I am in agreement with Sam that if we can do this in your home with no danger it would be the best. I did not say without trials but without danger. Let's us get the kids together. I want to leave all four of them together to start forming their own opinions and expectations during this time that we can address at the right time."

The children all seemed very happy to having Frank come home. I was amazed at having Tyler relate my coming home from prison for these other children. The night was soon over and we had gone to bed.

Bonnie asked, "Were you hurt when Tyler talked about you coming home from prison with the other children?"

I told her, "I was pleased that the innocence of our children has not been tainted as the world would have it. All mankind needs a hope to lift him from the despair of this world. I am glad that I am able to now teach about the eternal hope for mankind in Jesus. Did we decide to accept Bernie and Cherie's offer to go with them to their cabin at the lake on Saturday?"

Bonnie said, "I believe that it would be a good time. Bernie said we could show the boys how to cast from shore and we could all go out on the boat if it was warm enough."

I said, "I will call them tomorrow because I want them to come and preview their cabinets. Good night."

Al and I brought another load of cabinets to the factory in the morning. The ones that had been finished yesterday did not make it to shipping so there was one step saved. We took the hinges off and numbered the entire matched product so we could send the doors to get finished. We were in the thick of it when Celine stopped on her way to the office to know if we were going to camp with them. She was thrilled to see her cabinets almost done and was very happy with style and color. I told her to call us later with directions and what we needed to bring.

I later met with the salesman and line foreman about the samples we had to have ready for next week. It turned out that the biggest difference was in the sanding of the harder wood and the grain was critical. The discussion led me to ask how we trailed errors in the plant. The line foreman told me how to get that information at any time. I asked him if departments could manipulate the numbers to make production seem better than it was. He assured me that no one gained from that in the bonus system but if a piece was sent to be repaired in a department and still failed again it was given a double failure in the current system. I thanked them and looked up the current material needs listed for one of these items and what we were receiving for them. I took the cost versus price to see what the markup was currently. I then came up with our price with the new material and finish to be ready on Wednesday.

We were all in the car early the next morning with fishing poles in the trunk. I had no problems finding the spot and the cabin. The early morning fog was mesmerizing as we pulled the car down near the private beach. The glasslike surface already free from the fog was reflecting any object it had a view of. The green mountains stood on their heads in the lake under a lowered skyline. The calling of a pair of loons near the far shore rose out of the mist to greet us. Tyler soon had ripples dancing on the surface by throwing a stone into the lake. We were soon gathered around a wicker table within a screened in patio enjoying fresh coffee and fruit with Bernie and Cherie.

The rustic cabin was not meager of amenities with four season building with heat in each bedroom and an insulation package to conserve utilities. It had a laundry room, dining room and kitchen, family room with fireplace, baths up and down and three bedrooms on the second floor. In the back, there was a fish dressing table with running water for cleanup. There was a lot of natural wood throughout that had been used to combat cracking of the walls in off seasons when not in use. Top that with a three season screened in porch and a private beach and you could enjoy a long weekend. This was where she was going to prepare Bernie's can diet while we had their house torn apart for an expected two weeks.

The boys had great time fishing but let all the fish go that they caught. Bernie and I watched with great pleasure to see young Tyler catch two fish without help. I asked Bernie when they intended to start his own family and was surprised to hear that they would soon know if they were doing it right.

We had two sleepy boys when we got home for the night.

# Twenty-Seven

Pastor Mike seemed to know about Frank on Sunday as he made a point to offer his services. I only had time to mention his need for salvation before he was gone again. Samuel and Celine wanted to push the trust issue with Frank and not tell him where he was going to stay until we were all face to face. They said it would either cause a big scene or set the tone for the relationship's restoration. We did not want Frank to fail by our setting indistinguishable boundaries. We were offering help for his life and not our own and he had to make the right choices to succeed.

Both of the two men I had spoken to were carpenters before they came to the factory to work. They were both interested in hearing more about the start of the custom shop. Al said they were both trainable from what they knew now and both had their own strengths. I asked Al which one he wanted today and I sent him down to help finish the doors. We had several of the lower cabinets completed except for the drawers and they looked exceptional.

Dan and I talked about how the meeting had gone with Diana and he was pleased to hear what the plan entailed. I then asked him how he would have gone about placing a price on the new sample. He told me that he had never explained to me how he kept a log of each material that allowed for an average loss due to non-usable portions from each bunk of materials. He said he had started it when the company was much smaller but the time had paid for itself many times over. I would simply add that number and the amount of profit you want to try to make to the numbers you have. I have a number from Sarah on the equipment replacement costs to be placed on each piece produced and that is about thirty-five cents per piece and another twenty-five cents for taxes. I learned some of this the hard way when I did not make the profit that I thought I should.

I said, "If I follow what you have said and already have the numbers for, I would have to get seven dollars more for oak over the birch we are now doing.

Dan said, "That is if you do not want to make a profit. I would have asked for nine to ten dollars minimum. Nothing we buy is going down in price and this order could have options for future productions. I would usually honor the original price for the entire contract and accept any minor fluctuations of cost myself. No one would question catastrophic changes in the middle of a contract. Both parties have options in that circumstance of cancelling the order or the production. By the way, we will be visited this afternoon by the man who built this building. He is trying to retire like me but he is willing to give you a price.

I was pleasantly surprised to have Tyler and Bonnie stop by to bring me some pizza. They were both going to a play put on by Ryan's class for the end of the school year. This prompted me to ask Bonnie if she had found any child care facilities.

She said, "I am meeting with a woman I know from the church who asked me to pray about an opportunity she had. She has been a teacher in a small private school near our house. The owner is fighting a disease that does not allow her to teach anymore. She offered to sell the business including buildings and land to Ellen. I guess that there is a large safety approved playground with a high fence adjoining it to the building. You have to go by a manned desk to get outside. It sounds really ideal. She says she could double the current income by offering what I do for Diana."

"Would you like me to go and assess the buildings for you and Ellen?" I asked.

Bonnie said, "We were going to meet there at two thirty as the children went home. Mother is going to be at our house with those four so we could walk around and pray."

I told her I would meet her there and then went out to see Al. He was going to be going back to the house in the morning to start the drawers. He asked me if he could speak to me after work and at the house. I agreed to do that and went back to the office for a page.

I walked in to the office and Dan introduced me to the contractor who had done this building. I said to him, "I don't know if you are up to date with my buying the factory but my goal is to add a custom line of cabinets and furniture to what exists. We will add conveyors and such to receive materials and product for assembly in that area. Shall we go out and see what and where I am thinking as I keep talking. I believe I will need at least another ten thousand square feet adjoining from that corner. At the same time I want to address the loading and receiving dock that exists."

We all walked and talked about options to consider before we all went our own ways. I did mention to them that I had checked with the city and that it was just a formality to them because of the current zoning for the area.

I left the factory again to meet with Bonnie and Ellen at the school. The buildings were all modern with all the wiring already done for networking computers. The roofs were fifty year rubber fabric and no heating or cooling units were mounted to them. Those units were under a covered area in the protected yard. The cafeteria doubled as a gym when the weather demanded. I did get a gentle hint from Ellen that she could use a partner to help her get going. I asked her if we could see the projections she had used and talk about this some more but I had another meeting to go to.

I looked at the messages that had piled up during the day and saw that the people wanted to see the samples at nine thirty in the morning. I knew we were ready for that so I got Al out of the shop and headed for our house. Al could see that I was not ready to listen yet so he waited until we were in the garage.

Al started, "I need to ask you a few questions if you have the time. I found my ex-wife the other day. It was easier than I thought it would be once I looked under her maiden name. I steadied my nerves and gave her a call. She did speak to me for quite a while and she may let me know about the kids in the near future. I did not get the response I expected and she used a lot of the same phrases you have spoken to me. She spoke of having received Jesus as her personal savior as well as the children. She said it was a kind of love that I needed in my life. I told her about you and what you have done for me. She suggested I talk to you because it sounded like I could ask you and here I am."

I started, "I will not get involved if this is just a ploy to get back with your wife and kids. This the most important decision a person can make on this earth. When you accept that God sent His Son down to earth as a child born in a manger to a virgin named Mary and her betrothed named Joseph as who He is. Then you can accept that Jesus died on a cruel cross to take away your sins. Jesus never sinned on this earth but He was crucified in our place for the sins we have done. Now to whomsoever does believe these things about Jesus are true, God the father forgives ours sins and allows us to spend an eternity in heaven with Him instead of hell with Satan and the other nonbelievers. It is a free gift for the asking but we must be sorry for the sins we have done and do all we humanly can do to stop sinning in the future. It is nothing we can earn such as a release date from prison because we have spent enough time there. We cannot buy it nor can we do it for someone else. Jesus wants to be your personal Savior and the Lord of your life."

Al said, "I have heard some of the bible stories in a children's bible class when I was very young. I never went enough to hear anything like you have told me here. Something inside of me tells me you are telling me the truth and I want to believe you but I don't know if I can."

I said, "You will never be able to see all what I am telling you is true if you do not look with the eyes of your heart. It is with the eyes of faith that we can see him. We as humans will always let each other down but Jesus promises to never leave us or forsake us. God will never hold a sin against us if it has been washed away by the blood of Jesus on that cross. Jesus knew two thousand years ago that he was carrying your sins on that cross and He forgave you then. All we have to do is accept it."

By now the tears were flowing down Al's cheeks. I led him in a prayer of stating his new beliefs in Jesus and asking to be forgiven. I looked around as we were getting done and I saw Bonnie standing there with tears in her eyes as well. She said, "I think this calls for a celebration. My parents were going to barbecue some steaks with us tonight and now you can stay and join us. We have been praying for you since you came here."

We all enjoyed a great summer meal that night and then I had an idea. I asked Al if he had his ex-wife's phone number with him. I listened to the three rings that it took her to answer. We talked for a couple of minutes as I told her who I was. I then asked her to speak to her ex-husband and listen to some news he had to tell her. We let Al walk away from us as they were talking. He was soon wiping the tears away again as he handed me back the phone because he could not speak through the sobs. I told his ex-wife that we would call again in the near future and told her what church to look for on Sunday if she wanted to come to a safe and welcoming place.

Our customers were there at nine-thirty as we sat around my office. They knew Dan and the salesman so we all took a couple of minutes introducing ourselves and a little bit about where I wanted this company to go. We set the new oaken model in the room for them to see beside a birch one from the line. The stark contrast of the two grains of the woods and the color variation made a statement of two distinct decors as the company had wanted. They were well pleased with what they saw and wanted to know the cost differences. I gave them that information very boldly so as not to be mistaken as flexible. They commented that it was in the narrow range they wanted to be in for pricing the new line so they brought out a contract for me to look at. The number was hand written and initialed by both of us. They wanted to order seven thousand pieces over the length of the contract. Three thousand pieces at first and then two subsequent orders of two thousand were already written in. We all signed the contracts and then I gave them the routing number to make the deposit to. I asked Dan if he wanted to take these gentlemen to dinner with Gina but I had to go back to work. Once they left, I received some messages from Diana. One was from the prison about Frank.

I called the prison and made arrangements to pick up Frank right after two in the afternoon. I could not do it in the morning because of a prior commitment with Samuel, Ellen, Bonnie and myself to go over numbers for the school. I had told Bonnie that I would support her going back to work with Ellen if she wanted to. I even told her we could possibly become Ellen's partner if they could do most of the administration work because I was feeling stretched with what I had.

Ellen had a price from the woman she worked for to buy everything and a non-competitive clause for the amount of four hundred-eighty-five thousand dollars. We had some numbers for maximum occupancy for different times of the day and projected incomes at that rate. We had the projected cost for employees at full capacity and had five years of the other woman's operating expenses with the salaries withdrawn so we knew what we felt we could amortize at. The school would have to maintain sixty percent capacity to amortize a reasonable mortgage. I was sitting there taking this all in when I knew I was hearing the Lord tell me that we should not offer more than four hundred-sixty thousand dollars and that is what I told the others. I made one more statement to everyone at the table before I left. I believe the partnership should be fifty-fifty between Walker Enterprises and however Ellen chooses to protect her investment but I want Samuel written in as paid arbitrators for major disputes. If you and Samuel can come to that agreement and find adequate financing, then you have my support and I went out to the factory.

# Twenty-Eight

I called the prison and asked if I could delay the pickup for two hours. We could not get Pastor Mike, Samuel and Celine, and me until almost five o'clock. We were going to have Diana listening from just out of sight until we felt Frank was sincere. Bonnie was going to be there for prayer support and to keep the children occupied for a few minutes. We were all committed to bring Frank to a motel as the very last resort.

The contractor stopped by in the last few minutes I was there and gave me a loose estimate from which I could choose some options. I asked him if he could do it soon and he said he would start the excavation while he was waiting for the steel building to be made. One of the options that saved me money was to take a slightly larger building than I wanted that someone could not buy and receive a discount for that. He told me that if I committed to that building this week that we would be moving in within two months.

I picked up Frank and what belongings he had at four as planned. He seemed very uptight but he would not allow himself to ask me too many questions. I told him about the first meeting we were going to and with whom we were meeting. I told him a little about Pastor Mike and our church. I told him about Samuel and Celine and how they were going to be the primary counselors in the beginning. I asked him if he could work in a factory versus a carpentry job and he said he was grateful to have work because so few people would hire people with his background. I told him I did not know his crime and I did not want to know unless I have to. I told him that he was going to be signing a policy letter that allowed random testing for drug use with a no cause clause at the factory.

I walked Frank into the church at the agreed time and made some introductions as to who I had told him was going to be here. Pastor Mike led us in a brief prayer and then broke the ice by asking Frank what he knew about God and Jesus.

Frank said, "I do not have much of a background with religion. I know of God the Father and Jesus His Son. I learned this when my parents made me go to church. I can't say that I am a strong believer but I am not a nonbeliever either."

Pastor Mike said, "That is an honest answer at worse. I guess you know we are here because it is our intention to support you after your time in prison. The life you left three years ago has become a new entity from the mere passing of time. You have been in one of the most despicable arenas that life has to offer and I am sure you are different. However, you are the one who made the choices that got you in prison. You could make those same choices again and we could not stop you. Our offer is to help you learn how to make right choices. We have been told that you are an angry man. Is that true?"

Frank looked down at the floor and said, "I have lived most of my life angry at one thing or another. I went in to the prison angry but was given the opportunity to see the errors of my ways by the help of one guard. I will tell you about it someday if you want. I never hurt my family but I would do things that would hurt me."

Pastor Mike said, "You want me to believe that your family does not have anything to fear from you?"

Frank said, "I cannot give them back the three years from prison or the fairly miserable life we had before, but they do not have to be afraid of me."

Samuel made a motion with his hand and Diana came into the room. Frank stood to his feet but just stood there wringing his hands. Samuel asked Diana if she had heard all the comments or wanted anything repeated.

She said, "I heard it all. I believe he thinks he is telling the truth about never hurting us but that is not true. I stood before God in that room and asked for the grace to forgive you and I have done that. I do however hope you can show him how many ways he has hurt us. To be the one telling our children that there was nothing for Christmas for them. I can't throw a ball or do most of the sports they saw their friends playing with their fathers. I hope it is not too late."

Pastor Mike said, "It is never too late in God's eyes."

Samuel waved his hand again and two children came out to see their father. They were not as reserved as their mother as they went over to get hugs. The tears were now flowing freely from Diana's eyes as she watched her children with their father for the first time in over three years. Then we heard the question of the day from the youngest child, "Are you coming home with us daddy?" Frank did not answer but from behind him came the words of his wife who simply replied, "Yes."

Pastor Mike gave the entire family a warning about not letting emotions get out of control. He told the family to be ready to meet again on Sunday after church and that it was not an option for anyone. We closed in prayer and then went home for the night.

Frank had a very strange look on his face when he walked into my office to do his employee paperwork. I asked him, "Is there a problem you want to talk about?"

Frank said, "I had trouble falling asleep last night so Diana told me some things about you. She said that you hired her at the church without knowing anything about her and matched her old salary. She told me about the arrangement for the boys to be at your house until she can be home at night. But would you please tell me why I am here now?"

I said, "If I understand the question, you want to know why I hired you. It is a long story that I will abbreviate because we both have work to do. I was falsely accused of money laundering by the federal government. My partner had set me up to take the fall. I did several weeks in federal prison where I met some good men who had lost all hope. God intervened to the point where I got out of prison but it did not end until I killed two assassins as they tried to kill me and my family. I went on with God's help to buy this factory and I try to return the hope I have in God by sharing it with others. I will gladly tell you more when we have time but I need you in receiving so I can transfer someone out of there."

Frank said, "I don't know if thank you says all I want to but you will have a good employee as long as you need me. Show me where to start."

I took Frank to receiving because I wanted to know how much oak I had room to order. I had him start training on the saws that prepared the rough wood for the rest of the process. I then went in and ordered some material. I asked Dan what he thought of the offer on the new building. He said that the cancelled order was a fantastic deal and the fact that it had taken him almost a year to get into his building was incredible. I called the contractor and told him that if the company would take another ten thousand dollars off the price I would order it today. He said he would call me back within the hour. Dan looked at me and said, "You know when to listen to God don't you?"

I said, "I hope I am right because I can't do this on my own. I went with Bonnie and her friend Ellen that is the teacher at the church to go and investigate buying a school. The owner is sick and the two women want to do this together. As we talked about it, I got a very clear number spoken to me from God and they are going to make an offer on it today. They are all meeting at Tim Simonds office today. They have already spoken to the city school board and they are going to become a bus stop so they can do what we have been doing for Diana."

Dan said, "I am glad God found a willing vessel for His works in the two of you. Could you spare me for the rest of the day? Gina and I like to go riding around the lake on quiet days like this."

I was just getting settled in front of my computer to check inventory when there was a quiet knock on my door. It was Diana and I told her to come in. She had a couple of messages to hand me and then she hesitated for just a second. She started, "I don't know if you realize what you have done for me and now for our whole family. The word thank you is not enough for what I am feeling. I pray that we can repay you some day but for now, I am asking God to keep His hand of favor upon your life. I was told that Al has accepted the Lord and is talking to his family. There are very few people who will do what you do willingly. Well, I just wanted to say that."

I told her she was welcome but that they did not owe me for the blessings that God was giving them. A couple of minutes later she put a call through to me and it was the contractor. The company had accepted my offer and we were on our way to a new building the following week. I was thanking God and asking for His wisdom to keep this all going when there was another knock on my door. A salesman and Bonnie were at my door. They came in together so I stood and kissed my wife hello. The salesman quickly said that a handshake would do for him as we both chuckled. The salesman quickly got to the point and asked me if we could accept an order for six thousand pieces like he showed me a picture of. The picture said it would be clear maple and clear birch for materials of which each kind represented half the order. The note on the bottom gave the last price the factory had made them for. The company wanted a price confirmation and if we could get them five hundred of each per month for six months on Monday. I asked him to find the line foreman for me and to come back with him.

I then gave my attention to my wife who just jumped up and said, "They took the offer. Ellen and we are going to assume the existing mortgage that has fantastic rates and we will have need of less than fifty thousand dollars to close the deal and begin working the school. I am so excited doing this and Tim is writing up the partnership the way you wanted it. I took the liberty of telling Ellen that the four of us should get together for dinner this Saturday so we are hosting a barbecue in our back yard. I heard you talking with the salesman as I came in. Is everything okay?"

I said, "Everything here is fine but I need to be careful not to over commit to work we cannot get done. Congratulations on your deal with Ellen and I look forward to meeting everyone on Saturday. I do need to get this ready for Monday so I have to go back to work."

I barely had time to get to the reports on the former runs of the prior orders when the salesman came back. We discussed how long it had been since we had made the other orders. I asked the line foreman how many pieces we could put out in an average day and how some of the other runs were doing on the line. We were ahead on all but the newest orders and were going to ship some large quantities next week. I took the time to ask him if we had any problem areas on the line. I also mentioned my idea about training some people to the point that they could be put where we had a temporary problem. He told me that creating some people who could be moved around would help him solve nearly every problem on the line. I asked him to give me some names next week and let him go back to work. I thanked the salesman and asked him one last question. I asked him if he thought the company was expecting a price increase to which he said yes.

# Twenty-Nine

I was looking at the drawers that Al had made this week in my garage. The dove-tailed corners were a clean tight fit and the bottoms seemed to have no movement at all. It was some excellent work. He had written a word in the sawdust on a table that I could still read as Jesus. He had all the fronts ready for finishing so they could be attached. I always used heavy drawer slides and he had them on the drawers as well.

Bonnie was in a festive mood when I went in and she handed me a glass of wine as I sat down. She said, "I did not realize how much I missed working with children. I have had most of the formative years alone with Tyler and Ryan but now we can put them into our own school. What a blessing from God that is."

We shared each other's company over a tender and flaky haddock fillet cooked in lemon oil, olive oil, and breaded to keep it from drying as it baked. We then sat down on the couch together to watch a movie the boys had picked and made popcorn to share. The boys woke me up so I would quit snoring. I took the time as we got ready for bed to thank God for the times I was sharing with my family and no longer in prison.

Ellen came in the next morning and introduced her husband Ted to Bonnie and me. We were soon in the back yard so the kids could all play as we talked. It turned out that Ted had to travel on a strange cycle for the company he worked for. He might be gone one to two weeks per month and did not like leaving the family behind. He was a mechanical electrician that would repair, replace, or simply maintain equipment that could not be handled without his going to the other companies. Many of the companies could not stop production on normal work days so he was there during down times. He said that when he considered the real expenses of his job that it did not pay him well. He had recently gotten a computer for their house so they could at least see each other even if they could not touch.

I asked him, "Are you an electrician by trade or do you only know machines?"

Ted answered, "I still maintain my electrical license by recording all the hours I work in this state. Why do you ask?"

I said, "It may not be the right time to ask with our wives starting their school but I need someone like you in the maintenance department. On top of all the work that has to be done daily I just ordered a new building to be attached to the factory. I am expanding the factory to include a custom side to build cabinets and fine furniture that we will sell and ship."

Ted said, "I think you are wrong and this is the perfect time. I know what my wife can do but I miss her and the kids a lot while on the road and I would love to be here when they begin as support."

Ellen cut in, "I did not know how much you were missing us and I was trying to keep a stiff upper lip when you were around so I wouldn't draw you down. I don't know what Sam can pay but if it means we can be together then we will do it together. Money is not a good reason to separate our family. I wasn't expecting God to join us together so completely but I know when He is at work in our lives."

We were all fascinated at how the morning had gone. We enjoyed each other's company for a couple more hours as we ate and prayed in thanksgiving to God's blessings. We said we would see them in church the next day as they left.

The church had several visitors in it the next day. I had picked up Al on the way and he was sitting next to me with a new bible. Frank came in and sat with his family near Samuel and Celine. Al was looking around when he let out a gasp and got my attention. He asked me to go with him right now. I stood to go with him and saw a woman with three children standing in the isle at the back of the church. He went and spoke to the children who did not look as young as I might have thought them to be but I knew they had to be his. We all came back down to sit for service and said we would all speak afterwards. The three children had to sit in the row in front of us but they looked at their father often. Al's wife saw that I was showing him how to find the verses and volunteered to do that. I simply looked at Bonnie and told her how much I loved what God can do.

Pastor Mike gave a strong sermon on the restoration of individuals and families through the blood of the cross. It had a special meaning to me as I looked at the families we had sitting all around the sanctuary. At the end of the service, I asked Samuel if they needed me with Frank because I wanted to be with Al and his family. They said that they knew Pastor Mike was going to be there so I could meet with Al. Samuel jokingly said that we were going to have to get more counselors if I kept it up. I told him to get ready because I didn't think God was done yet. As we separated, I asked Samuel to come by the office in the morning if he could and he said he would.

We brought Al and his wife to a fast food restaurant so we could talk. Al introduced Edith to us as we sat down at a table big enough for the nine of us. Edith told us that I could have knocked her over with a feather after I had called her the other night. She said that she had always had a faith in God but had not been able to influence Al. She was not ready to jump in with both feet but had never loved anyone but Al. From the conversation, there were not many bad feelings between the children and their father except for his long absence. There was certainly nothing wrong with their appetites as we managed to eat four big pizzas and some salads. It turned out that Edith had to work out at two jobs to make ends meet and relied on her parents to watch the children most of the time. The one thing that impressed me the most was the absence of animosity from any of them. Prison had changed their lives but Edith and the children had not gotten to the point of despair that Al had while behind bars.

We soon left and Edith said she would drop Al at his apartment so they could have a few private minutes before she had to go home. She had to go to work at a diner later so she wanted to get on the road soon. We all knew that we would be seeing each other very soon. We told Edith that if she came next Sunday we would barbecue at the house so the kids could play.

The next morning Al and I loaded all the fronts to the drawers and I brought them to finishing. I told him how happy I was with his work and we had to start thinking about the next order he was to build.

I went over the prior numbers with Dan so I could solidify the price on the pending new order. I felt that I wanted to remain competitive but I wasn't interested in working for free. I did the final calculations and called them as agreed. They felt the price was fair and they were going to next day mail the contracts for me to sign. I gave them the routing numbers for the deposit before hanging up and thanked them for the orders.

Samuel came by the office as I had asked. I asked him if I had any problems with cash flow and if I could use some of the reserves I had. He said that he would like to have a few questions answered first about work status and the standing of order delivery.

I said, "We are ahead on all the contracts in production except for two substantial ones I just got. One was an hour ago for six thousand pieces in six months and it represents sixty thousand dollars profit for that one. The one last week had seven figures of profit. When I say profit, I mean debt reduction as well as personal income. Our sales projections are great and our production is ahead of any of the last five years we did our commitment on. I am under contract to build my new custom shop adjoining this factory in the next two months. I don't know if you have heard but Ellen and Ted Richards have decided to go in partnership with Bonnie and me to buy the Kid's Freedom school four blocks from here. I don't know everything that God has planned for us but we saw Al give his life to Christ last week and his ex-wife and children were in church this Sunday. You have been helping with Frank and Diana so you know more about that then I do. I also hired Ted Richards to join our maintenance team so he can be at home instead of being on the road on that crazy schedule."

Samuel said, "I will go to Sarah's and see if you have all the information you need and then we can talk again. I don't know if I am the one who wants to discourage what God is doing all around you but I will give it an accountant's scrutiny. See you later. By the way, Frank has asked for a special meeting tonight and it will be at six at the church. He wanted you there if possible."

I told him I would be there and went out to see Al and how the cabinets looked completed. The pulls worked with just a simple push or pull and the faces aligned very well when closed. It was some great work. I told him I had to get on the ball with the next project's preparation. I found the line foreman and asked him to come to the office.

I said, "I have to have three men for some work outside the factory for up to two weeks. I had several large custom projects ordered when I bought this factory and one of them includes the remodeling of the kitchen that the cabinets we have made go into. I have Frank who is still in receiving and the two men who have been helping Al with the assembly. What will we have to have to help you cover the line and would this be the time to start the cross training of some of the men?"

He said, "It would be an excellent time to start the training. I also know that two of the shift splitters would like to come on full time. We could still use one more employee hired if possible."

I said, "I believe we should do all of the above because we cannot afford to fall behind right now. I will find some new people to try because I am sure we will have to cover some vacations when school lets out for the summer. I am going to flag an area on the end of the building that can no longer be parked in. We have dirt moving equipment coming for the new building tomorrow. Would you please hand out these reminders today because I do not want a mess in the morning? Would you please send in the head of maintenance as you go by their room and have him bring in his longest measuring tape?"

I had the dimensions that the contractor had sent me to clear for the morning. I had the maintenance foreman help me stake out the area as we spoke. I said, "I want to get you involved as soon as possible with the layout of the new building and what we need to consider in regards to the conveyors or if we are going to run this shop on dollies. I also want you to know that I have hired an electrician who specializes in motor electricity. We will be doing most of the wiring for the new building in house with his help. I know that you will find him a great asset to your team."

He said, "I have always wanted a true electrician on the crew. I personally believe that you should get the custom shop going with dollies or leave room for the forklift to get close. Once you have a system, then you can have some conveyors or ceiling tracks put in."

I thanked him for his help and support and we both went back to work. I went out to see Diana and asked her to set up employment interviews with several candidates this week if possible. Then I called Pastor Mike and asked him if he knew anyone out of work and he said he would send one person over today and that he would see me tonight.

# Thirty

I asked Dan if he was going to take some time off this week as the weather was getting hot. He said he might take two days off at the end of the week for some last spawning runs in a river to the north. I told him fine and asked him to sit in on a couple of interviews of people whom God may not have put in my path. He simply told me not to expect a perfect record when dealing with this many people.

The man that Pastor Mike had sent over was now sitting with Dan and me. I asked, "why are you here today?"

He said, "I got a call from Pastor Mike to come and see about a job. I am not sure what I want to do and I have several applications out there already. I have never worked with wood before but I am sure I could learn. I usually make a living playing in a band."

I told him, "We are interviewing several people this week and we will let you know if we want you to come in. Thank you for coming in today."

When he had left Dan said, "Some of them tell you they don't want to be hired. The secret to a good interview is for you to know what you are hearing and you are wise enough to not make too many mistakes. It is okay to make a mistake and have to fire someone."

I went home to say hello to Bonnie and the boys before going to the church. Bonnie said she would wait up because she wanted to talk to me tonight about the school. I told her I would not dawdle after the meeting. I was the last one to arrive so we went right into prayer.

Frank said, "I want to thank you all for coming. I would like to tell a short story from my time in prison and then ask your help. I have told you that I was an angry man most of my life. I failed to tell you how mean I was to people who were smaller than me and could not fight back. I brought that attitude with me to prison and would be mean to some of the smaller inmates. There was a guard named Officer Drews who kept telling me to quit before I got hurt. He kept telling me that prison had a way of getting that meanness out of me. I would not listen to him until I was at my work detail near the laundry one night. I was suddenly surrounded by eight inmates that I had been mean to while I was there. They all tackled me at once and I was soon lying face down in the hall. They wrapped a rag around my head and in my mouth so I could not yell for help. They taunted me to be mean to them now. They forced my hands in front of me and one of them stood on them. They asked me if I was learning anything yet about my meanness. I shook my head yes as the man did a little turn on my hands. I was warned to stay down for several minutes before returning to my cell. They taunted me one more time about having a good memory before they got off my hands and left. I could not close my hands for a week but I never said a word until now. The question I have for you gentlemen is why I am always angry?"

Pastor Mike took the lead and said, "Anger is a secondary emotion. In other words, you might get angry when you have been betrayed. To keep it very simple you get angry in any way that you feel you do not get what you want. You want to have enough money to pay your bills and your boss cuts your hours. You can blame God for your losing a day to rain. The excuses are endless and the answer is always the same. Jesus says we are to love every one more than ourselves. We cannot do that by ourselves so we have to look at Him on the cross. Jesus died on the cross to forgive our sins and make us lovable to God the Father. The relationship is the same. We cannot love anyone whom we do not forgive. We will not be angry with anyone we forgive. You can learn to not react in anger as those inmates taught you but God sees our hearts. He knows if we hold unforgiveness toward anyone and He wants that out of our lives. You may have to go back as far as your childhood but it all has to go. Have you ever asked Jesus to forgive you?"

Frank said, "No! I have never realized the need you are talking about."

Pastor Mike said, "We all have to come to the end of our own abilities to find what we never knew we lost. God created us to be His children. Until we come back to the Father's love by the forgiveness of our sins at the cross we will have a great big void in our lives. The love we accept from the father allows us to forgive and love our fellow men. When we believe that Jesus is the living Son of God and died on that cross to forgive all our sins, He is faithful and true to do it. Our part is to accept the free gift of salvation and to stop sinning as best we can as humans. We learn how to ask God to help us not sin and He shows us how to love each other."

Samuel asked, "Do you like your life the way it is? Would you like to find peace after all these years of anger? Only Jesus in your life will bring the true peace that is beyond our understanding."

There were tears gathering to flow down Frank's cheeks when he said, "I want to change. Just tell me how to start having what you and my wife seem to have."

We led Frank through a prayer of asking forgiveness for his sins. We had him invite Jesus to come and live within him. He then committed to live his life for Christ and the Father. We finished the night by praying into his and his families' life to become peaceful through forgiveness from the heart.

I went right home after the meeting and found that I had gotten home before the boys had gone to bed. I got on the floor and let them attack me while we watched a movie. Bonnie told me to not get them riled up just at bedtime and she sent them up to their room for the night. I jokingly told her if she wanted to be alone with me she only had to ask. When she sat up in a chair and faced me instead of sitting beside me, I knew it was going to be serious.

She said, "I know that God has opened the door for Ellen and me to buy the school. We are nearly ready to close and now Ellen is feeling guilty. She says that after looking over the numbers and start up costs that she is not comfortable."

I jumped in, "I saw those numbers and I know that the school can pay for itself. If you add just one third of the drop off kids that you can have legally you can do very well."

Bonnie said, "It is not the question of income. It is the part of half ownership in a venture she cannot contribute to equally. She thinks I should own more of it if not all of it. I have been praying about this since we spoke earlier and I know it is set up the way God wants it to be no matter how little she can give now. I don't believe that it was our intent to take a greedy portion of this project. I know that Ted is getting home tomorrow and I would like us to get together and settle this. Can we come by the office in the afternoon?"

I said, "Of course you can. I cannot leave because we break ground on the new building tomorrow. I also have some employment interviews scheduled during the day but I will make time for you."

I met first thing in the morning with the two people selected to cross train for the line. I had gone out and started to get some hard hats of different colors and I gave them red hard hats to wear. I then stopped by Al's area and gave him a yellow hardhat I was designating for assembly. I gave a couple of the department heads their blue ones and I had put a star on each side of the line foreman's blue one. I had orange ones for receiving but I had to leave a lot of the rest in white for now. I looked outside from receiving and saw a bulldozer being backed off from a trailer. I noticed that the parking was going to be tight for a while.

I had three quick interviews within the next hour. There was only one applicant who wanted to see in the plant so I asked Dan to show him the basics. When he got back he asked me a question that told me a lot about him. He asked me what it would take for me to give him a try. I told him to show up in the morning and he could have that try. He thanked me, shook my hand and said I will see you in the morning. I had him do his paper work and sign the company policy letter and told him if he wasn't on time not to come at all.

Bonnie was in the waiting area when he left so we all went back into my office. I opened us in prayer and then I started, "I have done a great deal of praying since last night and I know what I want to say but I would like to hear from Ellen."

Ellen said, "I have a heavy heart about the agreement we made about the ownership of the school. I feel that I need to concede a portion of the ownership because of how little we can give of the initial money. My dreams were bigger than my billfold."

I looked at her and Ted as they seemed to be in agreement. I said, "I want you to remember the first day I went to the school with the two of you. I saw two sisters in the Lord wanting to do good things for children together. I know what I heard from the Lord about the amount you were supposed to offer and how it was to be operated as a partnership of equal proportions. Do you remember that conversation? Did I say that you had to put in the same amount as Bonnie?"

Ellen said, "No, but I don't feel right about it."

I said, "That is too bad about how you feel. I suggest you prepare your heart to please God with the work you are about to do. I suggest you two go to see Sarah very soon to start setting up your accounts. Now go away and let me work." We all chuckled at my feigned attempt at being gruff. There were a lot of teary hugs as they left the room.

Dan had gone out to see the start of the outside work and came back to report how well it was going. He said that they would be bringing in the base gravel this afternoon. I told Dan, "They are just in a hurry to get more of my money. Are you going fishing tomorrow as planned?"

I contacted the people who had placed the next custom order from me and verified they were still interested. They were ready and asked if they could order one more set of shelves for a storage area in their closet. I told them I would now have to come out and measure as well as get an idea on their finish. I asked if we could come out tonight at five-thirty and that was fine.

I brought Al with me so he could see where everything was going. The first cabinets were going in the laundry area and they knew we could not match the existing so they said to come close and they would be fine with it. The new shelves would have to be made in two halves to get them behind the doors that existed. We would use the same finish as the others because they were hidden. I took a deposit check and we went home.

# Thirty-One

I had three men with me on Monday morning as we pulled up to Bernie's house. Bernie and Cherie were going to be sleeping at the camp until further notice. The construction dumpster was on the lawn and we were preparing to fill it. I told them they had to work together but I was asking Al to be the spokesman for the group. I told them that if the old cabinets or any parts like the sink could be given to Habitat for Humanity I wanted to do that. I told them they could not sacrifice too much time for the sake of salvage and just keep moving. I was going to have Ted come move the wires and add two circuits in the kitchen tomorrow. I had some miscellaneous lumber and the new window brought out to do the pass through to the dining room and install the window. I showed them where to put in the dust walls and then I went to the factory.

The pilings had been poured for the new building and they were grading for the slab. We were going to lose some more parking in the morning when the building steel arrived. I went across the street to our neighboring factory and asked if some of my employees could park along their back row by the street. I offered to pay for the privilege but they did not want reimbursement for a favor. I had the word passed through the factory so they would know.

Bonnie and Ellen were due to close on the school on Friday so I asked Dan if he could be here in the morning at least. As president of Walker Enterprises LLC, I had to be there to sign as the primary.

I had the salesman from a commercial woodworking company meeting with me this morning. I was in the market for a high capacity shaper for fine furniture and doors. He brought in a computer video of it working and all the shapes that could be made. It was also able to do tongue and groove moldings to use for wainscoting and flooring. The knives could be changed in about one hour to change style. I had not thought of the flooring market before but it piqued my attention. The machine was very expensive but could be leased for a trial period. The biggest drawback was our having to ship the knives for sharpening to the factory. I asked him to call me in about a week so I could investigate possible markets in our area.

I was speaking to my lumber broker later in the day and I told him I was looking at a flooring shaper to build a new line of production. He said that he had several markets for the processed wood but they would not be a full retail buyer. I asked him what they were paying so I could assess my production costs against it. As we hung up he said I should check with some floor installers in the area for our market pricing.

I stopped by to see the progress Al had accomplished through the day and found that ninety percent of the demo was done. The cabinets had been saved and were ready to be picked up as well as the old counter top. We were about to leave when Al took me aside and said, "I would like to speak to you when you have time. I would like to know if you are going to need a cook for the school because I have someone for the job."

I said, "Al, I am not going to run the school but I will certainly ask Bonnie tonight. Who did you have in mind?"

Al said, "My ex-wife has said she is interested in trying to spend time together again if she can find work in the area. She has years of experience in the nutritional field and has cooked where she works part time now for six years. If you had the need I would appreciate the opportunity for her to apply for the job."

I said, "I will let you know. Ted will be here tomorrow for the wiring and I hope to have the sheetrock finisher here the next day. Most of you will be back at the factory while he is here. Good work today. I'll see you tomorrow."

The next day I stopped by receiving with the line foreman so we could consider how much more production the plant was capable of. At this time, the receiving department would process all the incoming wood and do some sorting by lengths. We tossed around the idea of the placement of another man for sorting versus less sorting at receiving. No one wanted to sacrifice production time by having to sort on the floor. It would require more manpower to achieve the maximum of the two areas. There was the option of a conveyor doing some of the stacking by sending the shorts into a bin organizer versus stacking it all by hand. I thanked them for their time and said I would bring them a proposal in the near future.

I went outside one time to see the portion of slab that had been poured. I had not thought of it before but the contractor asked me what I was going to do with the steel that would have gone where I had a building. He said that he would take it off the bill if I wanted him to because he had to repair a building that had had a fire. We agreed on a price and that was all settled.

I finally had a few minutes of quiet time so I asked Diana to come to the office. I got to ask her if Frank being home was going well for her and the children. She said they were working together on how Frank was to discipline the children as the head of the household the scriptures of the bible spoke about. My only advice to them was to make sure the children knew why something was wrong besides just I told you so.

The closing took place on Friday in a conference room at the bank. The sale had to be timed with the assumption of the loan by Walker Enterprises LLC and T. E. Richards LLC and the cash payment for the balance to the former owners. Tim Simonds had to present both entities to the bank and the formal partnership as well for the satisfaction of the bank. It took a little time but it was worth seeing what God had ordained come to pass.

The wives had placed an ad in the local paper offering the start of their services. The school year officially closed the day of signing so they had to get some summer work lined up quickly. I knew that they were going to speak to Edith when she came to church on Sunday about working as a cook. We had also let my employees know of the available services.

I was beginning to think God was going to give us a little rest when I got a call from the warden at the federal prison asking me to meet with a new inmate on Tuesday. All he would tell me on the phone was that he had less than a month to his release. I told Bonnie about it as we talked that night. I told her also that in about two weeks we were going to take a long weekend at some lake as a family to relieve some tension before Dan left for good.

I ordered the shaper delivered for a minimum three month trial and the option of two more single year contracts to follow if we could keep it in production. I had two flooring installers that promised to try our product already so I went ahead with it.

The carpenters at Bernie's house asked if I was considering doing remodeling as another side. I told them that at this time I could only offer it with the sale of a custom order. I would have to get a multi-year job offer or wait to build up my management team. They said they would keep their ears open for me. I told them to take no work from Tony Gatzee or Frank Gavin on my behalf and would not tell them what I meant.

I drove out to the prison on Tuesday to meet Joe Black. I was led to the usual conference room and took a seat to wait. I heard a key from the guard side of the door and was then introduced to Joe Black by his case manager. I gave him my first name only and started, "Tell me a little about yourself and any possible plans for after your release in a month."

It was obvious that Joe had a chip on his shoulder when he answered, "I don't know why I should tell you anything about myself or my plans."

I said, "You don't have to but a friend of mine asked me to help you if I could. How will I know that if I don't know anything about you?"

Joe said, "You have a friend who wants you to help me. Can I know that friends name? I don't have any friends around these parts."

I said, "I am friends of the warden here and I have helped some inmates as they come to their release date with housing, work, and a support team. He asked me to come and meet with you."

Joe said, "You're lying that the warden asked you to come here for me."

The case manager piped in that it was true but if he didn't want my help he would call the guard.

Joe said, "Now wait a minute. I may want to hear what the man has to say. I don't have anything to go back to. My parents both died since I have been here and that was all the family I had. I served three years for the sale of drugs. I worked as a carpenter's helper on the outside and I worked in the wood shop here as a red hat if you know what that means."

I said, "I do. I don't remember your face but another guy named Al and I had the assembly bench nearest the rip saws. I now own a woodworking factory and I offer housing, work, counseling and support for you to learn how to make better choices in life. I would be the first one to turn you in if you came to work for me and screwed up. You would be signing an employment letter that allows me to have random testing for drugs with a no cause clause for the test."

Joe said, "I never used drugs but I was selling them on the street. I would like to know why you want to do this."

I said, "I was here for months when I was falsely accused of money laundering. I met a bunch of inmates who had no hope left for their lives and some would not accept help in a meaningful way. I heard an old adage that said: you can feed a man a fish today or you can teach him how to fish for tomorrow. You were picked for the opportunity to work for me by several men here at the prison and by God. Do you want to commit to the program that I am offering?"

Joe said, "I turned my back on God a long time ago but I am willing to try your program."

I said, "Then it is settled. I know your proposed release date and the people here will call me. I will see you soon."

As I drove home, I thanked God for the ability to help inmates like Joe even if they had a chip on their shoulder. It was all a part of the mental cruelty to be found as an inmate in prison. Joe had lost his hope and his trust while in the prison. Maybe we could help him get some back.

# Thirty-Two

Bonnie and Ellen could not keep up with the calls coming in about the school. They had to start doing a short blurb about what the clients wanted for services and then taking down phone numbers to call them back when there was time to talk. Others who had services before the closing brought their kids just like they normally did. Fortunately all the prior names were in the computer and helped abbreviate the turmoil. Three of the staff had stayed on so they were able to take the children in to rooms and start their day. The prior pricing for services was honored and used to help mothers decide what they wanted. The two women had expected to get a brochure ready before opening but it was not back from the printers yet. They quickly printed off the sheet that they had sent to the printers and used that for a handout. The printers also had new contracts that would give health information and emergency contacts and the extent of services they expected for a given fee from the school. Bonnie and Ellen had a clause put in the contracts that there probably would be material taken from the bible on any given day. Bonnie called the factory to see if Sam could get the printing to the school and he said he would get there as soon as he could escape.

Ted had one more job to complete at his employers before his notice to quit would be honored. He had wired Bernie's kitchen for Sam the week before and would do the trim when the paint went on and dried. He was looking forward to being home with his family all the time.

I was at the factory trying to deal with a couple of no shows and how to keep the line going. It was going to be a month before Joe Black could start so I got Diana calling in some more applicants for interviews. I went to Bernie's and brought back one employee who could fill a void as I got the printing. I dropped the guy off at the factory and asked him to check in with the line foreman for orders. I did have Bonnie check the brochures for accuracy with me before I left. I was only able to pick up one box of contracts but the women could get the existing children signed up.

The crane and welders were in the new building as they modified the pitch of the roof to make it run water all in one direction. We had not had enough rain today to stop the work but it was threatening to keep the last part of the slab from being poured and was another reason to get a roof on quickly as possible. We could not start anything to help ourselves until we could enclose and lock the new wing.

I had returned to the office to start making some drawings to scale of how to utilize the custom shop when there was a knock on the door. It was one of my no shows asking to talk to me. He wanted to show me a report of a motor vehicle accident he had been involved in on the way to work. It turns out that he had picked up the other no show because his car was in the shop and they were together at the time. I asked him if he was still physically able to come back to work and he said they had both been cleared by the ER doctor but it was almost noon when they got released. He had come to the factory because it was his fault that they were both late. He had a rental car now and they both wanted to come to work tomorrow. I thanked him for coming by and asked him to bring in the ER release for them both so we could make a copy to put in their files.

My plan for the new shaper was having me take a look at where I wanted to do the custom assembly temporarily. I was now looking at a long strip of floor on the back wall for the process. It would require forty feet to do sixteen foot flooring if I wanted to do some that long. We would have to pass by the working process if I put it there. The other option was right beside the receiving dock and we would have to modify that area some to do that. Dan told me that in the past he had rented a cold storage area from the neighbors to keep the raw materials coming from the broker. It could hold four bunks of three types of material under a roof and lockable. We both went over to see if it was still available and rentable. The owner was very agreeable but wanted a copy of my insurances covering my inventory off site. I told him I would have him sent a copy by my insurers and get him a check.

Now I had more options in receiving to do the shaper beside it. I was observing several boxed up pallets being gathered on the side above this area and asked what they were. The guys told me that the first one thousand pieces of the latest contract was being picked up by the truckers in the morning for delivery. I asked them if there were often materials there and they said it was necessary if the product was not picked up in a timely fashion. That led me to ask if the trucking outfits were hired by us or the other companies. They said by the other companies were the most common but the cabinets I had in the racks was using a lot of the normal space. I told them that I was going to move them to the job site tomorrow and some of that would be cleaned up.

I went by Bernie's house on the way home and found that the kitchen was painted and ready for the cabinets. We had made and finished some trim to go around the pass through and that looked fantastic. With a three inch overhang on each side of the wall you had ten inches to put dishes on. The guys intended to finish the outside trim around the window before going home today. I said, I guess that means I can bring the cabinets tomorrow for you to put in. We will put the upper cabinets in so the trim for the inside of the window will be against it. I will go back and get some on my truck and leave them in my garage for early tomorrow. Good work guys."

It took two days to put in the cabinets but we were soon back working on the new order in my garage and I put one man helping Al. I had Bernie and Cherie meet me at their house on the night all the cabinets were in. I had made them promise to not go home until I called them and they went along with it. I was inside the kitchen when Cherie could finally see it. She just covered her face and cried. She said, "This is even better than I had dreamed possible. I am so glad that I listened to a couple of your suggestions to give me what I really wanted. I can just picture the ivory colored counter tops with a beige sink molded in. And look at the dining room from here at the window. Do you know when they are going to do the counter tops?"

I said, "They were here yesterday to measure so they should be in by the first of the week. Do you know if the appliances are in yet? You should be able to move back by the middle of next week if they are."

Bernie said, "Everything is in and they will deliver them the day after I call to tell them we are ready. We still need to decide what we want to do with the floor."

I said, "Do you think that you would like solid wood floors in the kitchen and maybe have it flow around to the dining room? Maybe a medium brown stain on some nice ash would look nice? I have ordered a shaper to make hardwood flooring and you could get an installer to put it in."

Bernie said, "Let us think about it and we can talk about it some more this weekend when you and your family come for a barbecue at the camp. We have several things I want to talk about with you so please come."

I said, "I will ask Bonnie when she gets home from the school and I will call you tomorrow. Good night for now."

The new building was now water tight with a completed roof and four walls. The door that had come with the kit was without an automatic opener but we could use it and lock it. I had ordered two bunks of lumber from my broker to build some storage area and the raised work areas. They thought that they would be done insulating in a couple of days and we would be on our own. The two month estimate for construction had been done in five weeks. Ted was going to start full time this Monday and was going to complete a new sub-panel for the custom shop that he had gotten started.

Bonnie and Ellen had never thought that they would have almost a hundred children within two weeks. They had hired Edith and she was going to start full time Monday. They had hired a couple of young women back from the original owner who exchanged childcare for some of their salary. The one thing that was found to be needed was an elongated day to get more people to be able to work until stores closed at six o'clock. The child care would probably have to be offered for twelve hour coverage of any days. They had sixty applications for the school year already that they had to examine to place twenty children in the four grades they taught and some preschoolers as well. One of the reasons that Bonnie agreed to go to the camp was for the down time as well as being with some friends.

The boys brought their fishing poles again when we went out to Bernie's camp. The weather was overcast but was not enough to make you stay inside if that was what you did all week. The four of us were in chaise lounge chairs near the boys as they fished. Bernie brought the two of us a beer as we started to talk. Bernie asked, "What school was Bonnie getting home from the other night when we were looking at the cabinets?"

I said, "You haven't heard? Bonnie and Ellen Richards bought the 'Kid's Freedom School' and are now running it. Why don't you tell them about it Bonnie?"

Bonnie said, "Ellen came to me in church and asked me to pray about her buying the school that she worked at because the owner was sick. We prayed about it, made an offer that was accepted, and have been running it for two weeks. We will not start formal school hours again until fall but we already have one hundred children for the summer. In the fall, we will become a place where children can be left to go to the city schools and picked up from there after the buses leave them off. We have already gone to the school board and have become a designated bus stop."

Cherie said, "That is so exciting. How early will you take applications for your school?"

Bonnie said, "We are taking applications now. Wait a minute, are you telling us something about the future?"

Cherie just smiled and the grin on Bernie's face was priceless. We congratulated them on the good news. I said, "You were concerned about the smell of the wood finish the other night making Cherie sick when we were talking about the ash flooring weren't you? Well you really don't have to worry about that with the new finishes on the market. The smell would be all gone in less than a week if you can open some windows during the curing time."

The afternoon took on a spontaneous gaiety between us as the talk of how a baby changes your entire world and the way you look at it carried the theme. We called the boys in to lunch so we would not have to worry about them. They told us that they had only caught two fish all morning. Bernie said that he wanted to show the boys something in the back yard so they followed him. A couple of minutes later, Tyler came to get me so I could see it. He brought me near a balsam tree that was on the back line of the property. He signaled me to be quiet with his finger over his lips as we watched a fat Mrs. Robin bring some lunch home to her chicks. We left her alone and I asked Bernie if he wanted me to start the grill.

After a steak barbeque followed by strawberry shortcake, we were ready to just sit for a while. The boys went into the back yard and came back with a small garter snake. I asked them if they wanted to see more of how nature acted as I took the snake over by the lake. I threw it about twenty yards from some weeds by the shore and told the boys to watch closely. In about three seconds a large mouth bass came up and broke the surface as it ate the snake and then disappeared. The boys were fascinated and I asked them if they remembered the hawk that had caught the snake in the park. I told them that even snakes had to be careful about where they went. The boys both wanted to catch the fish but I told them it would have to be another day.

# Thirty-Three

Al had stayed at my house working until I had gotten home so he could speak to me. He asked, "Are you happy with my work and how much I get done?"

I said, "Of course I am Al. I have told you on several occasions just how I felt. I am thinking that I will have you as foreman in the assembly area. What makes you ask these questions now?"

Al said, "It is not a bad thing. Edith and I are getting along so well that I want to ask her to marry me again. I want us to be a family as God would have us. She put money down on an apartment here in town today and she can move right in. I want us to be married or not in the same house but I really want God in it for us."

I said, "You know that you have my support whatever happens. I know that Bonnie and Ellen are both happy with the work that Edith is doing for them. I have another inmate that is coming out in a couple of weeks and I could put him in your apartment if this works out. I just love the way God orchestrates our lives if we let him."

I had the area cleared by receiving for the new shaper that was coming in the morning. We were going to have a trainer for up to a week to get us basically familiar with the machine. I wanted to see it make furniture and door moldings for the custom shop. I had a piece of furniture ordered by the warden's neighbor and I wanted it to be a prototype of things to come. Ted had run conduit and wiring over to the site as per specs and would attach the service disconnect once it was in place. We were ready for another change.

Bonnie called me in the middle of the day to tell me she had a new girl working for her that was very nervous. Edith had said yes to Al's new proposal of marriage and she was as giddy as a teenager. I told Bonnie to congratulate her for me and we would talk later. What I did not know yet was that they wanted Bonnie and me to be their witnesses before God at the altar when Pastor Mike married them.

We ran some temporary lights to build the work stations and storage areas in the custom shop. I had decided to bring a table saw and build a receiver table for the custom area for changes that were needed once something was started. We were also going to have a smaller shaper to do butt joints in the furniture making. The maintenance crew was in charge of getting ventilation and heating to the new wing by the time we needed it.

I was called to the office one day to meet with someone I did not know. He was very well dressed and I invited him to sit down after he told me he was Bob Davis. I said, "What can I do for you Mr. Davis?"

He said, "You may call me Bob. It took me a while to find you but I got your name finally from Bernie Segal. I am negotiating the purchase of the building you were working on for Frank Gavin. Please don't panic yet, I am not Frank Gavin. I own several buildings here in the city and you can check me out if you want to. I am negotiating with the federal government as I told you. They seized the building by law to settle some of the costs to prosecute your old friends. It gets very complicated to clear all old assignments against a building taken this way but I am a patient man. I do however agree that the planned renovations were very well thought out and the ratio on returns would be good. I also checked you out in regards to the renovations. I want to know if you want to go back and finish the work you started as the general contractor. I know the original permits allowed for nearly two years to do fourteen million dollars of renovation. I believe that I could have the work upgraded and still done for around twelve million dollars. You would do the work of keeping everyone in line and on time. I would pay you to pay the others but there would be no duplicating of work. I would pay the usual ten percent fees for handling the subs and materials and I am offering twelve percent profit and not the usual twenty. I would write one check to your account per month as per invoices and progress verification. Is this something that you would consider because I want to get started as soon as I own the building in about two months?"

I said, "When you mentioned Frank Gavin my stomach churned. That was a very good project and the neighborhood was in line with the plans. My life is very different now and I would have to give this some serious prayer time. I know I can do the job but I now have this factory to run. How soon would you have to know my answer?"

Bob said, "I would like it in a week and I want you to know that I do this all the time. There would be more offers if this one went well."

I said, "Why are you looking for someone new now?"

Bob said, "That is a fair question. The man I have been using has no attachments to an area and I have him lined up for a property in Florida. He then wants to retire there at the end of that job. I will have him get in touch with you if you would like to meet him."

I said, "I would really like to meet him ASAP so please take my card to have him call me or come here. My last question to you Bob is, do you believe in God the father and His Son.?"

Bob said, "I try very hard to have him lead me in His paths and I believe you are on that path with me for at least a while. Please call me with any questions. God bless and have a great day."

I was dumbfounded to the point that as he left, I never stood up. I watched him leave the room and let out a low whistle. Dan looked at me and said, "I didn't mean to eavesdrop but that was fantastic. Do you not think that the hand of God is on that offer? That is over two and a half million dollars on the table in two years."

I said, "Dan, I am not sorry that you heard the numbers but I trust you to tell no one my business. I see the hand of God returning the original blessing but things are very different. You are scheduled to leave here very soon and I could only do this if I had a manager here and on the job site. I have to pray and see how God fine tunes the rest of His plan. I need to make a quick call to Pastor Mike and Samuel."

I asked the two men if they could join me for an hour or so around two o'clock today. I also asked Bonnie to come if she possibly could. I took the time until they all arrived to weigh out some options

on paper. I made two columns titled for and against and started to fill
them. In the middle of the process as I prayed, I heard the Lord ask
me if I trusted Him. He said if you trust me you can throw that piece
of paper away and I did.

The three of them got there right at two o'clock and we made
small talk until we opened in prayer. I started, "Thank you all for
coming on such short notice but my nerves needed prayer support. I
was visited this morning by a man named Bob Davis whom I do not
know. He is buying the building I was remodeling for Frank Gavin
from the government. He has asked me to take on the job as General
Contractor and do the job for him. He is a believer and I think that
God is returning the original blessings to me. He laid all his cards on
the table and wants an answer in a week. I need you all to take this
before God and confirm what he has already told me. I do not want to
mention numbers because I don't want anyone to consider anything
but obedience to Him in your prayers. I believe that I would have to
hire a manager for both places for this to work but I need to pray
about all of this."

I answered a couple of direct questions from them and then they
all left. I was sitting there quietly when Dan spoke, "I would be
willing to help you train a manager for here as either a consultant or
part time employee. I have only taken a few days off and I get bored.
We have decided that we would like to tour our country but I would
gladly delay that to make your life better."

I said, "Thank you Dan. I want to give God a chance to reveal the
rest of His plans. I don't want to give all my income to the
government as taxes any more than you wanted to so I am going to
get Sarah involved in this also. She will be able to tell me how to
connect all the dots in cash flow."

I went home early and was met by Al in the garage. They loaded
the entire order into my truck to take to get finished. We would
assemble the finished work there. When we were done and they were
about to go home, Al asked if Bonnie and I would be their witnesses
in nine days at their wedding. I told him I would be proud to do that. I
would put off getting Joe Black until the following Monday so the
apartment would be ready.

I was playing toss and catch with the boys after supper when the boys found another garter snake and wanted to take it to the lake to feed the big fish. I told them we would be kind to this one and let it grow bigger. I told them that Bernie was back at the house in the city for a while now the kitchen was done. Bernie had stated the last time that I saw him that the next work done to his house would be paid for because my bill was paid in full. I had him pay for the counter tops on this job and he was still happy with the terms.

I had a special time of prayer with Bonnie as we prepared for bed. She asked me if I was comfortable with working on a building with ties to Frank Gavin. I told her that it would be owned by Bob before one thing was done to the site. I had the job under control when we got shut down and I know without a doubt that I can do it. I just need to know more of God's plan before I give him an answer.

I set a time with Sarah in the morning and went over to get her expertise on my situation. Sarah said, "It is my opinion that you are on the edge of paying tremendous amounts of taxes. I can give you several areas that I would consider if I was in your shoes. We should really upgrade your vehicles to better models. We could increase your giving to the church and such. I can go over a list of items that should be directly connected to the company. You could change one line item in the calculation of the scrap we burned to increase its value in the eyes of the law. I have told Bonnie to keep track of all the childcare that was traded for labor by her employees to show the loss of income as a donation. You will probably have to start investing in some other projects in a couple of years after we have all these new ones on the books. I heard tell that you are hiring inmates to work right out of jail and we can take a tax credit for each of them. Your most direct deduction is what you pay your employees as wages. It may be a good time to get Samuel in here to start a retirement plan for your employees that you contribute to. I have all the numbers plugged in for the interest on your loans and the depreciation on all the buildings. We will have to bring up some of the ages on some of the machines to depreciate them from Dan's records but I can do that easily. Now tell me why this is so important today?"

I said, "I have been approached by someone to take the job back of renovating the building I was doing for Frank Gavin. He is a believer and owns several properties in this area. I believe that I would have to hire a manager for both the factory and the construction job to do this but it is a huge amount of money over two years. It is over two and a half million dollars and I do not want the headaches to just give it to the government. I can hire two managers and still make nearly one and a half million dollars. That number can be increased if I hire carpenters on my payroll and I sell the cabinets for the entire building. Now do you see why I need to know?"

Sarah said, "If you start this, I can show you how to disperse this in ways that you will keep most of it. It will be by investing and tax credits that we opt for. I believe that God is pleased with you now Sam. I'll talk to you soon and I am going to look into the credits of generating electricity from the burning of your wood and still get the benefits of the heating and drying you have from it for now."

# Thirty-Four

I was watching a very expensive machine being brought in from a truck to the home it was going to have for at least a few months by receiving. It had come so late in the day that we would not even hear it run today. I was called to the office to find a man speaking to Dan. He was saying that Bob Davis had asked him to come by and Dan simply said that he needed to speak to me. He was obviously a working man with calloused hands and a good hand grip.

I said, "I am Sam and you say Bob sent you over?"

He said, "I am also a Bob but people call me Bobby so there is less confusion. I have worked in this area for Bob Davis for the last nine years. I helped him decide that you seemed to know what you were doing on the Gavin site. I read some of the articles written about you but I was not surprised to hear you were completely exonerated of all crimes including the last episode at your home. The workmanship was not that of a crook. I know that he always pays his people well and I have put a bunch of money aside so I do not have to work until I die. You will never have to ask what he is thinking and will listen to reasoning other than his own. This is a real offer from an honest man and I hope that you take it because I suggested you."

I said, "Thank you. I hope to see you again someday."

I went out to see the two carpenters I had working with Al. I had the one that asked if I was going to do construction steady to come to the office. I said, "Do you still like carpentry better than the factory?"

He said, "I would be lying if I said different. I used to have my own company with a few men but I always seemed to get ripped off just as I was getting ahead. The unions also made it hard to get someone that was good on a steady basis. At least I can get a paycheck every week and feed my family. Why do you ask?"

I said, "Do you remember what I said it would take to get me to do carpentry regularly? I told you that I would have to get a job that would last for a couple of years and change my management to fit. I have that opportunity at this time. Tell me about the scope of work that you have done and how many people you supervised."

He said, "I have done some big commercial jobs where I had to follow blue prints to the tee or recognize the need of a revision. I believe I could supervise up to ten men of union skills and the laborers needed. Are you seriously considering me for the position?"

I said, "I only have to say yes to the job if I want it. I have yet to decide if you and I would be enough supervision or if I would have to put one more man over you. The job is a twelve million dollar job to be done in two years. It will set the stage for doing similar jobs in the future for the same man or others. I want Al in the assembly foreman position at this time. We will have to go out tomorrow and put this order in place for the clients so be ready for that. I have to call them and let them know we are coming. I will talk to you soon but I do not want you talking about this because I have not taken the job yet."

All of my support including Pastor Mike felt that God was leading me to take the job for Bob Davis so I called and met with him away from the office at work. I started, "I thank you for sending Bobby over to meet with me and he could not praise you enough. I checked with the city and spoke to tenants that you have and they could say nothing but good things about you and how you are a man of your word. I believe that God has me on a path to help working people by being their boss. There is nothing worse than a hopeless man. I would be very interested in your offer if I can ask for a couple of things."

Bob said, "I am very glad you chose to come to work for me. What few things do you want to ask?"

I said, "I had hired all the carpenters and supplied them for the work before and I want to do that again and bill them to the job. I also want to build any and all kitchen and bathroom cabinets and sell them

to you at fair market value. I can get you chances to see our
workmanship and it would come with a personal guarantee. If you
will do that I am ready to come on board."

Bob said, "I was impressed with the cabinets you made for Bernie
because I went to his house to see them. I would be glad for you to be
your own subcontractor as long as your insurance covered you for
both. I am also in need of the cabinets for Bobbie's current job if you
want the work. I will have him get you the specs so you can get
started. We will need them in less than a month is that okay?"

I said, "It certainly is for me and I thank you. I look forward to
hearing from Bobby soon."

I went back to the factory praying I was in God's will. I did not
have much time to get a manager for the factory and I was waiting to
see who God would move forward to fill the position. I didn't know
how quickly God was going to answer that prayer. I went to see Al
and asked him what he needed to do to get a driving license. He
smiled and said, "I have a license it is a vehicle I do not have."

I said, "I am going to fix that right away. I will have you drive my
truck for the company and you can keep it at your apartment. I want
you to deliver and install these where I took you tomorrow so you can
have a couple of days off with your wife next week. By the way, I just
sold several kitchens and bath sets for you to build assembly foreman.
One more thing, do I need a tie on Saturday morning?"

I went out and found a new truck and had them get it ready for
delivery early in the morning. Sarah had told me how to do the
paperwork to get the maximum use of the purchase. We were going to
do similarly with a car for Bonnie and possibly give her car to a
needy family from the school. I was ready to leave for the day when I
got a call from Pastor Mike who wanted to come and see me so I
waited for him. He came into the office within twenty minutes with
another man.

Pastor Mike said, "I would like you to meet Kevin Brown. He
stopped by our county pastors meeting this morning and
immediately thought of you. I will let him tell you about himself."

Kevin said, "I have been in the area for several days looking for
work. I used to run a woodworking factory down south before Katrina
went through. I listened to the promises from the company on how

they were going to rebuild until I was out of money and had to start looking for employment. I was in prayer last night and God told me to visit with these pastors in the morning which I did. I am now sitting in front of you but I do not know why."

I said, "So Pastor Mike did not tell you why you are here now?"

Kevin said, "He just told me to get ready to see the hand of God at work."

I said, "I have been praying for a factory manager for about one week. I need to split my responsibilities to two people I can trust so I can continue to help people as God would have me. I do not want to keep Pastor Mike waiting as long as we would have to talk so can I drop you somewhere in a few minutes and he can go home." He said that he could come back in the morning so I agreed on nine o'clock. This had been a full day of blessings.

I picked up my new truck as I took Al to install these cabinets and shelves for the client. I sent all three of them because I did not want to leave it over the weekend. I went back to the factory to meet with Kevin and Dan. We took a quick walk through all the areas and ended up near the new shaper. Kevin was familiar with the machine from his time in the south.

Kevin started, "I looked back last night and found that I decided to look for work just as you began to pray for a manager. We had different lines we produced but we did a lot with flooring. I ran that shaper for a while as I worked my way up the ranks in the company. I am very interested in seeing how the custom work will fit in. I have never made a piece of furniture but a good manager knows how to use your employees. I see that several of the women in the factory worked at gluing up panels. They do well matching grains in the woods usually."

I asked, "Do you know what kind of salary you would need to come to work with me and I emphasize the fact that I will be here a lot. Dan is going to do some of your training also because I bought this from him."

Kevin said, "I would like to really hear your offer. I have been earning sixty-five thousand dollars but we have to rebuild our home life where ever we go because there is nothing left. I have two sons and a wife that are staying with friends this week while I am up here. I would consider less to get some employment."

I said, "Would you consider seventy-five thousand to start. I will call a real estate agent from our church and see if there are any houses you might like."

Kevin piped in, "I am not in a position to buy at this time."

I said, "I don't want you to concern yourself about that. Let's just see where the hand of God is taking us. Do you need three or four bedrooms?"

I called our real estate agent Terry and asked her if she had any nice three bedroom houses that could be moved into quickly. We were soon on our way to see two houses that just happened to be near the school. I followed Kevin around as he looked at the two houses. When the door to number two opened I heard him gasp. It was beautiful and modern with a fresh brightness from a lot of windows. The back yard was not as big as ours but was adequate. It had a large master suite complete with full bath downstairs and had one and a half baths with two bedrooms up. I looked at the spec sheets and found that the listing was nearing one year old. I asked Kevin if he thought his wife would like it and he was sure she would. I told the agent that they had a cash offer for twenty thousand dollars less than list and we needed to close in less than two weeks. Kevin just gawked at my abruptness but said nothing. I told her to call us as soon as possible or I would call another agent. She asked me if she could make a private phone call and she would get us an answer if possible. She came back into the room and said congratulations, you just bought a house. She wrote a contract for Kevin to sign and we were gone.

Kevin said, "I have never seen the hand of God move so powerfully for anyone before. I think I will enjoy working for a company that works for God. Thank you for what you just did."

I said, "I will take no credit for the blessings that come from God. You can thank and praise Him like I do."

Kevin said to Dan, "Have you ever seen Sam in action with God? I have seen several miracles in the short time I have been here."

Dan said, "You would have to stay the weekend if you wanted to hear just part of them. I am guessing that you now own a house."

I said, "Don't you two have work to do? I've got to go out and find out why that shaper is still not working."

Kevin followed me out and started to go down a list of steps to make what style I wanted. He moved the company rep out of the way and made some adjustments to the knives. He then slowed the speed of the feed and fed a piece of wood into the shaper. It came out the other end looking the way it was supposed to. It made me smile.

# Thirty-Five

Al was a nervous wreck as we stood at the altar waiting for Edith to come down the aisle. There was only a few people invited to the wedding and there was no formal reception planned. If people wanted, they were coming to our house for a quick barbecue before the newly remarried couple left. It was a very nice ceremony that gave the biblical promises for a couple. It was the completion of the true vows of a man, a woman, and God to live for each other. We had a front row of fidgeting children but they behaved as they got to witness something few children ever got to see.

Al had given me the key to the apartment before the ceremony so that I could get Joe Black on Monday. Al said that he was leaving everything I had bought so he would have what he needed to live there. "When I get back I will see if I can pick him up for work for a while," Al said.

Pastor Mike's wife Mary joined us for the barbecue and got a tour of our house for the first time. She was vibrant and witty now as she spoke more words than I had ever heard her say. She was fantastic with children as she got Al's two to come out of their shell a little and play some toss and catch with a football. Everyone was gone by mid-afternoon so Bonnie and I went car shopping.

Bonnie could not see how having a nice car could save us taxes but she liked the idea of more comfort in a car. We looked at a couple of cars that were not kid friendly until we looked at the big sedans. Bonnie did not like the one full sized sport utility she drove. She said she wanted to be comfortable and not aggressive. We settled for a well equipped Cadillac sedan in an azure metallic blue color. We told the dealer we would pick it up on Monday after I negotiated the price and they were going to treat the seats against staining as well as the carpeting. She had picked a single mom that traded child care for labor to get her old car. It was ten years newer than the one she was driving.

Monday afternoon found me picking Joe Black up from the prison. He did not have many belongings which was true of most of the inmates. I said, "I have you an apartment near where I live. In a few days you can find someone who will pick you up for work or you can learn the bus schedule. The last person here moved out Friday but had used the bus system from the third day he lived here. I bought the furniture and stuff that is there for you to use. I have not had time to get you food yet but we will before the night is over. I am going to have you put your stuff in the apartment, meet the landlord, and then I will take you to where you will be working."

Joe said, "What makes you believe that I want any of this. This is starting to sound as bad as prison."

I said, "You may think so now, but you need some structure to help you learn to make the kind of decisions that will keep you from going back. You have not had to make any decisions about what you want to do with your life for years. You told me that both your parents died while you were inside so you have no support group to help you determine and achieve any hopes that you may still have. There are several people at the factory who are willing to listen and give you choices in your life including the man who just moved out. We were in the federal prison together as you know and he just remarried his wife on Saturday. We all have a faith in the Lord Jesus and you should have it to."

Joe said, "I don't need religion to make it in life."

I said, "I didn't say religion. I said a personal faith in the Son of God who has forgiven our sins and now lives in us as a guide to the will of God. Jesus taught against the religions of His time. He wants to be your friend and the strength that you lean on instead of your own."

We arrived at the apartment and did what needed to be done there. The refrigerator was clean so we had to go shopping. I pointed around the corner to a convenience store that was open around the clock that he could walk to. I showed Joe around the plant and introduced him to the line foreman. I told him that Joe had been a red hat at the last place he worked but I wanted him to get used to what we did first. I left him there and went to see what needed doing before I went home.

There was a note from the salesman that one of the companies we served wanted to order ten thousand pieces over two years if I could hold the price. He had the printout I needed attached to make that decision from. I told him to confirm it and to get us a contract from which to work. I thanked him for the good work. I went back out to get Joe and told the foreman about the order. Then we had to go grocery shopping.

Bonnie and I were talking in the living room about Joe. She said that he was the youngest one so far. I told her that it meant that our influence would last longer for him. She told me that I had become an eternal optimist. I told her that as far as the eternal with Jesus was concerned, she was right, but I still knew that mankind was fallible. She said she loved me but she had to get some rest for the days at the school. I reminded her that we both had to find a couple of days to get away and soon.

Kevin was back on Wednesday with his wife and children. Kevin introduced me to his wife Gail who was far more petit than Kevin. She was a red head and I smiled the first time I heard the Southern drawl. I asked her if she was ready to become a Northerner like the rest of us here. She stated that she would tolerate us if we did not have hurricanes and laughed. I told Kevin to show Gail around and then I would bring them to the motel.

I looked at Dan and said, "I really pray that you are not offended by my choosing Kevin for this job. I know that you were willing to sacrifice going on your trip for me and that means that you are a true brother in the Lord to me. I wanted to say that before I asked you to do a quick inventory of materials and if we don't need anything else just order two bunks of ash for this week and two more for standby in a week. I also know that I will be using a bunk of cherry for some cabinets I have sold."

Dan said, "I am not offended in the least and you will get me out of the doghouse with Gina about maybe postponing our trip. I'll let you know when the lumber is coming."

Al was also back on Wednesday and was trying to get the shaper to do window moldings. I told him that Kevin was going to be back after a while and he knows this machine. I asked him if he had any questions about the cabinets we were building for Bobby. I gave him a quick recap of how we got the work and he congratulated me. I told him to come and see me in the office so we could talk.

I said, "I have told you how much I appreciate you and I want to show it. I am giving you the truck to use as your own within reason. I am getting you a company credit card for gas and in the case of needing something for the installation of a job. I might have you get things for other departments once in a while because you are going to have the only one outside of this factory. Diana will have one to send out in emergencies and will have to be returned. Every item bought has to have a receipt brought to Diana even if it is with your card to be charged correctly to an account. I am also giving you a dollar per hour raise to make up for the rent you are no longer using. I have some general announcements I am going to make to all the employees at two thirty so we are shutting down around two for the day. Thank you and bring your people up to receiving before two thirty."

I had told the line foreman about the early shutdown so everyone was ready for my speech at two thirty. Samuel had come early so he and Diana could have a look at some forms that were going out today. I got my notes because I didn't want to forget anything and walked out to receiving with Kevin and Samuel.

I started, "I want to thank everyone that works here for doing their job so well that we are not behind on any orders. I said when I came that I would show my appreciation in a tangible way and I am going to tell you about that in a few minutes. First I want to let you know that the custom shop is really taking off with a bang. We may train some more of you in the future but I would like to introduce the foreman for that area. Al, would you come up here and stand by me so people can get used to you. I also have decided to go back to my roots and I just took a two year building renovation job that I will be starting in about two weeks. I cannot be in two places at once so I have found some help. We all remember hurricane Katrina from a while back. The next gentleman you are about to meet lost their home and the woodworking factory he used to manage in a matter of hours. He is here as the new manager of All Things Wood and I would like to introduce Kevin Bailey to you. Kevin, would you please come up here and stand so people can see you. There are other people that are new here and I am going to have them just raise their hand. We have Ted Richards that is an electrician on the maintenance crew. We have Joe Black who joins us in production so when you get a chance, say hello to these new employees. Now for the tangible part I want you to know about. Samuel, will you be ready to speak to these employees in a couple of minutes. Samuel is here because he is going to teach you if you need the help how to manage the retirement program I am starting for each of you. I had to ask Dan what a bonus looked like in the past to determine what to invest for you the first time. I have some envelopes with your names on them and the form that Samuel will need to have filled out. There is a slip of paper in there with your personal amount of bonus to start your funds. The retirement package will require no vestment time so the money is yours now and forever. I have given you ten percent of the gross you have earned from me to this date. I will continue to put in two percent if you do not save more on your own but I will match the next two percent if you do save and you would have a total of six percent going to the funds. I am now going to have Kevin say hello and then Samuel will work with you for a while. Again I say thank you for your help."

Kevin said, "I am very excited at the opportunity to join in the management of a company that wants to grow and is doing something about it. I started with my old company on the machine that just arrived here and worked at several levels before I became the manager. I will be able to understand what most problems are when you come to me to get them fixed. Sam will be around a great deal of the time and Dan has agreed to work with us as a consultant. I look forward to meeting you all as time goes by. Thank you!"

Samuel said, "I am here to work for you. I want to teach you about investing and I will need the forms back in by Tuesday at the latest to open all the accounts. The questions on the form will tell me how aggressive or conservative you want to be with your money. I also have a box for you to check if you do not understand mutual funds at all and I will come here and teach you. I will be here for a short while yet so some of you can see me today. Questions on a daily basis are to be given to Diana and she will let me know. Thank you!"

# Thirty-Six

I was surprised on Sunday to see Joe Black walk into the church with Al and his family. I went over and said hello and welcomed him to the service. I am sorry to not have had much time for you this week but I will have more time coming up. You will also see Samuel here today and you will be getting to know him much better as a counselor. Come and let me introduce my family and some other folks. Kevin and Gail also came over to meet Bonnie. Gail told Bonnie that she had been a teacher and if she needed more help to let her know. God was putting together a team to be reckoned with in our city.

I took Al on Monday and went to Bobbie's site to see where the cabinets were going and verify the measurements. Bobby gave us a quick tour of the complex he had going and then gave us a look at the specific units. We were talking when a subcontractor came up and asked Bobby if his father had decided on the color of a unit. I said, "You failed to mention that Bob Davis is your father when we spoke."

Bobby said, "I apologize but I did not lie to you at all. I let my dad work the politics and I make the noise. I did pick you to replace me in this area of the country because I want to go back to where I grew up. He wants to continue in this area but we actually bought the unit in Florida together. It is over twenty stories high structurally but the contractor went bust. We got the property for pennies on the dollar and we are going to modify the original plans to a medium price range rental unit that will tolerate this economic state until it reverses and we may sell it or add to it. I believe that dad intends to call you today to start next week. We may have to find out what it costs to ship your cabinets to Florida because I will need more than eighty sets of kitchen and bathroom cabinets."

On the way back to the factory, Al said, "We may not have room enough to do furniture if you keep selling cabinets the way you do. I have a model of the door worked out for you to see for the piece of furniture we have sold now. I also found a lighter glass to put in it to keep the weight as reasonable as we can. In mahogany it really looks good. I wondered if we could make use of the door design for some kitchen upper cabinets but Edith says doors are to hide your mess in a kitchen."

I said, "I am thinking of enclosing some of the upper shelves of a book case with that style door and solid doors on the bottom. A six foot bookcase with four upper doors with glass would be beautiful. The middle would be open and the bottom would have solid doors. I will sketch it out for you in the near future to try it in mahogany again. I am checking with my materials broker about getting our hardwood finished plywood at wholesale. I am also having Dan call other brokers to see if our pricing is the best. Tell me how you feel things are going between us at this time?'

Al said, "I know you told me that you wanted to give back my hope when we first met in prison but I had no idea how blessed I was going to become. I know what King David meant when he said to follow hard after God and he would follow hard after me. There is no way for me to thank you but I know that you did not do it for your own glory. I am trying to show Joe Black the door to the same blessings. I think you made a good choice when you asked Kevin to be manager."

Bobby was correct and there was a message to call Bob Davis waiting at the factory. He was doing the final closing on Thursday and was going to get the new permits on Friday so we could start on Monday. He had a list of subcontractors for me to call that they used. I would be responsible for them completely as we had discussed but he trusted all the people on the list. He checked off all the ones who had looked at the blueprints I was working from and had done estimates to budget from. I knew more of what to expect this time around. He asked me the name to put on the permit and I told him that it was Walker Enterprises LLC.

I checked with Diana about how many of the forms had come back filled in for Samuel. She said that three quarters of them had come back. I went out to the foremen and asked them to help convey how important it was to do these all at once. I made a call to Sarah to see if she had everything she needed for me to start next week. She said she would check and that she might have to hire more help if I kept up this pace for much longer. I told her to just think about how much sooner she could retire with the money we were paying her as I laughed with her.

I had three men that were going to the new job on Monday and the man I was going to put in the lead position. I was going to have to use some union carpenters if I could not hire some soon. Bobby thought that he could have two of his framers come and work for me as we got started. We were training guys in the shop all the time now and we needed more employees still. I went to Kevin and asked, "Do you know how to contact some of the employees from your old shop that might want to move here?"

Kevin said, "I had some really good employees down there and I could make a couple of phone calls including one to our pastor to try to locate some of them. Some of them may not be comfortable coming to a mostly white factory."

I said, "We have the people who have come to us for work with no regards to color. I have the name of a Black man that is in prison that I have to go and meet this week. I will hire, pay, and promote a man for his work done. Bonnie is getting more Black children at her school than was ever there. I know that biases exist but I will not condone it in the factory. Let me know if we can help some of your former employees. Do we have a pricing report Dan? I need plywood right away."

Dan said, "All indications are that we should stay where we are. You might save a few dollars per bunk but we would have to find our own trucking. I ordered you two bunks of cherry plywood and one of maple and it should be here any minute. You are saving over fifteen dollars per sheet from last week. If we get cornered on pricing a job we could get some three rib plywood for less money. It works fine for vertical use but not for shelving. I did have Kevin watch me get the inventory sheets and he listened in to the call for materials. I think he is more up to speed than when you first came. I also asked the broker if he knew of any trucks going to Florida with some room on them. He is going to have some of the biggest ones give us a call."

The next morning found Kevin, Gail, and myself doing the closing on their house. We put the property in their names and I was the mortgagor until they could convert the loan to their names in a few months. Friends were going to ship the very few belongings to them until I decided to have them go down and see some of his old employees and bring the stuff in my truck. He left right after the closing so he could be back on Monday. I would share Bonnie's car for a couple of days. I went to the local prison to speak to Tim Smith that afternoon.

I went to the room I was directed to and waited. I heard the familiar jingle of keys and stood up to meet the man. The case manager from before came into the room followed by a mountain of a man that had to tip his head to come in the door. I said, "Hello Tim, I am Sam and right now I feel like I am a scout for a basketball team but that is not the case. Have they told you why we are meeting today?"

Tim had smiled at my attempt at humor and said, "They only told me that you were going to make me an offer for when I get out in three weeks. What do you want with me White boy?"

I said, "Let's get one thing straight right now. You can address me as Sam or sir but you will not speak derogatorily to me and I won't to you or this will be a short session. I came to meet with a man named Tim Smith about a proposition I have for him. Tell me a little about your work history please and if you have a family waiting for you to get out."

Tim said, "I apologize. I had no reason to do that to you Sam. I have been around the building trades most of my life. I can do some good finish work for my size. I left a wife that has lived with my brother and his family since I have been here. I had a serious gambling problem and I left them without anything. What kind of offer do you have for me?"

I said, "I come with an offer of housing, work, and counseling on how to treat your family and people around you. I am not sure if you would be in my cabinet shop or in the field working as a carpenter. I need to know that you can play nice with people or I will help them bring you back here. You would be subject to Christian counselors as I direct to help you make right decisions. You would be signing a letter that you could be subject to random drug testing with a no cause clause. Are you interested in this program?"

Tim said, "Could you tell me why you are doing this first?"

I said, "I spent time in a federal prison when I was falsely accused. I met a lot of men who had no future and no hope for a change. I come with the hope and a chance for change if you want it."

Tim said, "Yes I would like to take you up on that offer."

I said, "Okay! The prison will call me as you are about to get out. I need your permission to find your wife and get her involved in this program. She will have to meet with the counselors also. I will get some input from her on housing. You need to be ready for a mostly White crew to work with. You will hear from your case manager soon. Good bye."

During the time that I was at the prison, Pastor Mike and Mary had been at work. They had organized a secret house belongings restoration drive for Kevin and Gail. They had made arrangements to have access to the house while the closing was going on. They moved in donated beds and bedding, dining room table and chairs, sofas and recliner, entertainment center, and even had some pots, pans, and dishes for the kitchen. They brought a used game boy for the kids and other toys. They even had a desk to place in a corner. They had towels of every size so they could settle right in. They had made arrangements for Gail to meet the real estate agent a couple of hours after the closing to go to the house. Gail was able to walk in and find this entirely done in secret. A couple of minutes after she walked in, Pastor Mike and Mary walked in and welcomed them home.

Gail said, "What have you done?"

Pastor Mike said, "We just wanted to give you a little help after what you had lost. Just think of it as a welcome to the neighborhood from God and friends. Just let us know if there is something you really need and we will see what we can do."

I was returning from the prison in Bonnie's car and thinking I
could ride around in something like this if I had to. I stopped by the
factory to make sure that I did not have any fires to put out. Dan told
me that we were shipping the very last of an order and had not had a
response from the company to our salesman about wanting more. I
told him that God knew what he was doing and not to worry. I went
and got Bonnie from the school because we had invited Fred and
Paula out to dinner. They were going to have the boys for four days
from in the morning until Monday.

Bonnie and I left the boys off in the morning and put their car
seats where they could be used if they had to. We drove a couple of
hours to get to the lake where we had rented a cabin and planned to
relax from the pace we were both keeping. The soft whispering of the
wind in the pines behind the cabin and the gentle waves washing onto
the beach gave a relaxing tempo for the time we were in each other's
arms. There was a canoe that could be used at the cabin so we went
across the lake the next morning. About half way across I told Bonnie
that pushing a pencil was making me soft. The evening was spent in a
nice restaurant where we cherished the catering to our needs. We
were told that there was a spa nearby that we might enjoy and decided
we would go tomorrow. We built a small fire that night and listened
to the night birds all around us. The spa was everything that they had
said it would be. We each got a massage and then had some cold
drinks by a pool. We had one more night to spend at another
restaurant before the facts of life would envelop us again. We took the
long way home on Sunday and stopped at a church we found on the
way home. No matter how good the words of the preacher are, there
is usually nothing like your own family of believers. We finally got
the boys from Fred and Paula's and went home.

The boys had to tell us all about their weekend before they would
settle down for the night. We made some popcorn while we listened
and then we all went to bed.

# Thirty-Seven

I took the four men to the Davis building to get started first thing in the morning. There were a lot of safety issues with openings for elevators and such that needed to meet OSHA regulations immediately. I had Ted come over and make sure we had enough power to get started on temporary circuits. I was going to try doing the work with just my carpenter, Travis and I in the beginning. I had material come from the same store that I was using the first time and left them to fix the safety issues. I went to the factory to make sure that Kevin had made it back.

I walked into the office to find Kevin at the computer and a Black man in a chair near the desk. I said, "Good morning every one! Who do we have here?" as I stuck out my hand to the Black man.

Kevin said, "This is Robbie James from the other factory. Robbie ran the shaper for me for the last two years. I convinced him that we would pay for a bus ticket back if he did not want to work for you after he got here."

I said, "Please tell me about your work and family situation."

Robbie said, "That is a short story. I was at the factory for a total of four years before Katrina. My wife and three children were in a rental house that went underwater and there was nothing for us to salvage. Kevin says you are a shaker and a mover with the hand of God on all that you do."

I asked, "Is that what he says about me? I will have to remember to thank him the next time I see him. I just got this shaper delivered and I really don't know what it will do yet. I want a lot of this molding made for furniture doors and I know there is a market for tongue and groove flooring."

Robbie said, "After I have set up the machine for a run, I can do almost three thousand linear feet of flooring in ten hours of running. In other words, it takes about one hour for set up and then it will do more than three hundred linear feet per hour."

I said, "What would it take for you to not need that bus ticket? I would like to hire you to run that shaper."

Robbie said, "I was getting ten dollars per hour at the old factory. I can't work for less. My wife worked for a daycare center to help us keep up with the bills as it was."

I said, "I can't have you working here for that amount or I couldn't sleep at night. I will start you at fourteen dollars per hour with the promise of another dollar at the end of the month if you can make that shaper do what you say you can do. If your wife wants to work here in production or if she would rather work for my wife at the school, one of us would hire her as well. If that is agreeable we will get some paperwork done so you can go to work. I need to know also what it will take to get your wife and children here."

I asked Kevin to take over with Robbie and make sure we had him a motel room for tonight if he needed it. I then started by calling the real estate agent to see if they had a rental for Robbie and family with three bedrooms. She jokingly asked me when I was going to start in the rental business. I told her when she brought me a deal I could not refuse. She asked me if I could meet her in an hour. I told her I needed two but I would meet her at the location. I quickly called several of the subs that were going to work on the Davis building and asked them all to meet with me there in the morning.

I met with Terry as we had planned. I was standing at the first building of six in a row that were all three stories tall. What were not buildings was parking lot with tiny islands of grass between. The general appearance was moderately clean and most of the buildings appeared cared for. Terry had me look briefly at the outside and then brought me to an empty four bedroom unit. She said that this apartment went for fourteen hundred dollars per month and had three of them on the first floor of two of the buildings. The next floor was all three bedrooms that were renting for one thousand-one hundred-seventy-five dollars and the top floor had two (two) bedroom units that rented for one thousand dollars and three (three) bedroom units. Each floor had a coin operated laundry with several washers and dryers. Terry said that she had a folder with all income and expenses at the office. The total income was over a million dollars per year and had ninety percent occupancy because the state subsidized the renters.

I asked, "Why is this property for sale?"

Terry said, "The owner wants to go and be with the rest of his family in another state. He let things slide until he is about to lose this back to the bank. The state helps enough people with their rents that this should be a gold mine. The other reason that I am telling you about it is that there is a lot of tax credits available to a landlord with this kind of units. They do most of the investigation about any possible tenants and you just have to accept the next name on the list. If the tenants do not pay their portion by the fifth they get an eviction notice from the state. He also owns a set of buildings that are only one and two bedroom units for the elderly and disabled that is also for sale with the same program."

I said, "Terry, can we do some of this at our house some night soon. I have to use my daylight hours very wisely right now. I have a new crew that is not being supervised at this time. Could you come over to the house tonight with your papers at seven?"

I was impressed at how the guys had systematically started outside near the parking lot fence and made their way to the third floor already. The laborers had come from the union and pitched in around ten in the morning. Ted was putting in the last temporary electricity on the fifth floor when I saw him. I found that most of the temporary office was still functional with the old desk and a couple of lights. It would work as a gathering place for the time being. I checked the phone and it came to life with a dial tone. I took the list I had from Bob and made arrangements to get the elevators examined so they could be used. I half came out of my skin when the phone rang. It was Bob to tell me what my phone number was that I just answered. He ordered a phone in the company name and suggested I get a portable to carry around on the site. While I had him on the phone, I asked him about the state rental program on those units and he said it was fool proof if the amortization was reasonable. I thanked him for the help and asked him if he wanted to be at the meeting in the morning. He simply said that I should set my own ground rules for the subs and he would support me.

I went and got some cable to lock the gate with and got some keys made for Travis to open up with. It was near the end of the first day and we were off to a positive start. I showed everyone what I expected in the way of reporting their hours to me if they wanted to get paid and asked the union guys to be there at eight. The new permits only allowed us to work from eight a.m. to six p.m. on anything that made noise.

I went by the factory for my own peace of mind. Dan came over to me and said I had not lost my touch. The company we just finished with had called to ask for some simple modifications from their previous design and wanted a quote on fourteen thousand pieces to be done in thirty months. They also wanted to have a quote on cherry as the wood to please some different interior designers with a possible run of five thousand to start. I just said thank you God.

I asked Kevin where Robbie stood at this time. I was told that he was in a motel tonight and was going to speak with his wife to see how they wanted to move. He had run several hundred feet of mahogany molding for my doors today. He is going to set up for some two and a quarter inch ash flooring tomorrow. I had receiving making us two and a half and three and a half base to process tomorrow. I don't think receiving is going to be able to keep up as they are when he gets into production. I said one step at a time for now but we cannot have general production held up either. We may have to get another laser rip saw for receiving. I am not ready to go backwards yet and we will do what needs to be done. I made one more quick call to Sarah about the tax credits for those rentals and she said that it was one of the best investment strategies out there today.

Bonnie was a little tired at the thought of Terry coming over tonight but she was as willing to help as many people as we could. When Terry knocked on the door, she was met by Bonnie and a smile. Bonnie said, "You will do anything for my husband won't you?" They both laughed as we sat down at the dining room table.

Terry said, "I brought the numbers on both sets of buildings. These numbers are congested but I have been guaranteed that finite numbers are available. It shows the rental income for the five years they have been rented as well as expenses and so called profit. He would not disclose his amortization ratio but says it makes him a living. I called him today to see who has his mortgage and a big portion is in HUD with no interest recapture clause and is assumable to a qualified buyer. I was surprised at how little equity he had amassed in five years."

I said, "If you look at the first two years it appears he was only paying the interest payments and got a late start at earning equity. With the market the way it is, he is not going to get rich before he leaves the state. I will make a point to go to our bank tomorrow and see if I qualify to assume the mortgage at face value with the same terms and then we may make an offer."

Everyone was off to a good start in the factory in the morning and I asked Kevin to find out about a laser saw and how we would place it in the mill. Kevin wanted me to know that he could not say thank you enough for the help they had received since he had come to town. I told him to thank the one who deserved all the Glory. I then went to the Davis building to meet with the subs. I asked Travis to get the men going and then come back to meet the subcontractors with me. The room was really too small to hold all of us so we grabbed a sheet of plywood to put the blueprints on.

I introduced myself and honestly admitted that I was taking Bob's word that they could do the work. I had a general timeline in my head and told some of the trades that they were crucial in staying on that timeline. I told each one of them that I reserved the right to put other tradesmen on different floors to help keep this project on cost and timely. I do not expect that I would have to do that but I want you all to know that I would. I have copies of all your rates for the duration of this contract and I do not know if any of you have the contracts ready to sign yet. I only get to hand in one bill per month and will pay out only one time per month unless you come to me with your reason. I will not accept forgetfulness as an excuse. I need any invoice that you want to be paid for to be here by the twentieth to get paid on the first. I also have a sheet that you will fill out for me each week that will give a date, number of tradesmen and laborers that you had on the job per day. I intend to leave the most honest paper trail that even the government can understand and not question. I expect a copy of invoices of materials identifying that it came to the Walker Davis job. It is not that I don't trust you but I have a history with the federal government that I am not going to allow them to harm me or my family again. Are there any questions so far about what your paperwork will entail?

I would like you to meet Travis who will be here even if I can't. I need to know if the air handling people are here. A man in uniform stepped up and said they had taken enough basic measurements with Bob to have some trunk lines already to go. Please start your men right away I said and I will get your projected timeline. Electricians are you ready to start. A man said that they were going to get their main feed conduits to designated panel areas first. I told him he could start and he could give me projected timelines as well. I did the same with the plumbers and steel framers. I thanked them as a group and then finished with each one as a trade.

I met with Travis last. I said, "I don't believe I have to tell you how important all this paperwork is. It has to go to two other people before anyone gets paid. Once you get it to me, I will ultimately be responsible. I need to have you keep a mental note or start using a pocket pad to verify the number of men on the job site. I will buy you whatever you want to make your system work. I will call the lumber yard and tell them you can use the account but it has to be identified going to the Walker Davis site. Please try to get the entire building secure by tonight. Tomorrow we will go to my house and get my old job box that we can lock the tools in. We can also get some of my tools to put in it. You have my cell phone number don't you?"

I stopped at the lumber yard and did the paper work for Travis. I then continued to the bank to meet with my account manager. I asked him if I could find out about assuming a HUD loan. He said that he could make an initial call if he wanted me to. I asked him if he could find out about the two sets of buildings I had looked at. He told me that he was all too familiar with the project because he had originated the loans for HUD. He said that he was sure that HUD would like to see a new owner of the complex. I asked him how much was assumable and if he thought I might qualify. He got on the phone and talked to three departments before he got an answer. He was jotting numbers on a pad and then asked the person to fax him the proposal.

He said, "I think that I believe you when you tell me you are working for God. I got sent to the head of HUD before I was done. You can assume all that is owing and fifty thousand more at the same terms to help you buy the two sets of buildings. I only had to tell them that you qualified to do the loan. Do you have some inside information to give me?"

I said, "You only have to believe in Jesus as the Son of God and live your life for Him. I will be in touch in a couple of days."

# Thirty-Eight

Terry set up a meeting with the apartment owner, Bonnie and me for the next day. We met at Terry's office to negotiate for the buildings. I had already offered Terry and her boss less than the normal fees for such a transaction and they had accepted. The owner was introduced and Terry told him that we were interested in both sets of buildings. He asked us what we wanted to know and I told him I knew all about his loans and how they stood. I told him that I was not going to make him wealthy but I would help him leave town. I offered him forty thousand more than he owed and told him I would pay the realtor fees. I told him that I had the financing arranged and we could close shortly. He started to say that he would not settle for that amount and I told him I only had to wait about one more month and he would not have to be paid by me. I told him that he had taken enough rent money off the top that he should have saved that to go away with. He glared at me from across the table and I said, "Do we have a deal?"

We both signed the contract that included the fact that we would close on the first and all rents were due to me. Ten thousand dollars would be kept in escrow at the bank until we all knew that he had not taken any of the rent due on that month. He had to show that all taxes were current including property, federal, and state taxes due from his employees at the apartments. All pertinent equipment for the operation of the business including the tools in the maintenance rooms and the offices were to come to me and a nondisclosure form about the formalities of our sale was to be in place for two years.

Bonnie and I stopped at our bank and gave them a copy of the signed sales agreement. The manager said if we hadn't talked to the guy yesterday we never could have closed by the first. You better get Tim Simonds on this right away so the papers can be examined and new ones prepared.

Bonnie went back to the school and I went to the factory to check on that. I found a classy looking door leaning against my desk when I went in. Al had completed the door to the one side and it was exactly as in the picture. Now that it was glued it was strong as we would need. The other one was also made but he only brought one out to me. Kevin said that it sure looked good to him and matched the picture completely. They also had one set of lower cabinets ready for Bobbie's job and they looked great. The uppers were going to the finishers this afternoon.

I asked, "Kevin, what is the story with the shaper and receiving?

Kevin said, "It took a good part of the day to get a quantity of molding made before we stopped the run. Robbie is running two and a quarter inch ash at this time. He will have caught up with receiving in the early morning. I called the salesman on the laser saw and he will be here by five tonight. He said he had a used one that was in excellent shape for half the money if we were interested. I think we could move some shipping racks to the rear of the building by custom and have the two saws side by side to use the same waste conveyor and sorting bins. I would like to tell you what Dan and I have prepared for the production bid so you can call tomorrow."

We were going over the pricing process when the salesman showed up. We had him wait a minute as I gave my final two cents on the pricing with the two materials. I asked Kevin if he followed how we derived the price and he said he did. We got the salesman back and he started with some of the changes that were available on the new saws. I asked him if any one of them made them more productive and he said no. I asked him about the used saw that he had mentioned to Kevin. He said it was identical to the one we had and came with a bunch of extra blades. He said the used saw is exactly half the price of a new one. He asked if we needed the saw because of the new shaper and I had to tell him yes. He said that if I bought the saw today, he would extend my three month lease on the shaper to one year for free. I simply said sold and when can you get it here.

Bonnie and I were going over what was happening at the school as they hired teachers and took applications from parents. She said, "I have found that the more driven the parents are, the less well behaved the children are. I have some six year olds that the parents are applying to colleges for them instead of having them as a child. If we are able to get to the children in a way that they trust us to know them as a person, they will perform miraculously for us. We have parents that are not learned themselves and I wish we could take more of their children to teach. The numbers show us that we should eliminate a classroom and make a room for infants to have higher income. I would like to find a way to get the income high enough to give some scholarships to the school."

I said, "Let's start praying to that end and see what God does."

Travis was trying to locate a crane to fly some materials to different floors for the subs. He had one that could come for one day in the morning but would have to leave at the end of the day. The two of us told the subs to have all they could on site for the morning and bring some dollies if they had them. We had some lumber ordered to place on the upper floors. We built some protective covers to put in the windows that we removed to let the materials in so as to not damage the jambs. I was looking at the blueprints for the upper luxury apartments when Bob stopped by.

Bob said, "You seem to have caused a stir among your subcontractors the other day. Good for you! I don't know if you know this or not but I have bought several pieces of large equipment that I used to have to rent. If it is available or if it would solve a dilemma you could use it. I own a Lull lift that will go up thirty feet at the forks with a payload of nearly a ton that is doing a lot of sitting still that I believe that you would find very handy at this time."

I said, "I have rented a crane to fly up all that the subs can get here for tomorrow but if we could get it to the third story with the Lull it would be very helpful. I need Bobbie's number to see if he can help me store some cabinets if he is not able to put them in yet. The factory is just jumping with the addition of the tongue and groove flooring I just added to production and storage is a commodity."

Bob said, "I will call your factory with the times I can send my truck for them. I appreciate the fact that you did not ask for any money to order the cabinets but if you prepare me an invoice for them, I will pay you on the first to help with your cash flow. I expect a small invoice from here also for the time to secure the building. I am going to get the gate repaired in the back lot immediately for security. I am going to speak to my architect and see if we could put some hardwood flooring in the kitchen dining areas in some units. I sense that you are going to attack more than one floor at a time at this site."

I said, "I want to form the shapes of the apartments upstairs as soon as possible. I don't know if you have marketed the second and third floors yet or if you have a generic plan that you use for us to give that its shape. I would then end up on the bottom floor. I also need to know if the storefront is as it was in the original or what so I can get that underway. The city does not want the sidewalk hampered in snow season so we cannot work there this winter."

Bob said, "The architect has done a couple of revisions to the front in design so we may be wiser to start that immediately after snow in the spring. It would be very costly to set it all up twice. The elevator inspector said that some siding was coming off the protective canopy on the roof and should be sealed up and repainted right off to prevent any more damage. If you would have someone look into that, I would appreciate it. I am going to get you the placement of the mall bathrooms down here so I can get rid of those unsightly Port-Lets and I will speak to the plumber if you have any trouble with him about making them work. I'll talk to you soon."

I had Tim Smith's wife come to the factory right at one o'clock. I said, "I hope you didn't have far to come to meet with me today. Do you have any idea who I am at this time?"

She said, "No! You may call me Mary Jo if you wish. Tim just said that I should listen to the offer you have for us and that is why I am here."

I said, "Tim told me that he had left you in dire need when he went to prison. He also admitted that he had a gambling problem that caused that need. I am known for helping inmates as they come out of prison. I offer work, housing, and Christian counseling including how to handle the money you earn. He told me that he was willing to commit to me on my terms when he gets out."

Mary Jo said, "Praise God! I can't believe that you got Tim to commit to Christian counseling. This is the first time that God got Tim's full attention by having him go away for a while. It will all have been worth it if he puts his trust in the Lord for his life."

I said, "I told him that I would get your input on housing because until the first of the month I do not have an apartment located yet. Do you have furnishings if you have an apartment or will you need some of those things?"

Mary Jo said, "I haven't told him yet but everything except a few clothes is gone. I will look around and see if I can find an apartment and get back to you. Thank you very much."

I said, "The only other question for you is do you work at times?"

Mary Jo said, "I have worked in a daycare in the past but it closed down."

I said, "If you want to do that again just let me know. My wife runs a combination school and daycare near here called Kids Freedom School and they need more help before the school opens. Take one of my cards here so you can call me or her."

We had moved several shipping racks to the back wall and were trying to get the laser saws beside each other. We were trying to see if they could work from the same bunk and do the entire process by having the two saws doing two types of ripping. In theory it should work well and get material out for both production and the shaper. It would have been a little easier to have one tail to the other if our needs were more consistent. It had taken a couple hours to just position the machines and it would be noticeable in production very soon. Even the custom shop was waiting for the cherry panels for doors and cabinet faces. They were precutting the sides of the cabinets from the plywood to keep moving. I had not seen this coming but we were doing our best to rectify the situation.

I called the salesman to my office and told him I needed his help. I said, "I need you to go on line or to catalogs and list the prices of all the different cabinets you can get me. I need you to differentiate those with half inch sides from those that have three quarter inch sides like we do. I need as many sizes as they offer and materials they come in. You may be able to print off most of this but I need to produce a price list for our products that is competitive. We will eventually be able to print out a list of sizes by materials when I have reached my goal. That is what you will be able to quote estimates from in the near future."

I had the man who wanted the hutch replica come to see the finished product and see if he was happy. It was a beautiful piece of furniture and both Al and I were proud of it. We had made it as the picture portrayed it to the fraction of an inch. He said, "I am amazed at the details you did to this, and yes I want it. Can you deliver this on a weekday so she is not home when you bring it?" We set up a time for two days from now and delivered it. We did take several pictures of it for the sales catalog. Now I wanted to try a bookcase.

# Thirty-Nine

The crane came and set up at the Davis building in the morning. There were several trucks waiting to be unloaded when the Lull was delivered. We used the Lull to get the trucks unloaded and let them leave by putting materials on bunks we fabricated. The sheet rockers put their steel studs on three floors primarily. Conduit was sent to the top floor and to the third floor. Lumber was put on the fifth and third floors also. Plumbing piping for waste and sprinkler system was scattered throughout. The last to go in was the ventilation trunk for all the floors. It was starting to look like a construction site by the end of the day.

I left there to go meet the managers at the two housing complexes. The manager of the bigger units ran what was known as Butler East. They lived in a unit and supervised activities such as the two maintenance workers on site. When I got there they were both in their own apartments and not out working. I knew that had to be reevaluated in the near future. The manager took care of complaints and the collecting of the family's portion of rent as well as emptying the quarters every night from the laundries.

The managers of Butler West had similar duties. Neither manager did deposits but rubber stamped the checks or money orders to be picked up. They both had a simple quarter rolling gadget to get them ready for pickup. I made myself a mental note to order a rubber stamp with the correct account numbers on them.

Sarah was not surprised to see me after our last conversation about the rentals being a good investment. I gave her a general idea of what I was buying and she said she would get it set up by the first. I would need one more account from the bank for general expenses but could use the other employee account to pay these few people.

I called the company to give them a price on the specs they had given us. I told them that the general cost increases of materials and production that we needed an increase of twelve percent to build them in the same material and thirty-five percent for the change of material to cherry. They said the increase was not unreasonable from three years ago when we last priced them. I told them to send the contracts and a moderate start up fee and we would put them back on the line for production.

I drove by the school to see it full of children and noticed a person at the house adjacent to the school. It was a large two story house with a porch on the side. I stopped for a minute to say hello as a neighborly thing to do. The lady was a little elderly but still got around very well. We spoke for a few minutes and said, "I may not be your neighbor much longer. I want to sell the house and go live near my grandchildren. They are old enough now that I can help care for them and they would know me."

I said, "I did not see a sign that your house was for sale. I would be very interested in buying it if you are serious. I know what it is like to be separated from your family. I thank God every day that I get to kiss my boys and wife good night. Do you really want to sell the house?"

She said, "My children have great jobs in another city. It would be much more advantageous for me to go near them. I haven't listed it with an agent but I was thinking I would ask one hundred thirty-five thousand dollars for it because it needs a few things repaired."

I asked, "May I get my wife and look inside in a couple of minutes?" I quickly went into the school and had Bonnie come outside for a few minutes. We found the house quite charming with three small bedrooms on the second floor with a full bath. The downstairs had a kitchen that flowed to a dining room, full bath, a large living room, and a large bedroom. All the fixtures were dated but functional. The carpet needed cleaning but was intact in a rainbow of colors. I said, "When did you think you wanted to sell the house?"

She said, "It would be nice to move while it was still nice weather. Do you want to buy the house?"

I said, "If you are ready to sell, I will buy it today. I have a very good friend who would help you write out a contract and you could have a lawyer look at it before we signed it. Does that sound like a good idea?"

We told her we would be back in two hours to do the contract and she could check with her family in the mean time. When we got outside again, Bonnie asked me what I was doing. I said, "I stopped to say hello to our neighbor and the conversation drifted to her wanting to sell and move nearer to her family. I heard God say that this would make a perfect place to keep the infants safe and away from the bigger children. You asked God to increase your income didn't you so you could give some scholarships to the school. I think I told you to lay your petition before God and watch Him work. I will get Terry to meet you here in two hours. I will give her the info to put on the contract. Then you let her take it to her lawyer for consideration. You can see if Ellen likes the idea also. I'll talk to you tonight if not before."

Travis was starting to create the bathrooms on the lower floor for the plumber. The sounds of pipe being threaded and hammers pounding allowed me to watch unobserved for a few minutes. Partitions that were not adjoining a neighboring unit could be studded with wood making it easier to put handicap railings in so that was what we chose to use. We had the steam fitters place their sprinkler main where it could be joined at a later date and not have to remove the partitions. Timing was vital during the early phases because some trades had to move from bottom up and others from top down and mistakes were costly. Travis and I went to the office to go over strategy and status like we did every day. He had me remind the plumbers about their reporting sheets and there were words said. He said that he had never done that for Bob before and could see no reason to do it now. I told him that he answered to me first and those were my rules. He said that it was a useless rule and he wasn't going to do it.

I said, "I am going to tell you a short story. I started this job once as a partner to Tony Gatzee. I was the one that was jailed wrongly when Tony was laundering money. I spent months in a federal prison before I could prove in a tangible way that I was not fixing the books. Those records got me out of prison along with a couple of other things that happened. I want those records for a legitimate reason and you will comply."

The plumber said, "I thought I recognized your name from somewhere. I even know the rest of the story at your house. I will give you what you want in the way of numbers. Thanks for telling me without some foolish threat thrown in. I wondered why some areas had some work done that followed the current plans and now I know."

As I got home, I found Ellen at our house discussing how to utilize the house with the school. They had some sketches drawn out on the table when I came over. I asked how many infants and toddlers can you put in the house. They thought they could have up to a dozen with a staff of four. The other option is to have no more than four infants and ten toddlers with the same staff. The returns are higher than the school or regular daycare if we needed a staff of five. The lady took the contract to her lawyer but was smiling and talking about seeing her grandchildren. We should know in a day or so.

The next day found me forming a price list with my salesman. He had made a nice ledger sheet with comparables listed and had a place for us to plug in a price in four types of wood to start. Our main woods were maple, birch, oak, and cherry but we would give a quote for them in hickory, butternut, ash, and even mahogany we usually reserved for furniture. I took the list of cabinets we had used for Bobbie's order and totaled it up from three price lists. Our price was in the middle but our overall quality was superior in many ways. I told him that I would help him expand some option details for when he made quotes. I suggested he contact some of the local builders to get a feel of how we might be received.

We also had a floor finisher/installer that was going to do several rooms in a house under construction with our product. He was going to pay us market value if it worked well or we would make it right with him. Robbie was very confident that he would be completely happy with the product.

Custom was back in good shape and the guys on the two rip saws were starting to work very well as a team. We were building up a stock for Robbie and the production line. It worked very well with Al giving a list of panels to be produced for the cabinets on order and they were getting made in time to keep everyone on schedule.

I called Bobbie to discuss the prices he had used in his estimates for his units. I was very much in line with the pricing and they were getting a better cabinet. I asked him when he wanted the next load and he said he would send a truck on Wednesday morning around nine. Now I could give Bob the invoice for the cabinets and the startup at my job.

Kevin said, "I went to the bank you told me and they were expecting me. I am going to close in about one week and they are going to alloy everything you used at the closing from the original seller and save me hundreds of dollars at this closing. I should start a journal on all the things God has done through and for you."

The first of the month was quickly approaching and the closing for the apartment complex was all set to go. Kevin had closed on his house and returned the money that I had used to help him. The school was going to be the buyers for the house next to them but the properties were to be owned as two units as per advice from Tim Simonds. The Walker Enterprises LLC ownership was going to be for two complexes with one mortgage by the same advice so that the possible future sale could be for just one unit. I was going to use one of the empty units in each complex for Robbie and family and Tim Smith would come out of prison to the other. Tim was going into the custom shop and Mary Jo was going to work with the infants for Bonnie.

Bonnie and I got to see Bernie and Cherie when I brought some flooring samples over for them to see. Cherie was finally getting over the morning sickness and was working on the nursery. They liked the open grain contrast of the ash with the maple cabinets in the kitchen. Now we just had to find an installer.

For the time being, Travis was doing all that had to be done while I was away from the Davis building. We had the ventilation subs and the sprinkler sub getting the top floor ready to frame. The plumbers had to finish from the ground to the top as well as the electricians with the supply lines. I had gotten two invoices for material the subs had brought for me to pay. I combined those with mine for the cabinets and the hours to date to give to Bob.

I made a point of getting Sarah, Samuel, and me together for a strategy session on some looming payments. I had been using all the monies as I wanted to but I knew I needed a focus for the end of the year. I had a cash flow that was staggering if I stopped leaving it in God's hands but I knew I had the stewarding responsibilities and wanted to draw from the wisdom of my friends. Sarah said we would have to plan the apartment's expenses to maximize profits. I jokingly said that I didn't know I was making any after I paid her bill. I was going to try to put some money in short term investments but Sarah said there were some ways to actually save tax money while still having the money available for use. She and Samuel could take care of that for me as directed. We decided to meet again right after the first and the closing.

# Forty

I was sitting in an office with the head of alternative energy for the state. I was being told a bunch of facts about the benefits of a wood burning electrical generator for the factory. My concern was the amount of water it would require to generate steam to power the turbines. I was not up to date on the water supply of the city and I thought it was illegal to disturb the natural flow of streams and rivers. I was told that if the water recaptured after the process was returned to the same water source it could be used for the generating of electricity. I was told that whatever amount of electricity I put in the grid would first have my consumption taken off and then would be paid for the balance. I had to pay for the complete start up costs and the sale of the excess and some significant tax incentives would be my recapture rate. I was told that I had to bring him a detailed plan of the size of generator, source of water and return practices, smoke and ash filtering system, as well as a proposed purchase agreement for the electricity for a minimum of twenty years when I wanted to apply for a permit. It would be a minimum of four months to get a permit to start the project.

I left there confused as to why anyone would want to get involved with that kind of a project. I would have to let Sarah explain it to me better. I knew that the amount of electricity that I paid for amounted to more than six figures a year and was a direct expense on the date it was paid. I would no longer have that expense to deduct. I went to her office to see why I would spend any time thinking about this any further. Sarah said, "This falls into a special category of tax credits and depreciation. You would have all the costs to amortize for up to twenty years which is different than some businesses. You would also get tax credit for the entire costs again. I don't know if you understand that an expense may be used against the business income but the tax credit is deducted from the actual taxes you owe. The tax credit has a greater value and can be used for any of your taxes owed. That is why the people coming out of prison and those from the south have to be accounted for. You can get up to twenty-five hundred dollars tax credit for each."

I was meeting with the flooring installer about putting in Bernie's floors. He was very happy with our product and had done a second house with the ash flooring. He said he would be glad to if he became our official installer for the orders we sold installed. I told him I was willing to give him the primary position but I was going to look for a backup to not lose a sale on account of timing. We agreed to what we had to charge for his services above our price. I told him to remember to not bite the hand that fed him when he was sent out to measure a house for us. He said he wouldn't do that. I asked him if he had ever done hardwood over a slab and he said it could be done two ways. He said it would cost more to do that.

Bonnie and I were at Tim Simonds doing the closing on the apartments. It was not the friendliest closing but the owner did what he had to do. Tim had a copy of the bank account with the ten thousand in escrow as per the contract. He had a bank copy of having paid all withholding taxes for us. It was one month from having paid the property taxes for the year so we passed on having him pay for one month. The bank had a check for him for the other thirty thousand and we owned some more property. We went out to see the two managers and gave them each a new stamp for the checks. They were also given a book of deposit slips to prepare as the checks came in. We took the checks they had been told to hold on the first for us to pick up. We told them that we would like to meet with them and the maintenance people at ten and eleven the next day. We had been provided a list of all the tenants in both buildings when we had told them who they were going to pay on the first. The list gave the state paid portion and what the tenants paid us in balance. I gave them the name of Robbie James coming in to the big unit and Tim Smith in the smaller unit so they could give them the keys.

Al had made a duplicate to the hutch we had sold and started a book case to display in the waiting area. I was having a web page made to show our products for sale that included cabinets, flooring, furniture, and anything by design.

I went to the prison in the afternoon and got Tim Smith now we had an apartment for them. I said, "Do you fit in a normal bed because I don't have one yet. I was going to stop on the way to the apartment and buy one and some other stuff."

Tim said, "I do well in a king size bed. Have you met with Mary Jo recently? I stopped calling to try to save some money for her when I got there."

I said, "You did not have much left to your name. My church had Mary Jo come over and set some stuff aside to be delivered today and I went with her to a consignment shop for more items. We will have you all set up in a couple of days but you will be picked up for work at six-forty in the morning by one of my employees. Your rent is okay for a month and you will have time to straighten that out. Mary Joe is already working for my wife at the school. You will meet Samuel and Celine on Sunday and they will set up your first counseling session. Let's see if they have a bed here you like."

We picked out a simple bed with only a support frame and a matching set of night stands. I got them to knock off thirty dollars and then paid them. By the time we got to the apartment, most of the other stuff was in place. It was a little comical at how Pastor Mike had to look up to meet Tim. Tim said he didn't know how to thank everybody for the furnishings. Pastor Mike told him to consider this a welcome home from his new family and God. There is even food in the refrigerator Mary Jo said.

I met with the managers at the times set. I went over what I wanted them to do and how. I told the maintenance guys, "I was not impressed with finding you in your apartments during work time. I believe the outside appearance important as the inside. I know both buildings are now going to have to pass the state tests and I expect you to work or quit. I will be back in a couple of days, let's say Monday at the same time and I want a comprehensive list of what you do here. Please include at the time someone vacates and if it seems that I expect too much we can talk about it. You can also give me a list of things we could do differently and make it easier to do your job and that may include some tools. On Monday I want to see the actual maintenance rooms and all the tools I have received on inventory." I took several more checks with me from both places and some quarters.

I dropped by to see Sarah and see if she was going to keep the rental accounts or if she wanted me to find another way. She said, "Once I set up each building as the controllers, I just have to plug in name assignments to each. We have an entry for state payments and a balance payment and they will become total income. I will have a place for the laundry money separate on the spread sheet. We usually go to the bank at least three times per week for other transactions so we will just do your deposits after posting rents."

I said, "The laundry money is some of the only cash anyone can steal because of the honor system with the managers."

Sarah said, "All coin operated machines come with a counter in them. If you remove all the coins, you can register the counts from the machines every once in a while. You will then know whether or not they are honest. Be certain to give me the payment information for HUD as soon as you get it."

Travis was working with the plumber on isolating the water supply to the first floor to get water to the toilets. The framework was up with plywood for sides during the construction and had cheap doors on them. Bob did not like port-o-lets on his jobs and we wanted these four toilets to work during most of the two years construction. They just had to install one more area valve to get them functioning.

With the help of Kevin's pastor and Robbie's family, we had two more men located from the old factory and they had come up with Robbie's wife and belongings to meet me. One had been on a laser rip saw and the other was in the sanding department. Kevin was there and he agreed with me that we had a good team on the saws at this time. The man said he would do whatever we needed until an opening came up on the saws. We found out that both were single and their needs were simple if they came to work for us and then we made them an offer for work. I told them that I was fresh out of apartments and would talk to them once they found something. I would put them up in a motel for the night and asked them to come back in the morning.

I heard a knock on the door and found my salesman there. He said, "I have had fifty-three contacts from the web page in one week. I am over my head with people wanting their houses measured to put some kind of flooring down. I have sold three book cases this week and we don't have a contracted way of delivering the furniture so I don't have a shipping price to add in. I was working on the continuation of one of our customer's contracts and I don't have time for them. I haven't called back six people for cabinets. I don't want to get fired but I could anger some of these people by not being able to remain timely."

I said, "We can use the installer to measure some of the serious inquiries and I will look for someone to join our sales force. I got too many horses and not enough carts with that web page."

The man in the office from the southern factory spoke up, "I can measure houses for flooring and cabinets. I was a small contractor before I went into the factory to work and I could help there for a while if you need me to. I can also detect problems in what a client may be trying to do to his house. I can install both cabinets and flooring so I can do estimates over the phone."

Kevin simply said, "I think God still likes you."

The man that was going to sell was a man named Gary Ruggles and I asked, "I supposed you didn't come with many clothes on this trip?"

Gary said, "There wasn't any to bring. Katrina took what I had and the way to replace them. I see your other salesman is in clean casual clothing so is that what you want for me."

I said, "That's all you will find me in even on Sundays. Let's get you to a store and get you a couple of changes of clothes. We will get you a pad and such from Diana's stock as long as you have a tape and a smooth tongue we should be back in business in no time."

On the way over to the mall, I stopped at a car dealership and picked out an economical pickup. It was a couple of years old but had very few miles on it. I dickered with them for a few minutes until they came down nearly two thousand dollars and asked them to have it ready to pick up in about an hour. We picked out a couple of single color shirts for Gary and some blue denim jeans. We added some comfortable steel toed shoes, a belt, and a dozen socks to the cart. We checked out and went back to the car dealer. I said, "You do have a license don't you."

Gary said, "Yes, but not in this state. It seems it would take a freight train to slow you down when you get going."

I said, "I always take Sundays off to be with God and family."

# Forty-One

I spent Monday morning at Butler East and West with the managers and maintenance people. Once inside the maintenance rooms I asked them if all the tools were there because I had a lot more on the sales listing. I was told that the previous owner took some home during the last week before the sale. Both riding mowers were gone and some power tools as well. I asked them if they wanted a bagger on the mowers to help keep things clean. I was told that they had taken the other one off because of many tight corners on the little islands of grass. They liked little mowers that mulched most of the grass with no discharge the best. The one tool that they both seemed to want was an electric snake for cleaning clogged pipes. They agreed that they could share one with no problems. I had the maintenance men take me to the laundries and record all the machine counts of quarters as we empted them. I made it clear what I was doing and why. They all indicated that they wanted to keep their jobs and I told them that they were going to get a chance to prove it to me. The last thing I asked them was where they were in their pay cycles as I had them fill out new employee hiring packs along with the drug testing clause. They were all due a paycheck this Friday so I had to make sure what each was getting as well as their apartments. The original owner was not going to get much of those ten thousand dollars in escrow.

I was back at the factory right after lunch and caught up with Gary and the other salesman. Gary had taken a deposit on a large house being renovated and projected to be ready in three weeks for flooring and they wanted a quote on a totally custom cherry kitchen. Gary had the list of regular boxes and the specialty cabinet size and description. I asked the first salesman to pursue the contract as a primary concern and get Gary the most solid leads. Gary said he was going to measure two sets of cabinets where the people were ready to decide in the evening with the people home.

Tim said he was enjoying himself in the custom shop and he and Mary Jo were enjoying being together for the first time since he had gone to prison. I asked him to keep an eye out for trouble in the apartments and tell me about any problems. He said he needed to speak to the landlord and find out about the rent pretty soon. I told him I would give him the name so he could call him soon.

Travis had the bathrooms all working and I went to get some cheap fasteners for the toilet paper. The plumbers had brought in a used slop sink that hands could be washed in and I put a paper towel dispenser over it. Bob had been glad to see the Port-O-Lets leaving on their truck because of one time when someone had dumped one in a building and it had cost him a lot of money to clean up the mess. The subs were all proceedings on schedule and the plans had very few problems so far. We had reduced the number of men at this time because there just wasn't work for them to do yet.

I met with Sarah and Samuel as we had scheduled on managing the funds to make the big payments and how they would affect the income this year. Sarah said that most of the payments could be pushed to after the first of the year. She said that she had run two strategies in her computer and that it would be very advantageous to have all the companies have their fiscal years end with the calendar year. By doing this, she could show some big loses for this year and carry the loss to future years. They told me how to get some tax free interest income on the money that we started to set aside for the payments. I asked her if I should start looking into the generator more seriously and if the electricity used at Butler East and West could also come off first. I also asked her if we could show the scraps of wood with a greater value if they were burned for the generating. She said that both could be but she would have to look and see if it would be better to pay for the electricity for the Butler buildings. If they are paying you less than the going rate for the electricity used, you may want to keep the expenses for the buildings. The wood going into the generating could be shown as an expense but we already have it in the production mill at what I expect to be a higher value to the bottom line. I believe that you should look at it very soon.

I made one last call to meet with Terry in the near future. I left the factory and went by the school to see if they had a contract to purchase the neighbor's house yet. Bonnie and I went and knocked on her door before we went home. The woman said that her lawyer had been out of town but had gotten a look at her contract and found it very fair. She had picked it up in the morning as she went to the hospital to volunteer and we could sign it with her now if we wanted to. She said that her family was looking forward to having her come to live with them until she found herself something she liked. I asked her how soon she wanted to close and then move. I suggested we close in two weeks and then she could have until the first to move. She was happy with those terms and I felt better with a contract in our hands.

I called the man who I had spoken to about the wood burning generator and asked him if he had a company he could recommend. He said there were a Swiss company and a German company who both made a good product. He gave me their web sites and I told him I would be in touch soon. I looked at both their products at work on their web sites and liked the German product better. I sent them an e-mail and asked to be contacted as soon as possible. I sent an e-mail to the other company as well to be sure I found out all I had needed of to make a good decision. I had heard back from both companies by the end of the day.

Terry came to the office in the morning and asked me what I needed.

I said, "I need two things if you can find them. I need to buy the property adjoining our lot to build a wood burning generating plant. The property loses some of its value with the brook running in the middle of it but I need that brook for a water source. The other thing is that I may be interested in some rental properties that are not in the program for some of my employees to live in."

Terry said, "You want to hire me as a buyer's agent and try to buy that property behind you? I do have a couple of nice four and six unit apartment buildings for sale at my office that is not in the program."

I said, "I do not need the entire acreage but I need the section with the brook that abuts my line. If you find the owner, I will go with you if you want. I would look at the other listings later today if we can or you can call me."

Bob's truck came and took the last of the cabinets for Bobbie's job. We now had a book case and china cabinet on display in the waiting room as well as samples of the four types of flooring that was normal. We had sold three of the book cases just from the web site and now we had to get to the point that clients could use credit cards on our web site. I went to our bank and checked out our options for credit cards. It turned out that once the people were ready to stop shopping they could go to a link at the bank that was secure from hacking and copying to use any major type of card. They included an imprinter for the factory as well for the use of cards. Mary Murray was helping us set up the web site catalog and links for payments. I was taking the factory into the world of technology. The other link on the site gave them a way to leave us a request for information in person that Gary would usually follow up with.

I visited Travis at the Davis building to see if they were getting us some areas ready to work in. The subs were making good progress with the main lines and soon would be compartmentalizing some areas for us. Travis had marked out some of the units on the floor for use in the future and also to give the subs delineation factors to work from. I was behind in getting the data into the computer as far as tracking the progress but I refused to network to my house to work at night.

I passed by Butler East and West to get checks and see how the grounds were shaping up since I spoke to them and got them some tools. The yards did look better and they had done a few minor repairs to the exteriors and touched up the paint. I took some more checks and a lot of quarters from each manager. I had gotten with the bank manager about the missing tools, pay checks, and other shortages to charge against the escrow money. I got the information documented and presented it to the bank for payment and they sent him a little under two thousand dollar difference left in the account.

Terry and I met at the building with the six units that were for sale. It was a three story building with two (one) bedroom units on the third floor. It had two (two) bedroom units on the other two floors with coin operated laundries on the bottom two floors. We discussed the income and expenses for that building before we went to the building with four units. They were on the same street but not near each other. This one had a large four bedroom on the ground floor and three (two) bedroom units on the other two floors. The laundry for this building was on the ground floor. Both lots had ample parking and were about ten years old. The pricing did not reflect the needs that the property had. I told Terry that I would take the sheets and get back to her if I was going to make an offer. Terry said that she had found the owners name at the tax office and was going to make contact soon for the property that abutted mine.

I was visited by the woodworking equipment salesman in the afternoon. He said that he had become involved with helping a bank recapture some of their loss from a plant that went bankrupt. He had a couple of large panel sanders and he also had a machine for making the dowels for the backs and bottoms of chairs. It had to be programmed for the length, shape, and number of pieces and worked with minimal observation. He had brought some of the things it would do and we had nothing like it in production. With this machine, we could make kitchen chairs complete. It could be bought for one third of original cost and was less than two years old. He said that he could supply knives and such if we bought it. I offered him ten thousand less than asking price for the three items and he said he would have to call the bank. I let him use the phone at my desk to make that call. It took several minutes before he was done but he came back and said they had taken the offer but I would have to pay to have them moved. I was finally going to have my sander at my garage.

I discussed the two apartment buildings with Bonnie that night and we looked over the numbers that Terry had given us. It was still early in the evening so I had Bonnie call Terry to see how much they got as rental agents at their office. It turned out to be twenty-five percent for a new rental and seven percent of rent collected during maintenance months. We plugged those amounts against the other numbers to find what the buildings could be purchased for and still stay solvent. We also had to consider the money that was on deposit for security and last months rent because they were not under the state program. Those security amounts were to be in a different account by law in this state to be settled at the time of vacancy. The state had an arbitration board available for disputes between landlords and tenants. That account would have to be justified before the time of closing with tenants in the apartments now. We decided together on the number we could offer on the two buildings.

# Forty-Two

I got a call from the German manufacturer of the generators that he would be able to stop to see me for a day as he went back to Germany from an installation project. I asked him to please do so and call me again when he got in town. He said that his itinerary projected a one o'clock landing in town and he would contact me then.

Terry had found the owner of the land and I was going to meet with him in about an hour at my office. Terry was also bringing the two contracts for the two buildings for us to sign. I had called Tim Simonds and had him protect us as best he could in this kind of a sale and Terry now had those contracts to present. I was looking over those contracts when the land owner came by to speak to us. Terry had not met him in person yet so we all introduced ourselves as we started.

The owner said, "I have not decided to sell any of that large parcel yet and this meeting comes with no predetermined factor that I will sell. Terry says that you are interested in this lower part that has the small year around brook on it. I suppose you know how hard it is to meet the regulations regarding the undisturbed flow of water in this state as you try to develop it and I would like to know why it is of interest because of the water."

I said, "I am a kind of dreamer or visionary in my endeavors. I try to improve the state of mankind in all that I do. I want to use the wood that I am now burning for heat and use it to generate electricity first. This is one time when the state allows you to take water from a stream if the water you recapture from the process goes back into the original brook minus the steam that escapes. By purchasing your property I can use the cooling steam to still heat my factory and the dryers in the finishing department. The residue would return to the brook after filtration."

The owner said, "The entire process sounds very costly."

I said, "It is my guess without having found a piece of land yet that it would be about one million dollars and would take twenty-five years to get most of your money back. That is why most people do not want to do anything like this and I am not sure if I am ready to commit to it yet. I expect to meet with a German manufacturer this afternoon to get their portion of the costs."

The owner said, "Would you invest your money if you only had a lease on the land. Part of the permitting process requires open area around buildings for natural drainage and safety factors. I would consider giving you a twenty-five year lease with permanent rights-of- way to the site if you cannot come off from the back of your land. I would protect that lease and give you an option for another twenty-five in that protection. You could have your project and I could maintain my open areas."

I said, "I am very interested and if you would work with Terry on the amount of rent you would need, I could gather up the rest of my pricing. I thank you and we will be in touch very soon."

Travis was doing very well keeping things moving at the Davis property while there was so little wood working to do. He would organize the papers that I had to enter into the computer as far as progress and billing for Bob. I was in hopes to start putting the electricity and plumbing in the fifth floor apartments very soon. Bob had chosen some good subcontractors over the years prior to our meeting.

I made sure that I was around the office by one o'clock. I had Gary give me some input on what orders he had not taken a deposit on yet. He said, "I sold that big flooring job the first day I went out and I had them come see the cherry cabinets we had for Bobbie. We are waiting for the architect and the owner to give us the final details and we will get a deposit from them. The installer is picking up the first load of wood flooring tomorrow for there. I went out to see several more homeowners but two of them do not have anyone to remodel their homes to start the work. I saw the homes and it is straight forward remodeling and if you give me the word we can bid that work as well to get the kitchens sold. The others need to get home improvement loans for us to get the work so I am waiting on them. The furniture sales are good and Al should have two of the book cases ready to ship this week. I sold another one yesterday to be done in a medium brown maple. I told them yesterday that there would be a seventy-five dollar delivery fee to go the twenty miles and they didn't bat an eye."

I said, "Keep up the good work and don't forget to keep that truck serviced on a regular basis. I believe that you have been using the card that Diana keeps to get gas and you bring her petty cash receipts as well. If you are going to stay in this state and work for me you have to get the correct license for the state. I will get you the pictures of some of the other items we want to put on the web site as far as furniture for sale."

That was as far as I got to speak to him because the German man had taken the liberty to arrive at the factory unannounced. He said, "I apologize for not calling but I took an airport rental car with a city map and located you very easily. The furniture in the hall is what you make. Those are very good replicas for factory work."

I said, "Thank you! We do everything from production woodworking with pieces for other companies to assemble to custom cabinets and flooring as well as a line of furniture. My sales have doubled in the first year I have owned the factory. Let's talk about your product."

He opened up his laptop and started by showing a CD with several of their plants in operation. They were very automated and could use wood chips simultaneously with our blockings and sawdust at the same time. Their sensors would adjust intake air blowers to keep the heat fairly well regulated and turn everything to clean ash in the burning. The steam went through the turbines and went back into the vats for reheating. They were very efficient in their use of their heat. I asked him if it would tolerate my drawing some off for heating the factory and dryers without decreasing their efficiency too much. He assured me that he had several plants doing that in Germany and on very cold days they might lose ten percent of capacity generation.

We went outside to see the area that I was talking about leasing with him and he said that we had plenty of room for a five hundred kilowatt generator. He said that that was four times what I could use at capacity usage. We spent a great deal of time discussing operation, maintenance, and replacement needs for long periods of operation. Then we got really serious and I asked him how much I was looking to invest in this project and how long it would take to get it on line. He said that I was looking at six to eight hundred thousand dollars before it was connected back to my heaters and would take four months from ordering date to get it here and four to six months to have it fully operational. He said that they supplied all the engineering for the permit including the emissions from the burning. We had reached the end of the day but he said that he would come back in the morning before getting on the airplane again.

I had a call from the warden while I was talking to the German but it had gotten too late to call him tonight.

Terry called me early in the morning and said that the owner of the land had called her and said that he would lease us the property at fifteen hundred per month triple net. I told her that that was reasonable and acceptable. She then told me that the owner of the two apartment houses had accepted our offer for the two buildings also. When the German came by in the morning I was able to tell him that I had procured the lease on the property and I wanted to tighten up the numbers if we could and also the expected maintenance costs to operate for a number of years. He said that he would send me back a written prospectus as soon as he got back to Germany.

The warden asked me if I could speak to two inmates due out at two week intervals in a couple of days and we agreed upon a time. He also had looked at our web site and asked how the book case would look in cherry to match the rest of his office and I said it would be fine. He asked if I wanted a deposit and I told him I did not need one from him for this one. I told him I would call when it was done.

We had an official farewell party for Dan and Gina at a local restaurant with almost all the employees attending. We all knew that they would be back after their trip across the country but there were many tears shed that night. I had extended the invitation to the rest of the elder board and others from the church that had lived out a lot of the story along with them. The employees had chipped in and bought him a great fly rod set with a case.

# Forty-Three

The office seemed totally different as we gave Gary one of the desks to keep his client information in with the other salesman. He had gone back to both of the clients that needed to find installers as well as remodelers and we ended up with both of the jobs with the remodeling done on a time and material basis and the cabinets had already been quoted. We could do the electrical that was needed but I never had my men do the plumbing. We now had it so Tim Smith could cover if Al was not in assembly. We had two other men as well as Gary part time to do the work on these houses. I had found the same sheet rock man that had done Bernie's work and he said that he would do the work that we had to do somehow.

Travis and I were scheduled to lay out the next floor down starting today. We had people nearing the end of the top floor work with the metal studs and the electricians were starting to run their conduit. The sprinkler people had to test the lines on that floor before we could hang sheet rock completely to the ceiling in the unit separating walls. The plumbers had completed most of the floor and their lines were tested. I had to go to the closing on the house beside the school late in the day so I left Travis with a laborer.

I met Bonnie, Ellen, and Ted at Tim Simonds office just at four o'clock. The woman only had to give us the deed to the property that the lawyer had made prior to now and receive a check for the house. She agreed to be out before the first of the month and we would dispose of anything she left in a manner that we saw fit.

Earlier in the morning I had to stop by the house so the sander could be put in my garage for a while. The other two machines were going right to the factory. I had never seen the rung maker so I was curious to see how big it was in real life. I had the other salesman call some of the people that we knew made pieces with rungs and if they had a good supplier at this time. There were two possible markets at this time and they were sending us samples to duplicate.

On Friday we were at Tim Simonds office for the second time this week. These closings went similar to the Butler buildings. The seller had given statements with his accounting at the time of the sale and we were leaving five thousand for each building in escrow with a bank for final settlement. I would do as we had done with the other buildings but this time we had to deal with each tenant individually as far as a security deposit. We gave the owner no credit at the time of sale for rents that the people were behind on. I knew that I could use the information to have them evicted if I had to or make a settlement of some sorts with them. These had not been as much fun as the one with the woman moving to be with her family by the school. It was never good to deal with a businessman who was failing at what he was trying to do. I thanked God that I wasn't in his shoes.

I had received a box from Germany by next day air with an accumulation of information that we might need. I had Kevin and the head of maintenance in the office going over some of the pros and cons for the project. One of the things that concerned me was the need for parts always meant at least a two day delay and repair time. The opinion was that Ted was going to be my biggest asset when and if I put this thing on line. We were not going to remove any part of the present burner and we would only have to manually change some valves to light it back up and protect the factory from freezing and losing our driers. The directions also called for a heating/non-generating function that served during times of repair and examinations so that it could be back on line in a matter of an hour or two. This was going to be different than buying an apartment house.

Robbie had some cherry pulled from the narrow bins and had made a large amount of cherry moldings for book cases and we were going to make a china hutch out of cherry for display as well as what I needed for the warden. I had Terry and her office working on getting people up to date with their rent or times of vacating. I needed three apartments for the employees I had and two more people coming out of prison. Terry had one of the men that she felt sorry for come and put in an application for work. He had a family and was really down on his luck. I actually had him go to the Davis building and work as a laborer for Travis until I had a position inside. In about a week, we were able to present the bank with the amounts of the security deposits and some missing equipment against the escrowed money. I formed the new security account with Samuel as a separate tax free account to satisfy the state. Terry and Sarah were working on setting up the two new buildings as we had the Butler accounts to keep them current. I prayed that we all would have the Wisdom of Solomon with all this activity.

Bonnie and Ellen had started the year with four vacancies in the entire school. She already had five infants in the baby house as we called it and there were forty to sixty children getting on busses on any given day. Edith was overseeing the nutrition program at the school including the breakfast of several of the bus students. The state had allowed the school a grant to help offset some of the costs for the children's meals. Al and Edith were looking to buy a house in the area and not pay rent anymore and Terry was working with them.

I was honored by the city as Businessman of The Year at a city wide festival held outside in the fall of the year. The points that had been evaluated for me to win over some of the other people were numerous. I had to be employing people on a steady basis from all walks of life. I reached out with products or services outside of our community at least in part. The standards used in our company had to be above the norm of just getting by. We had to reach out to the humanities in our area for the betterment of our communities such as we were doing at the school. The last point was that I had overcome some adversity in my life to get to where I was now. I had never been as humbled as the day the mayor and Bernie Segal came into my office to tell me about it. Bernie had nominated me and made the presentation of my case before the judges in the community. I tried to turn it down but they said I had no say in receiving it. I had to stand on a stage in City Park and tell something about why I was doing some of the things that had won me the award. On that day, I was able to stand beside my wife and friends amongst many city officials I did not know and give them a short story.

I told them, "I took the time to look back over the last year and it felt like a lifetime had passed. I didn't like remembering the time in prison but I found a God given compassion for people while I was there. I didn't like the fact that I had killed two men even if it was to protect our lives. I was humbled at how God had started with Dan and Gina selecting me to buy the factory. That was the beginning of the basic tool that God had given me to help people. He had made me directly responsible in continuing the source of income for over a hundred people now. We were able by the use of the school to give a testimony of the love of God to a lot of children. I was extremely humbled by the working of His hand in the lives of Kevin and Gail and how they now blessed us after their own personal losses from Katrina. We had been able to change the lives of four inmates so far, three families from the South, and we looked forward to doing it more. Yet, the greatest blessing was my family being under one roof at night wrapped in the arms of God.

About the author

Armand P. Ferland was a multi-faceted business owner. He now spends his time writing, and resides in St. Johnsbury, Vermont with his wife of 42 years, Dorothy.

www.ingramcontent.com/pod-product-compliance
Lightning Source LLC
Chambersburg PA
CBHW070727280626
47159CB00023B/2849